DEADLANDS

BOOK TWO OF THE DEADLANDS DUOLOGY

DEVIN THORPE

For Draven,

This world bent you, but you refused to break.

TRIGGER WARNINGS

This story contains potentially disturbing or offensive content that may be
harmful to some readers. Examples of this include:

Child loss

Blood and gore

Extreme violence

Death

Grief/Loss

THE STORY SO FAR...

Drakini isn't what you'd call a "normal" human.

When Silenius Sylvian, child king of the Areopagus, declared a military draft, Drakini's life was thrown into a world of predestined plots much greater than her finite mind could understand. At only sixteen years old, she was forced into a world with only two options: Hunt, or be hunted.

With the help of an imaginary hellcat only she could see, Drakini was able to survive a bloodbath the gods preordained. With her trusty shadow soldiers (figments of her schizophrenic imagination), Wisteria, Grite, Havik, Osprey, and Lu Bu—Drakini evolved into a trained killer—a Huntress in a world full of monsters.

But surviving the military draft was only the first chapter in Drakini's story. After defeating the treacherous Count Viren, leader of the Undead, a sinister secret hidden in the Skaarian Isles' mines was unleashed—a monster known as the Wendigo.

For centuries, the Sylvian kings have suspected a foreign land that remains, to this day, uncharted. Decades ago, a brigade of conquerors were sent overseas to find the lands and claim them in the name of the Areopagus.

What awaited the conquerors in these Deadlands can only be described as a living nightmare, known to Deadland natives as a species of invincible demons.

In a desperate attempt to bring the fight to the Wendigos on their homeland, King Silenius Sylvian has sent the Hunter Corps, of which Drakini is the first female member. Their instructions are simple: Invade the Deadlands and eliminate any threat the Wendigos pose.

But paper doesn't bleed, and Drakini and her companions will soon learn that some demons are better off left to rot in Hell alone.

CONTENTS

READING ORDER

Deadlands is Book Two of "The Deadlands Duology" and stands as a sequel to *Huntress*.

However, both *Huntress* and *Deadlands* serve as immensely important stories to my overarching series, "The Bloodbound Trilogy," which consists of *Bloodlust*, *Hellhound*, and *Bloodbound*, in that order.

I don't do this to confuse readers, rather, I've written these books to enhance your reading experience. Think of it like this—the Marvel Cinematic blockbuster known as "Avengers" would have little ground to stand on without "Iron Man," "Captain America," and "Thor," preceding it.

Because of this, I can most certainly assure you that you'll enjoy *Huntress* and *Deadlands* without ever reading "The Bloodbound Trilogy," but I can guarantee that you will enjoy all these books more if you read them in their proper order, which is:

1. Bloodlust

2. Huntress

3. Hellhound

4. Deadlands

5. Bloodbound

In this context, *Huntress* can be more aptly viewed as Book 1.5 of "The Bloodbound Trilogy," whereas *Deadlands* would serve as Book 2.5.

Inside *Deadlands* in particular is a plot twist I've been planning since first releasing *Bloodlust*, my debut novel, but you won't understand it or feel the nostalgia if you fail to read *Bloodlust* and *Hellhound* first.

Okay, that is my one and only tangent—consider yourself warned.

EPIGRAPH

"The best way to keep a prisoner from escaping is to make sure he never knows he's in prison."

- Fyodor Dostoevsky, *Crime and Punishment*

PART ONE

1

FIRST-TIME SAILOR

Hot, hot vomit shoots up my throat and out my mouth, feeding the ocean below with the contents of my stomach.

"The gal's at it again," Pip laughs, mocking me.

"Don't see how she has anything left to upchuck at this point," Calico states calmly. "She hasn't eaten in days, but her stomach still manages to find scraps to sacrifice."

Even after my projectile vomiting ceases, my stomach and chest dry heave in anticipation of something that will never come.

"Little fawn can't get her sea legs under her," Pip chuckles, always laughing when he talks. "If she keeps this up, she'll be throwing up her liver and lungs by the time we get there."

"It was a mistake to draft her," Ghost mutters, mostly to himself, always talking to himself. It isn't the first time he's expressed his disdain for me. He's made his position on my selection clear with every opportunity that's risen.

I grip the handrail of the rocking ship tight, squeezing my eyes shut as a wave of nausea flips my stomach like a pancake. I want to defend myself verbally, but opening my mouth will only result in me gagging further, so I clench my teeth and pray inwardly for this storm of queasiness to pass.

I wipe my mouth with the back of my hand, which still has dried vomit on it from minutes ago, when I found myself throwing up for the dozenth time since the ship set sail. It doesn't make any sense how being afloat across the ocean spreads such sickness throughout my body. What makes even less sense is how my companions within the Hunters aren't possessed by similar fits of nausea. You'd think they were each raised as sailors with how their bodies respond to the crashing waves. I, on the other hand, spent my life landlocked in Fyrefell, only to realize too late that I'm apparently allergic to ships treading large bodies of water.

"Looky looky, the Cur is bringing our little princess a rag to clean herself with," Pip laughs, though I fail to see the humor in the situation. I suppose I'd laugh more too if the gods made me as ugly as they did Pip.

A gentle hand touches my back, rubbing it comfortingly. I lift my head back over the edge of the ship and twist my eyes to see who stands behind me.

"Here," Cur whispers, his eyes looking down at me sympathetically. In his hand is a moist towel which he offers me discreetly so I can clean up the mess I've made. It's dark out, especially so because it's the night of the new moon. All we have to light our way is the pathetic twinkle of the North Star, which currently hides behind the overcast clouds above. Still, despite the darkness, I can see the look of kindness Cur exchanges as he does me a favor I haven't earned.

"Thanks, Cur," I manage to whisper through clenched teeth. I take the towel and wipe my lips, then the back of my hand, all while Cur hovers over me, strategically blocking me from Pip and Calico's sight.

Still, Pip taunts him for his sympathy. "Look at that, the damn dog is trying to make a friend! Don't mistake his kindness as acceptance, Huntress. He's just a Cur, he ain't no Hunter. Alas, I suppose even outcasts deserve friendship."

It was just my luck to draw night watch with Calico and Pip, the two Hunters who treat every day as if it's initiation day for me. Granted, none of the Hunters have taken a liking to me as of yet. But these two treat disliking me like their full-time job.

I don't know why I expected to be treated the same as everyone else in the Hunters... I am their first female member, so it only makes sense they automatically see me as inferior to their current ranks.

Ghost, on the other hand, is only up here because he spends all day in the belly of the ship hiding from the sunlight. Night is the only suitable time for him to breathe fresh air and exercise flight.

In truth, he could fly to the Deadlands if he pleased, but doing so would strand him there all alone until our ship arrived.

He is the first member of the Godhand I've met.

Well, ex-member, if I'm to believe his origin. The black-haired, red-eyed Undead is a quandary of sorts. From what I've gathered, he turned on his own species when the Hunters came for them, then exercised his Rite of Supersession. Turns out, there's more than one way to join the Hunters. An individual can be recruited, as I was, or they can demand a spot by battle. If a challenger manages to defeat a Hunter in single combat, they inherit the Hunter's position, and after taking the Hunter's Creed, they become a bona fide member of the Hunters Corp.

Ghost is the only member of our current ranks to have exercised this rite, and many members still hate him for it.

"You know, Cur isn't actually my name," Cur whispers so Pip can't hear him.

I look up at his dark, sincere eyes, then at his clenching jawline. A strong breeze slides across the waters below, then scales the side of the ship. It blows Cur's bangs out of his eyes as a cold chill scuttles down my body. "I mean, none of us use our real names," I reply, unable to look away from his charismatic eyes. "That's why they call me Huntress... Because none of us use the names we were given in our past lives."

"Cur isn't a nickname, dumb girl," Ghost interjects, his superhuman hearing allowing him to eavesdrop on our conversation despite our whispers. "It's a derogatory term we use for Lycans. Kind of like how we call you 'bitch' behind your back."

"Damn bloodsucker!" Pip shouts, annoyed by Ghost's cruel transparency. "Why'dya gotta always ruin our fun? Now the bitch knows she's a bitch, and that ain't fun for nobody!"

I sigh, not surprised.

"How is 'Cur' derogatory? I've never heard that word in my life," I say to the Lycan who hovers above me, but it's Ghost that answers.

"It's like calling a dog a mutt—no—a mongrel." Ghost's voice shares little emotion. Every sentence he speaks sounds like he's disappointed with the words he's saying.

"There'll be plenty of time for him to tell you his real name if we get off this damn island the child king is sending us to," Pip says.

Calico adds, "Best if we don't get emotionally attached to our tracking dog... If the reports on these Wendigos have any validity, I doubt wolfboy will be accompanying us on our trip home."

I see a tinge of sadness in Cur's eyes, so I instinctively grab his wrist and whisper, "Don't listen to them... I'd love to know your real name."

"It's fine," he replies coldly, pulling his arm away from me. "They're right... No point getting to know one another. I'm only here to pay off my debt to the crown, then we'll all be parting ways... Best if we don't get attached."

He turns and starts to walk off, but I scramble after him and grab his shoulder. "I'm not like them," I whisper in his ear. "If you need anything... Anything at all... I'm—"

My voice cuts short as the ship lurches sideways violently. I'm thrown off my feet as something beneath us explodes. Cur falls atop me, instinctively placing his hand behind my head to cushion my fall. Pip squeals as he falls off the barrel he sits upon, the axe across his lap nearly splitting his head in two as he lands. Calico, despite being the most graceful of us all, is unable to remain standing. I see his body sliding across the splintery deck as the ship begins to capsize.

The only one of us unaffected is Ghost, who now floats in the air staring down at us with his ruby-red eyes. Countless voices scream out from below the deck, each of them ripped from their sleep from the seismic boom.

I watch splinters of wood fly above us in slow motion, realizing this wood once belonged to some part of our ship's broadside.

I should be scared, I tell myself inwardly.

But with Cur's body on top of me, shielding me from whatever destruction we've encountered, I've never felt safer.

As the ship rocks violently from one side to another, water splaying over the sides, wooden shards raining over us, I focus on the warmth of Cur's body, listen to his calm heartbeat, marvel at his gentle touch.

Voices scream.

Water floods around us.

Wood creaks as it splits in two.

Our ship is sinking.

Scared?

I should be terrified.

And yet...

I've never felt safer.

2

TUMBLEWEED

The Areopagus isn't known for its naval forces, but King Silenius Sylvian spared no expense in erecting Sun Treader for our journey. Unfortunately for Sun Treader, no ship made from oak and treenails could endure hitting the underwater coral reef we've struck, and so its hull cracked, then exploded under the pressure of an ocean seeking entrance.

What's even more unfortunate is the fact that our half dozen lifeboats were strapped to starboard, the same side that has already capsized beneath the vengeful riptide.

I'm disoriented. Like our ship's hull, my brain is dissected in two as my instinct to survive sets in, countered by my instinct to rescue the trapped members of our Corp. I inhale deeply—breathe in Cur's natural scent as his body continues to shield me from the ensuing wreckage.

I place my hands under his ribs and push, separating our bodies so I can slip out of his grasp.

I appreciate his gesture, but I'm not a girl who needs saving.

I try to stand but the deck's exponential slant instantly throws me to my back. A wheeze of air exits my lungs as I thud against the trembling wood. A wave of salty water washes over me, entering my mouth as I pant for air. It enters my lungs and I choke as my feet flip over my head. I'm falling backwards, all while Cur calls my name desperately in the distance.

Maybe I'm a girl who needs saving after all, I think to myself as my lungs vomit saltwater back up. It pours over my lower lip and onto my leather jerkin.

I'm like a piece of tumbleweed caught in a tornado. I continue to flip, unable to grab hold of anything that will slow my inexorable, clumsy jettison toward the side of the ship that's already capsized.

Somehow, by the grace of gods, my hand latches onto a cargo net transfixed to the main mast. Something pops in my shoulder as my body's weight is suspended; a jolt of pain follows the pop, causing me to scream involuntarily. I want to hold onto the cargo net like my life depends on it, because it does, but all the willpower in the world cannot dull the agony shooting through my arm.

My fingers slip, and I let go of the cargo net. I plummet into the ocean below, still wheezing for air despite saltwater being the only thing available to me.

The black, frigid waters swallow me whole.

3

CUR

The only light to guide me in these dark waters is the yellow tint displayed from my glowing eyes—the same yellow glow that once radiated from Wisteria's reassuring gaze.

There were no swimming holes in Fyrefell, no places for me to practice the art of flailing my limbs to keep afloat in bodies of water that have no bottom. Even worse, there was nothing to condition my mind to the feeling of being sucked beneath waves despite my hands propelling my body frantically toward the surface. It is a maddening experience—to be utterly out of air as my lungs convulse for something my mouth can't provide.

My body has been flipped by the raging waters so many times that I no longer know which way is up. And despite being told by fellow Hunters that all bodies innately float, that isn't what I experience now. In fact, I experience the opposite. It's like the ocean has its own source of gravity—one that wishes to drag me into the freezing depths where no Wendigo will ever endanger me.

In a way, this is nature's way of giving me a merciful death. Though my hand reaches out to be saved, it's as if the Almighty Ocean knows what waits for me in the Deadlands—begs my soul to stay here so I no longer have to endure the terrors that exist outside these waters. And if I was any other human, I'd likely relent to the ocean's wishes. But the constant glimmer of yellow extends from my eyes, illuminating the dark waters around me, reminding me of the hellcat that dwells inside me.

What would Wisteria say to me, if she could see me now?

Get up and fight, child! she would scream.

What feels like ages ago, I asked her why... Why fight? Why try? When I've been defeated physically and mentally so many times, why even bother?

To which she replied, *Because you are Worthy, Huntress.*

She knew what I was capable of before I ever could—could see past my many shortcomings, my weaknesses, my failures... And still, she believed in me.

And though she is no longer here to protect me, no longer here to encourage me, I can feel her spirit residing inside me. It sets my limbs aflame with a passion to survive, to get up and fight.

And so I fight.

Though my enemies aren't physical beings, though they are only waves, they put up a damn good fight. In some ways, this is worse than being buried alive. When several feet of dirt seal your coffin shut, there is no optimism of ever clawing your way to freedom. You don't even have enough room to writhe in protest.

Here though... Here, you have all the freedom in the world to fight back, yet the more I fight, the more the riptide exhausts me.

And the more exhausted I become, the more my muscles burn, further demanding oxygen from my lungs—oxygen which my lungs can't provide my salient efforts. It's like one of those damn finger traps Myre gave me once... The more I pulled, the tighter the restraint became. It wasn't until I learned to relax that my fingers were freed.

But I don't have time to relax now. My head is light. My vision narrows. My heart can beat no further without the nourishment of fresh air.

In the darkness of this endless abyss, I see something... A spotlight of radiant, white light shines to reveal a set of stony double doors. A sense of dread pulses from their sinister nature; a malevolent aura beckons to me. "Drakini," a voice whispers from within the impenetrable, sealed gateway. The waters seem to be pulling me closer to the gates as the doors eagerly await my arrival. No matter how hard I flail, I can't overcome the force that pulls me, repeating my name over and over.

Until...

Something—someone—some guardian angel—grabs hold of my nearly lifeless hand and pulls me back toward the land of the living. I'm delirious, one foot in this realm and the other in the afterlife. But just as my body threatens to release all hope, I feel the water's surface break over my head. Air avails itself to me in unlimited quantities, and I suck and gasp and wheeze until my second foot leaves the realm of the dead in favor of living once more.

"Huntress," a calm voice whispers to me as a man's arms wrap around my still-flailing body. "It's going to be okay," he reassures as I panic, flailing about as if the riptide still has a hold over me.

But it doesn't, I realize. There is no longer a force from below that grabs hold of my heels and pulls me under. There is only the strong, ever-present security of two arms anchoring me to the surface, and as I twist around, I see those arms belong to Cur...

"I'm here," he whispers as I fight like hell to stay conscious. "I've got you... I'm not going anywhere."

Last time he held me in his embrace, I pushed him away to show I don't need a protector.

But now... Now, I not only let him hold me, but I hold him back, afraid to face the consequences of letting go once more.

Through my labored breathing, I can't find the words to thank him, so I simply rest in his arms as the last of the Sun Treader dips below the ocean, never to be seen again.

Cur gently wipes my soaked hair out of my eyes and behind my ears, then places his hand on my hammering heart.

"Why did... you save me?" I pant, looking away from the sunken ship into his dark eyes. He makes treading water look easier than walking, and I silently envy him for it.

"Because," he says, a small smile on his lips. "You were the only one who treated me like a human."

The smile disappears from his face after uttering those words, and my heart sinks to hear them. "The others... they can be... cruel... But you mustn't..."

"It takes a lot more than a few nasty words to hurt me, Huntress," he interjects. "We Lycans are used to them. They go in one ear and out the other... But our only chance of making it to the Deadlands just sank. So I figured, what the hell, if I'm going to die out here, I might as well do it with someone who doesn't hate me for what I am," he laughs.

"We aren't going to die."

"Is that so? Pray tell, how do we survive this? Because last I checked, you don't even know how to swim, and we don't even know how many miles we are from a piece of dry land."

"We need to find the others... Dane... Dane will know what to do," I say, finally getting my breath under control.

"Dane was under deck when Sun Treader went down... Him and all the other Hunters. As far as I can tell, that asshole up there is the only other survivor," Cur says, pointing up at the sky. I follow his finger and spot Ghost's red eyes as he darts across the air above, silently searching the waters for any sign of survivors.

"Ghost!" I shout, raising my good arm to waive so he can see us.

"He knows we are here," Cur whispers as the ex-Godhand looks down at me. Cur continues, "Six... That's how many times he's looked at us since I pulled you to the surface... I've been counting."

Ghost looks away, almost as if he's in search of something better. "What's he doing?" I ask in disbelief, trying to rationalize the bloodsucker's behavior.

"Looking for better prospects, I assume," Cur states bluntly, like the idea of betrayal is nothing new to him.

"I know you see me!" I scream at the top of my lungs. Ghost doesn't bother turning around to acknowledge my existence.

"Forget that guy," Cur says, hugging me tighter. I can feel his legs kicking tirelessly beneath us, though he doesn't pant in the slightest. "Let's hear that plan... How are we going to make it out of here alive, huh?"

"No, fuck that," I growl, unable to express my emotions properly. "These fuckers have treated me like nothing more than a little groupie since I was recruited. I'm going to prove—"

"Do you know why I'm here?" Cur interrupts me, not willing to hear out my frustrations. "I mean, do you know why I'm the one being forced to sojourn with you Hunters, to serve as your tracker?"

"No," I answer, unsure what this has to do with Ghost's betrayal. "I, erm..."

"I killed a very wealthy man... A very important man... And I got caught... And I got sentenced to death for my actions... Only, the thing is... I wasn't actually the one who killed him." Cur's eyes are like the black sky above; I can see nothing but my reflection as I stare into them. It isn't that they are voids, it's that they are the opposite. Eyes that have seen darkness, and therefore adopted that darkness in order to fit in. Eyes burned by darkness, and yet, they possess inside them an infinite good. Almost like if I stare hard enough, past the facade he displays to the outside world, I'll see a gateway into a beautiful being—a man who desperately wants to be loved, even though he's only ever experienced hate.

"What do you mean... Who killed him then?" I stutter, mesmerized by his brutal, meaningful stare.

"My little brother," he says, smiling. There is a scar that cuts through the side of his lips, like a lightning bolt separating two clouds. When he smiles, I can't help but stare at it. "The man's name was Archibald the IV... He came from a long line of people who get what they want because they have more money than the king has power. Scorpos is ruled by the Areopagus on paper, but it has its own silent kings, and this man was one of them... Anyway, Archibald the IV had... dark desires, to put it tamely.

"One day, I came home to my parents crying... I'd never seen them do that before... It was so... surreal. And here was me, a Lycan in a family of humans... It was like I could almost smell what was wrong before they told me—like I could piece together exactly what had happened and envision it from the faintest twitch of my nose. I smelled the stench of intruders, the pheromones of my frightened brother, the sweat from an ensuing struggle... I didn't need my parents to tell me... I knew people from the Scorpos Temple had come and taken my brother...

"So without saying a single word, I left before my parents even noticed I was home. I left them to continue crying helpless tears, and I followed the putrid scent the kidnappers left on the wind—followed it all the way to the Scorpos Temple. But by the time I got there, Archibald the IV had already gotten his hands on my brother, and my brother had made him pay dearly.

"The brothel room was covered in Archibald's blood... My brother had bitten his... Well, I'll spare you the details... But when I arrived, I found my brother shivering in the corner of the room, naked, covered in blood. Archibald's body lay on the bed, dead and dismembered... It was like a Lycan attacked him, only my brother wasn't cursed by Dagon... That's when I got the idea... The idea to frame myself for Archibald's death and help my brother run free. I cleaned the blood off his body with the bed sheets and gave him my clothes... He was so traumatized he couldn't even speak, but still, he understood what I was doing when I started covering my own body in Archibald's blood...

"I knew both of us weren't going to make it out of there alive, so I made sure he did in my place. I lowered him out through the window, and by the time Archibald's men found me, the rest was history. After they learned I'm a Lycan, it was all too easy for his elite circle to cover up Archibald's egregious sins. I was sentenced to death for killing one of the most powerful men that's ever lived, and yet, the gods had other plans for me...

"Of all the people to show up at my execution, would you believe me if I told you Silenius Sylvian arrived as they tied the noose around my neck?" Cur laughs, almost as if he's still in disbelief at the order of events. "And not only that, but he showed up for the purpose of pardoning me... It took some explaining on his end, but after telling Archibald's heirs what he had in store for me, they were almost eager to let me go...

"And that leads me to the present, Huntress. I'm here to work off the debt I owe to Silenius—the debt for saving my life. Now, I know what you're thinking... What does any of this have to do with your experience in the Hunters Corp?" Cur laughs, trying to lighten the mood from the incredibly bleak story he's told.

"The point is this... Stop trying to prove yourself, Huntress. So what if these people fail to see what you bring to the table? Who cares if they can't see how valuable you are? What will their validation give you that you don't already have? Life is so unfair, but it's the unfairness that brings us our happiest moments. My brother didn't deserve what happened to him. I don't deserve what's happened to me. And you don't deserve to be treated like you haven't earned your spot here... But you're you, and that's enough. So let them call you a bitch behind your back... Let them call me a cur to my face... Who gives a damn! Life is just as unfair to them as it is to us, even if they don't show it. All I can tell you is this... You will never be happy until you stop looking for acceptance in places you were never meant to find it."

I am utterly and inexplicably lost for words. I have never, in all my life, felt so completed by another human being. When I look in this man's eyes, when I search his face, when I feel his embrace, I feel as though I am exactly where I'm supposed to be in this world... Like all the hell I've faced, all the tribulations I've endured, were to get to this exact moment in time and space.

I am speechless; I am breathless; I am under this man's spell. When I look in his eyes, I no longer see darkness. Instead, I see the dark side of the moon, a space of misunderstood opportunity, a place only those on a dark night like tonight can appreciate. And then I see that smile—that little scar that divides his lips in two—and I feel as though all in this world will forever be okay, so long as I have those lips to stare at. They erase all the trauma from my life, as if we aren't two stranded individuals treading water after a shipwreck. I realize I want to kiss them. In fact, I've never wanted to kiss a man more than I do right now.

"I, erm... My name's Drakini," I whisper, violating the solemn oath I swore to the Hunters to never reveal the name of my past life.

"What a beautiful name," he replies, drawing ever so closely to my lips, as if he wants to taste the name I've just spoken. He whispers, "My name is—"

"Over there!" a man shouts in the distance, cutting Cur off. The man repeats, "Over there! It's Huntress and the tracker!"

I see a silent look of disappointment wash over Cur's face as I'm pulled from the moment. I look over my shoulder and gasp, shocked to see several lifeboats paddling in this direction. Standing at the front of the closest one is a man I've grown to admire in my short time in the Hunters Corp. I scream with excitement, "Dane! We're over here!"

I spin back around to lock eyes with Cur, shivering with joy. "It's Dane! He's alive! We aren't going to die out—What's wrong?" I ask, noticing the romantic gleam missing from my savior's eyes. He isn't smiling anymore, as if the discovery that we will live to fight another day is the worst news he's received all day.

"Nothing," he whispers. "It's nothing."

4

THE MASKED MAN

I feel like a sewer rat pulled from a storm drain as Dane heaves me from the ocean, wanting nothing more than to collapse on my back and feel the sturdy, solid wood of the lifeboat beneath me. But Pip, Calico, Grimes, and Whistle reside in this boat already, each of them watching me intently as I evade certain death. I'd rather die than allow them to see me express my exhaustion, so I take my seat along the side of the boat. I sulk in silence, watching as Dane pulls Cur from the water next.

"Cryin' shame, innit?" Pip grumbles under his waterlogged breath. "Snotting Creator spared this whelp and her mangy mutt while real men like Dax and Urchin and Tripwire were dragged to the bottom of the fekking abyss."

"Real men? Last I checked, real men know how to swim," I spit back out of spite, staring at Pip with enough anger to set fire to his drenched beard.

"Did you hear somethin', Calico?" Pip laughs mockingly. "I coulda swore I just heard a cunt cry!"

I stand immediately, rearing back my left hand—the one that wasn't torn from its socket minutes ago—and throttle it directly toward the bridge of Pip's bulbous nose. My intended strike comes nowhere close to its target though. It's somehow batted away by Dane as he swivels away from Cur, graceful as ever, and knocks my fist off its course, then pushes me back into my seat.

"Enough!" Dane shouts, raising his voice for the first time since I've met him. Hearing him shout makes me flinch, like I'm being disciplined by a parent who didn't birth me.

We all instinctively shrivel in our seats and stare up at our leader as his expressionless mask gazes back at us. There are only two eye slits in the metal plate that covers his face, making it impossible for us to know the emotions he truly feels. Its silver exterior reflects the dark waters that ebb around us, and I can faintly see the bloodshot in his strained eyes.

No one in our cohort has ever seen Dane's face, which led to Hunters often joking about whether or not our leader sleeps, eats, or fucks with the mask on. Sun Treader's collapse leads me to believe he does, in fact, sleep with the silver plate covering his face. It's the only reasonable explanation for him to still be wearing it after the ship crashed during his slumber. Any sane person wouldn't have thought to grab such an item once awoken to flooding water and splintering wood.

I didn't even have time to grab my own belongings from beneath the deck. My rope dart, my helm, my clothes, and my rations are all gone, never to be seen again unless this ocean should succumb to drought.

"Look around you," Dane exclaims, his anger turned to a mix of excitement and mania. "Nearly thirty men just went into the water, and this is all that remains... Don't be mistaken men, it was no coincidence we made it this far before being deterred. If the demon we've been sent to kill exists, the forces of nature won't rest until they've put us in the ground. The Creator is watching our every move, because he knows we oppose his will. But oh how he will laugh if we tear each other apart before we ever see land on the horizon. We'd be doing his job for him, and we'll have failed our nation if we let this spiral into our downfall.

"The way I see things, we have two options," Dane says, half-sighing as he brainstorms a way for us to get out of this mess. "We have seven in this boat, and we have five in the other—that's twelve in all, plus Ghost, who seems reluctant to join us down here. Now, we can sit here an squabble about how Huntress is a girl or how most children are taller than Pip, or we could get to damn work finding what we came for.

"Rest assured, this is either the beginning or the end for us. Only our actions will dictate how far we make it. Otherwise, if you are hard pressed to join Dax and Urchin at the bottom of the ocean, be my guest. Less rations for me to figure out when we reach dry land. Now, if we're done acting like children, let's get some oars in the water and start rowing.

"Ghost!" Dane shouts, directing his attention toward the air. I locate the ex-Godhand hovering above, his glowing eyes a dead giveaway in contrast to the starless sky. Unlike when I called out for Ghost's attention, the damn bloodsucker submits himself to Dane's call humbly. Dane continues, "Your life is threatened now even more than ours, my pale friend. Without Sun Treader's hull, you have no shade for concealment when the sun rises."

"You read my mind, masked man," Ghost grunts from above.

Dane instructs, "Fortunately for you, and fortunately for us, flying is much faster than floating. I'd ask you to scout ahead and seek out the Deadlands. I have a feeling they are much closer than our map suggests. Where there is resistance, there is reward, and if this isn't resistance then I don't know what is! Find land for us, conceal yourself before day breaks, then find us once more when Luna rises tomorrow."

"At once, Commander Dane," Ghost growls, dialed in on his new objective. I've seen Undead take flight before, but I've never seen one move as fast as Ghost. One second he's there, the next he's gone, which provides meaning for his moniker.

"Pip, Huntress, you're on rowing duty to begin. Whether you want to or not, you'll be friends by the time we spot land on the horizon. There's no better way to bond than through difficult, excruciating labor."

Great, I think to myself. I've just drawn the short end of the stick—literally.

5

Salmon

"Row, row, row your boat, gently down the stream..." Pip sings under his breath for the hundredth time today. I don't know if he knows I can hear him; then again, I doubt he cares. "Merrily, merrily, merrily, merrily... Life is but a dream..."

His voice dies off, utterly defeated.

It's strange to see the humor beat out of him. Though we bickered like a married couple the first few hours we rowed, the exhaustion has drained all animosity we feel toward one another.

I want more than anything to give up my oar so another can take over, but I refuse to quit before Pip does. We've entered an unspoken competition, and I've come to learn Pip is one competitive bastard. He has one of the smallest bodies I've ever seen, but his willpower seems to be the size of a giant. I guess that's how it had to be for him to be recruited by the Hunters.

Regardless, I've spent the early hours of daybreak fantasizing about Dane ordering us to hand our oars over, but he knows as well as I that this is my only chance to prove myself to Pip. The dwarf is not the kind of man who concedes to others without evidence for him to do so. Hell, maybe the pip-squeak was right about me all this time... If he can row this long without so much as getting short-winded, maybe I don't deserve to be here as much as I thought.

But I took up this undeclared challenge at a severe disadvantage. Whatever happened when my hand gripped the cargo net, my shoulder remains ruined. Not only is it so swollen that I can barely raise my arm, but jolts of pain strike my side between the ever-present, dull throb that consumes my arm like a dying flame.

Because of this, I row my side of the boat with a single hand. Funny enough, Pip noticed my use of a single hand before long and took this as some sort of challenge against his pride. Without asking the reason for my madness, he began rowing with a single hand as well, unwilling to be bested by the girl he abhors.

And so we've rowed since Dane's command to do so, and we've seen the sun rise and crest in the sky in the meantime. My ass is numb from sitting so long, and my hamstrings are so tight I fear they will soon snap. My lower back stopped aching hours ago in favor of cramping, then spasming, now screaming in protest with every movement I make.

Additionally, my rowing arm is currently in worse shape than my injured arm with how much I've required of it. My hand feels as though I couldn't open it and release the oar even if I wanted to—it has cramped into a claw only capable of moving my oar back and forth through the water and air.

Still though, I've got to give myself and Pip credit... Not only are we in a competition with one another, but so too is our boat competing with the other, which is rowed by all five of their members. Despite me and Pip not switching places with others in our boat, we have led the race against our counterparts this entire journey.

Wasp, Lullaby, Graybeard, Katana, and Seance man their lifeboat diligently, especially for men that weren't trained to be sailors, but they have no skin in the game like Pip and I. To them, rowing is merely a chore. To me and Pip, it is virtually the same as hand-to-hand combat. Every rotation of our oars is another blow. Another step closer to besting our opponent. Any time he speeds up, so do I. And any time he slows down, I maintain my speed to show him who he's dealing with.

Any time I feel weak, I look to Cur for motivation. His eyes never leave me, even though I'm not much of a sight. He watched the first bead of sweat drop from my brow, and he has watched a waterfall of perspiration transpire since then. Though his face shows no emotion, I can feel him cheering me on inwardly.

He doesn't offer to take the oar from me, as most gentlemen would... He knows me better than that—knows I would take offense at the idea of handing this opportunity to another. Somehow, Cur understands me. He knows I want to prove myself to my companions more than anything, and even though he told me not to look for acceptance in the places I'll never find it, he won't stop me from doing so now. I silently love him for that.

"Row... row... row... your boat..." Pip whispers between sucking wind, his words synched to the motion of his paddle. "Gently... down... the stream..."

"Merrily, merrily, merrily, merrily," I sing out, whimsically joining him. The pain my body feels has tipped me over the point of delirium, causing me to laugh as I finish the lyric, "Life is but a dream!"

Pip joins me in laughter for once, chuckling, "My whole life I thought women were supposed to be good singers, but you've proven me wrong! I'd drop my oar right now to cover my ears if it didn't mean I'd lose to you!"

For once, I find his insult hilarious, and I roar with laughter to communicate that. Maybe it's the exhaustion, or maybe it's a change of perspective, but the joke is too funny to not laugh. Calico, Grimes, Whistle, and even Dane join in the laughter, all of them staring at me and Pip like the crazy bastards we are.

"You know, forget Huntress, we shoulda named this one Salmon," Pip remarks, looking over his shoulder at Dane, who's sprawled out in the back of the boat.

"Oh yeah?" Dane asks, still laughing from earlier. "Why's that?"

"Heard it said once that salmon swim upstream... Must be stubborn bastards, the whole lot of them! We don't have a current fighting against us, but I'm sure that if we did, this crazy bitch would insist on rowing against it. I bet trout and bass stare at those motherfuckers like they're the craziest sons of bitches they've ever seen. I know it like I know the tip of my prick, Huntress would fit right in with a buncha salmon..."

For a second, I can't even tell if the dwarf is insulting or complimenting me. But after hours of excruciating agony, I no longer possess the ability to overthink things, so I take the words for what they're worth and move on.

I reply, "You're not so bad at rowing yourself, for a man whose feet dangle when he takes a seat."

"She strikes back!" Calico exclaims, leaning over to clap Pip on the back, which throws him from his rowing rhythm. "She's got more fire in her than that whore you bedded in Gall, eh Pip?"

"That woman wasn't a salmon, she was a fekking Grizzly, and she had the hair to prove it, believe me boyo."

"Say, Dane... What caused you to recruit this girl in the first place?" Whistle asks, his noticeable lisp accentuating his words with a slight whistle.

Dane remains laying in the back of the boat, but he twists his head slightly at the mention of his name. "I watched every single fight in the child king's tournament, and I can certifiably say that girl was the worst fighter I've ever seen... I mean, she was baaaaaad."

I blurt out, "In my defense I—"

"I wasn't done," Dane chuckles, then continues, "I saw her get her clock cleaned several times over the course of a few days. Other draftees were belliwhopping her left and right. At first, it was funny to watch. Other recruiters would make jokes about her, and I'd share in their laughter... But what wasn't funny was how she always got back up... The laughter always seemed to die down when she got her feet back under her. The air would get tense as recruiters wondered how many hits she could take and keep going. Some of them would place bets on whether or not she'd give up, and I made a pretty penny betting she wouldn't.

"But everything changed the day she showed up to the arena, got the shit beat out of her, and then proceeded to fell an opponent twice her size... The recruiters, myself included, thought it was a fluke. Some random stroke of luck she'd never replicate... But then," Dane says, almost in a whisper as he sits up slowly, drawing everyone into his story. "But then, she came out the next day and won again... And the next day, again... And again... It's like she was Undead, the way she started winning after she tasted first blood. And it wasn't just the result of her duels that changed, the girl had turned into a fucking maniac on the battlefield.

"She'd come out throwing daggers, and when that got too easy, she started whirling them around on a chain. It was like a demon possessed the girl all of a sudden; I didn't even recognize her compared to the fighter she was days before. So needless to say, I started keeping tabs on her, started following her in her spare time...

"I came to discover she spent every waking moment in the practice fields, drilling her techniques against imaginary opponents. It was the most bizarre thing I've ever seen, and I hunt Lycans and Undead for a living. More than that, it was like she thought she wasn't alone... I'd catch her talking to people that weren't there, blocking blows from invisible assailants, disregarding the target dummies in favor of striking empty air... It was almost laughable, but her obsession and weirdness shaped her into the best fighter in her military sector...

"And then I saw something I wasn't supposed to see," he admits, his voice trailing off.

My face blushes and my growling stomach sinks as I sense where this is going. I want to cut him off, but I want to hear the true reason he decided to recruit me, so I bite my tongue and shut my mouth.

"I followed her the night before the draftees were sent to Skaar—her and her Arms Master snuck out of their military sector to spy on the Undead candidates in the north, I suppose so she could see what she'd be up against... Well, an Undead draftee caught them, but it wasn't just any Undead draftee... It was Count Viren's son, Ventur."

Cur leans over and whispers in my ear, "Take a look at Pip."

I twist my head and realize the dwarf has completely ceased all rowing, massaging his arm as he leans close to hear Dane's words. I can't believe my eyes... Am I hallucinating? His oar is resting in his lap. It's motionless. I've won the challenge, and my continued rowing is causing our boat to turn off course.

"This girl right here," Dane says, a shiver of pride in his voice, "This girl had the balls to challenge Ventur to single combat, despite never fighting against an Undead in all her life, despite getting the shit beat out of her by mere humans only days before... And not only that... This girl right here, a girl from a town no one has ever heard of, single-handedly beat the Count's son—beat him so bad that he never spoke of the altercation to his species out of sheer embarrassment.

"And that was the night, my friends, I knew our team had to have her as our newest recruit."

"Ah fek," Pip grunts, picking up his oar and shoving it into Calico's chest. "Nobody told me I was rowing against a crazy person... Joke all you want, I yield." The dwarf utters the words and immediately collapses, rolling onto the lifeboat's ground in defeat. He lays beside me, staring up at me with a look of bewilderment as I continue my rowing. Dane's story broke him. Hearing about my insanity stole his will to compete—shattered his soul.

"You gave it a good shot," Calico laughs, claiming his seat next to me. "Her inner demons are just mightier than yours, and that's all there is to it."

I continue rowing, relishing the pain and numbness that flashes through my body.

6

APOLOGIES

"I yield," Calico relents, dropping his oar. He looks at me with his separately-colored eyes—one blue, the other brown. His body is beyond soaked with sweat, the droplets cover his skin like early morning dew on a blade of grass. "Do what you want, girl, but you have nothing to prove anymore. There's little point exhausting yourself to the brink of death before we ever reach the Deadlands..."

"He's right, Huntress," Cur whispers, touching my back tenderly, but my body is too numb to register the sentiment.

I don't reply to either of them. Instead, I close my eyes and wait for Whistle to take up the oar. In all honesty, I stopped feeling pain hours ago. The monotonous rhythm of rowing has turned me into an automaton. At this point, I fear if I stop all movement, my body will cramp up and die, like a grasshopper who can no longer hop or a fish who can no longer swim.

Either way, there are only a few more hours left in the day.

"Listen to the mutt, Huntress," Pip grunts, still-half asleep. He's spent Calico's rotation resting and recovering from his battle with me, but he wasn't surprised in the slightest to still see me at it when he awoke. "The Wendigo will respect you no less for conceding... Besides, your shoulder needs tendin' to... Looks like a fekking watermelon."

"Huntress," Dane says, crossing the boat to be by my side. "Pip isn't wrong; we need to take a look at that shoulder. We brought you on this journey to throw daggers, not to watch you drop dead from rowing. Tell me, can you feel this?"

A jolt of pain strikes the right side of my body, causing me to drop my oar immediately. I spin around like a feral cat backed into a corner, hissing in pain as I attempt to defend myself against whatever entity attacks me.

But when I turn, I see no attacker.

In fact, nothing has struck the right side of my body at all.

Hovering over me is Dane, and all he's done is press his index finger to my throbbing shoulder. I look up at him, embarrassed by my guttural reaction. The injury is worse than I thought, if his mere touch was able to make me feel like I've been pierced by an arrow.

What would Wisteria think of me, watching me refuse to give up this oar as if my life depends on my pride remaining intact? Would she applaud me for taking a stand against these men who underestimate me? Or would she call me foolish, because every ounce of energy I spend now is one wasted?

"It's dislocated," Dane confirms, removing his finger. His feet stagger slightly, my violent reaction causing the boat to rock beneath us.

In truth, I don't know what that means. I've heard of bones breaking and muscles tearing, but this 'dislocated' Dane speaks of is foreign to me. It sounds bad, whatever it is, but I'm too tired to care and my throat is too dry to question.

"Luckily for you, your newest friend Pip just so happens to double as our medical assistant," Dane says, looking to the dwarf. Pip chuckles at the irony, cracking his knuckles as he rises from his slumber. I lock eyes with him, and something on my face causes Pip to blush.

"I have no love for that look in her eyes," he laughs nervously. "I can reset the shoulder, but I'd ask the fleabag to hold her back so she doesn't bite me."

Cur, upon hearing fleabag, rises from his seat. But he doesn't look to Pip, nor does he approach me. Instead, he lifts his nose to the air and sniffs, like a dog trying to find a suitable place to piss. At first, his nose twitches ever so slightly, then becomes aggressive as he snorts the atmosphere as if it's a drug.

Our boat is motionless now that Calico and I have both ceased in our rowing, but our companion boat has a considerable gap to close before catching us, so we remain content in the idleness.

"What is it boy? What do you smell, Lassie?" Pip mocks, talking in a high pitch voice like an owner calling out to their pet. Cur disregards the questions completely, his nose transfixed at whatever scent he's locked onto.

"You don't... Do you not smell that?" he mumbles, his senses seemingly transporting his conscience to another place altogether. I swivel toward the direction his nose points but see nothing but open ocean extending to the horizon.

Just as I look off in the distance, Cur shouts, "Now!"

Cur's hands shoot around my neck and torso as Pip grabs my right wrist, jerking my arm vertically and rotating it externally. I let out a vicious scream as a suctioning pop sounds from my shoulder. After hours of not speaking and sufficient deprivation of water, the howl floods from my diaphragm and becomes a demonic screech by the time it leaves my mouth. Pins and needles attack my arm, feeling as if an army of fire ants march along my skin. But after the initial shock subsides, the immense pain I've felt lifts almost instantly. Although my shoulder has no lungs, it almost feels as if Pip's jerking movement has allowed it to breathe once more.

I look down the length of my arm at the dwarf, who still holds my wrist reluctantly. His face has a humorous expression of horror and whimsy, as if he's trying to measure the anger I feel toward him.

Cur and Pip release me simultaneously, both backing away as I stare down at my hand, flexing it. I bend my elbow several times, then rotate the injured arm cautiously, flinching slightly as it clicks dully with every rotation.

"Well?" Pip asks, requesting feedback for his procedure.

I run my hand over the injury from my collarbone to my bicep, squeezing the swollen, bruised muscle. I whisper, my voice hoarse, "Much better... Thank you."

"You'll be back to throwin' 'em daggers in no time... Hopefully this suffices as my apology for... ya know, bein' sucha dick and what not."

"As I live and breathe," Dane remarks in astonishment. "Did I just hear Pip apologize for his wrongdoings?"

"Never in all my years did I think we'd hear such a thing," Whistle shouts gleefully. "Look to the sky, there must be pigs flying!"

Dane laughs, then continues, "If I knew all it took was a little friendly competition to earn your respect Pip, I would have had the girl challenge you to a duel the night we recruited her!"

"Woah, woah, woah, let's not get carried away here," Pip shouts defensively. "Her rowin' this damn boat in no way means she's a better fighter than me, not one bit! I'd bet on my axe over her chains any day of the week, ya hear? All I'm sayin' is... The girl's got gusto, and gusto's something we need more of 'round here."

This makes me laugh, though the laugh sounds like more of a low whimper because of my exhaustion. "Did you two... plan that distraction?" I ask, my voice croaking.

Cur and Pip look at each other, smiling stupidly. "Twas the fleabag's idea... The mangy mutt isn't half so bad as I've treated him either, and for that, he has my apology as well."

Despite using two derogatory terms in the same sentiment, Cur claps Pip on his shoulder, replying, "Considering how hard it was for you to say that, all is forgiven."

"A two for one special!" Calico shouts. "Say, while you're at it, I don't suppose you want to apologize for that business back in Bloodhaven, eh?"

"I'd sooner pick up that oar and go head to head with Huntress again," Pip says. "I shoulda won that game of Tichu and you know it. Damn God-hand bloodsuckers were countin' cards, so there ain't nothin' to apologize for."

"Cur?" I ask, staring at the tan-skinned man as his feet carry him to the front of the hull. Once more, his nose is lifted to the sky, sifting through the salty aroma of the sea. Pip and Calico's laughter dies down as everyone stares at the Lycan. I, on the other hand, stare at him hesitantly, looking around me to ensure another trap isn't being set to restrain me.

But there is no one lurking behind me this time, and even Dane averts his mask's hollow eyes in favor of watching the tracker do what he was employed for.

"Ice..." Cur mutters, mostly to himself, then continues, "Permafrost... Bitter cold... Damp earth... Hemlock... Yew... Juniper..."

"What is that, another language?" Pip remarks, looking around in confusion.

"It's land," Cur replies. He lowers his nose, staring off at the vast expanse of water. He turns to face us, a serious expression on his face. "I don't know how far away it is, but I smell land."

My stomach sinks as the words set in. This whole time, all I've been focused on was one stroke of my oar after another. I'd convinced myself reaching land was a problem I'd face another day. But now that it's become more real, my anxiety rises. Somewhere out there, close enough for Cur to detect, there is an uncharted wilderness lurking...

And after reaching its edge, there's no telling what monsters will be waiting for us.

7

ABOMINABLE SNOWMAN

"Sweet mother of Sylvian," Calico gasps as our boat strikes a layer of ice and comes to a standstill.

"Don't think we're in Areopagus anymore," Pip whispers, frost leaving his words to linger in the air.

The stalemate doesn't surprise me, considering we've waded through thin sheets of it for the past hour. The fact that we've reached a point where it is so thick that our hull can't break it, though, frightens me slightly.

Being from Fyrefell, there are many things in this world I've never seen. Snow falling from the sky to pile atop a frozen ocean, though... Well that's something none of us have ever seen.

Shivers run down my sweat-soaked back. My nipples harden like gemstones, peering through my entirely too-thin shirt like a set of eyes peering out into the world. I cross my arms across my chest to cover them and bury my hands under my armpits to preserve what little warmth they have left.

Calico lifts his oar and smacks it against the ice, leaving us to listen to a reverberating echo play endlessly in the distance like a low hum. Dane lifts his foot over the side of the boat and places it cautiously against the impervious ice, shifting his weight slowly, then all at once. As he gets both his feet on solid ground, he turns to us and announces, "I think we know now why they call it the Deadlands."

"I have never smelled anything like this before in my life," Cur remarks, snow crunching as his feet leave the boat. He looks around at the frozen desert, likely comparing it to Scorpos in his head.

I can see the goosebumps on the back of his neck. Cur was raised in unbearable heat, and now the gods have brought him to a place where the sun seemingly ceases to exist. Snow literally floats in the air, hanging suspended in curtains so thick it's impossible to see our surroundings.

It reminds me of a snow globe mother gifted me years ago—a little sphere of glass filled with some magical liquid that left flakes of fake snow floating over an apple orchard.

Lightning illuminates a mountainous range in the distance, but it does not strike the peaks like ordinary storms in the Areopagan Kingdom. Instead, it falls slowly from the clouds, almost like rivets of water falling from some portal amidst the stratosphere. The particles of ice hanging in the air cause the strikes to scatter in all directions, igniting the atmosphere with hues of purple and orange and yellow.

Thunder erupts not long after, sounding like war drums pounding to announce our arrival.

Again, chills barrage me. "What do you smell?" I ask, locking eyes with Cur's concerned bewilderment. He wasn't scared when we floated in the middle of an ocean as our ship sank, dragging any chance of survival into the depths. But now, I see incomprehensible fear written on Cur's face for the first time.

"Frozen death... But also..." Cur closes his eyes and shuffles across the arctic tundra, his nose somehow communicating things to him our eyes can't see. "I can smell a struggle nearby... Frozen sweat... Panic... It's Ghost, your Godhand friend... Yes, that's his scent... Frankincense and myrrh, like an underground crypt..."

"What do you mean?" Dane asks, his silver-plated mask starting to freeze over as condensation collects from his breath. His face is the only one I can't see, but if it's anything like the other Hunters', I'm almost glad it's concealed. It's one thing to see my companions trying to swallow their fears—but our leader needs to remain composed in uncertain situations like this.

"I can't be certain right now," Cur says, his inhalations snorting snowflakes from the air, causing his nose to quickly turn beet red. "I need to follow it to its origin, but something happened last night when he arrived. Someone... Or some thing... Found him... And whatever it was, it wasn't friendly."

"Lo, Hunters!" Graybeard calls from the ocean, their boat cracking a thin sheet of ice as it chugs steadily toward the frozen embankment. Seance and Lullaby row steadily until their hull thuds against a partition of glacier. "Bit cold for my liking out here... My old bones have a hard enough time getting around as it is. Always get a bad feeling in my hips and knees in weather like this!"

Graybeard used to have Dane's position as leader of the Hunters, or that's what I heard Pip and Calico discussing once. But this is not a group of men that will follow someone after their health deteriorates, and Graybeard is twenty years past his prime. I've never heard him speak without mentioning something about his arthritis or locking joints.

Seance and Lullaby stand at the same time, each of them breaking their oars over their knees. They toss the severed paddles to the side, leaving only the sharpened handles to serve as makeshift spears. This is not their first rodeo, and although we lost our weapons and supplies when Sun Treader went down, these are men who know how to turn ordinary objects into lethal munitions.

Dane pulls his trademark hand-cannons—things he calls revolvers—from their holsters, ejecting a chamber in their center, each one filled with cartridges that fire when he pulls the revolver's trigger. The weapons are things I'm told he built himself, unlike anything I've ever seen a fighter employ in battle. I've watched him put them to use in practice fields multiple times, each time equally as mesmerized by their abilities.

They have the deadly accuracy of a crossbow or sling, but they can fire seven shots successfully before needing to be reloaded. One is loaded with cartridges made from wood, the other with forged silver. With each of these hand-cannons, Dane is always prepared to face off against an Undead or Lycan, whichever crosses his path.

After spinning the center chamber of each hand-cannon to ensure it has seven rounds, he shoves them back in their holsters and moves to face us as Graybeard's retinue joins us on solid ground.

"Our tracker has picked up Ghost's scent on the frigid air, and his senses detect our Undead companion is in trouble, and I for one think we have lost enough Hunters for one trip. Ready yourselves... There's no telling what waits for us out there."

"If I may, Dane," Wasp interjects, "Must we move heaven and earth to find the Godhand? Last I checked, he's never stuck his neck out for a single one of us, and now you're asking us to risk our remaining troop to save the same monster we once hunted."

"Aye, I agree with Wasp," Pip grunts somberly. "The bloodsucker betrayed his own species to evade us outside Bloodhaven... If foreign hostiles snatched him up, we could be walkin' straight into their trap."

"I say we look for shelter... Night is coming, and if it's this cold during the day, the frost will nip at our fingers and toes until they turn black," Calico adds.

"If Nightfall taught me anything, it's that winter is merciless," Graybeard says, raising his sword hand to reveal two fingers missing. "And this cold here is ten times as bitter as it was there. We need fire... Need food an' water... Need—"

"You aren't leader anymore," Dane declares, pressing his gloved finger into Graybeard's chest. "Regardless of what you think about Ghost, he's one of us, and he possesses abilities we can't replicate. He can fly, he can scout, he can find shelter and resources in places our feet can't carry us. If we seek shelter for the night, the snow will cover any chance Cur has at tracking him down."

"And what if we're following the tracks of a dead man?" Wasp rebuts. "What then?"

"We can answer that question here and now," Dane says, his expressionless mask looking to Seance.

Without needing to be told what to do, Seance takes his sharpened oar and pierces his palm with its tip, then flexes his numb fingers to summon blood. It trickles slowly from the laceration, then covers his fingers as he clenches his fist. The eery man kneels to the ground, pressing his bloody hand against the snow-packed ground. Seance has always been a man of few words, so I listen intently as he displays the reason behind his nickname.

Over the howl of hail and distant thunder, he whispers:

"Take my blood as offering, oh spirits of the dead,

I ask a favor, therefore I have bled,

Are there any among you who hear my call?

Consume my blood, become my thrall..."

I stand in silence as anticipation creeps through my veins. Seance is what Dane referred to as a Necromancer—someone trained to speak to the dead. These men, Cur excluded, have all seen him use this power before, but this is the first time he's attempted something like this with me present.

At first, nothing happens. I inhale deeply, realizing I've unintentionally held my breath as I await some spectacle that defies the natural order of the world. The frozen air stings my lungs and makes me regret this unconscious decision instantly.

"Spirits of the dead, come join our sphere,

Make yourself known...

Any who hear,

Make yourself shown."

Lightning flashes as Seance utters the final words. The ice where his hand touches cracks, splitting in two as the ground beneath us shakes violently. Dane shouts Seance's name as the ground shatters beneath the Necromancer, sending him plummeting into the waters below.

I'm thrown from my feet as fissures separate the ice, severing it and causing it to split into separate icebergs. I thud violently against my injured shoulder, causing me to shriek. The falling snow whirls into a cyclone before us as we grow separated, the icecaps we stand upon drifting from one another.

It's hard to see through the raging blizzard, but as I lift my head and squint my eyes, I see the shape of a figure start to form from the atomic ice particles. A geyser of water shoots from the pool that consumed Seance, carrying with it his half-drowned body.

"These are the Deadlands, fickle man," a dissonant voice booms from inside the tornado of hail. "If you ask a favor of the dead here, so too will we ask a favor of you."

"Close the door, Seance!" Dane screams as the sub-freezing water throws him against a glacier. The Necromancer screams as the water continues to pound against his body, holding him perpendicularly pinned against the wall of ice. The blizzard slowly subsides, revealing an abomination made from nothing more than clumps of snow and ice, almost as if some demon has built a perverted snowman to use as its puppet.

"Looking for your red-eyed friend, I see," the abomination growls, contemplating the situation as the arctic waters drain the life from Seance with each passing second. "I don't know what part of the world you hail from, but here in the Deadlands, we dead do not serve as your errand boy."

"Release him!" Dane shouts, the only one of us to still be on his feet after the ice split. The abominable snowman twists his head whimsically as he stares at our fearless leader. His body is humanoid, composed of thorny tendrils of ice. His exterior looks like that of an armored knight whose body froze over an eon ago—a poorly chiseled ice sculpture meant to stand guard over this land like a troll protecting its bridge. Its shoulders and forearms are spiked with icicles large enough to impale a saber-toothed tiger. Its helm glows iridescent blue, like the shimmering waters reflecting the ice we stand upon.

"I see through that mask, feeble man. You may hide from these mortals, but there is no hiding from me, and there will certainly be no hiding from Steppenwolf. Go back to whatever land you've come from; that will be your last warning."

"Steppenwolf? Who is Steppenwolf!" Dane asks, though it is much more of a scream than a question.

"Your Undead companion was taken by the Ra-El," the elemental beast replies coldly, completely disregarding Dane's solicitation. "He has not joined our legions of the dead... Not yet, that is. But that may change by night fall, depending on how fast you find him... You there, girl," he says, his voice booming as he points to me of all people. "Those eyes of yours... Who gave you the Seer-Sight?"

I look around, as if I'm not the only girl present. So much is happening all at once... My senses are overloaded with what's transpired, and now this thing—this monster of ice and snow that materialized from thin air—is speaking to me, asking me questions I don't have the answers to.

I stutter, "I... erm... I don't..."

"Trust your instincts, Worthy One. This land has a way of deceiving mortal eyes. Beware your enemies, but beware also those closest to you! Do not trust the man with the double-headed coin... We wait for you in Draemir, we who suffer eternally. Lean not on your own understanding, and you might just make it out of here alive," he states plainly, like he hasn't just spoken on matters I'm incapable of comprehending. "Now, I've answered the Necromancer's question, so I will take him as my reward."

In the blink of an eye, whatever invisible force holds together this monster's bodice vanishes, leaving the ice and snow to lose its form and fall to the ground. In that same instant, the water which pins Seance to the glacier envelopes his body completely and sucks him back into the ocean without even a second for him to scream out.

I have no idea what to think, nor am I given time to process the elemental warrior's words. Seer-Sight... Steppenwolf... Draemir... Double-headed coin... None of it makes any sense! The prophetic words are like the key to a lock I haven't discovered, but I don't have time to focus on them.

Dane lunges frantically for Seance's flailing hands as they're pulled beneath the broken ice, but the water's current rips him from our sight before Dane can even reach the icy edge. The water bubbles, then goes still. We sit in silence for a long moment, each one of us in utter shock at what we've just seen.

The Deadlands have claimed the first of our forces, and deep down we each know this won't be the last life we lose to this hellish place.

8

DIVISION

"Fine, if no one else wants to bring up the goddamn elephant in the room, I'll do it!" Pip shouts as we trudge through the wintery wasteland, our beaten and battered troop putting their faith in Cur's sense of smell to lead us to safety. "We just watched one of our own get fekking sucked into the arctic by a... Fek if I know what that fekking thing was—a fekking snow demon!"

"I didn't sign up for this bullshit, man," Wasp whines, his teeth chattering. "Lycans and Undead, that's who I signed up to be hunting! Now the child king has us out here searching for boogeymen and tall-tales! That silver-eyed brat signed away our lives to come out here and freeze our cocks off!"

"Never seen the dead treat Seance like that," Lullaby mumbles to himself. "Never seen one so much as threaten him... This one just..."

"Swallowed him whole," Katana finishes, speaking up on behalf of the soft-spoken man. "And what was that bit about the girl's eyes? Demon was speaking about Huntress like he knew her... Called her the Worthy One..."

"Worthy of rowing a damn boat, that much I can tell you," Pip shouts, massaging his arms and shoulders as he recalls our competition.

"I told ya, Dane. I hate to say it, but I told ya," Graybeard interjects. "Ya made Seance go sticking his nose in an afterlife it didn't belong. Now he's food for whatever fish ain't frozen."

"Didn't sign up for this shit," Wasp repeats. The chattering of his teeth makes me feel ten degrees colder alone.

"What will you do now that you feel like prey?" Dane asks, turning from Cur's side to face us. We stop in our tracks, thoroughly divided by this place within minutes of arriving. It's reminiscent of the tournament, where Undead fought Undead and humanity belliwhopped humanity. Dane continues, "Will you act as prey does and run? Will we leave behind our slower counterparts so the faster may survive?"

"We ain't prey, damnit!" Graybeard shouts, his beard shaking the icicles that cling to his chin. "We need fire! Food! Shelter, damn you!"

"Has it not occurred to you these natives have everything you just listed?" Cur asks, speaking for the first time since we left our boats.

"I don't remember asking for your stinking opinion, fleabag," Graybeard spits, the frost from his breath traveling through the air to deliver the insult personally.

"Oooo, good one," Cur mocks. "Your words would almost sting if you hadn't spent every waking moment bitching, old man. Dagon's sake, you sound like a damn baby."

"What'd you say to me, dicklicker?" Graybeard says, stepping up to defend his honor.

"Oh, I'm sorry," Cur laughs. "I forgot old people are hard of hearing. I said you sound like a bitch with all your complaining!"

"I'll have your tongue for—" Graybeard shouts as he charges toward Cur, swiftly met by Pip and Dane standing as a barricade in front of the tracker. Together, the two take hold of Graybeard as he writhes to break free, shouting curse words at the Lycan like their utterance will bring him warmth. The struggle is put to an end when Pip shoves the man's hips, causing his feet to slip out from under him. Graybeard falls to the ground, panting and defeated.

"Even you, Pip? You'd take this mangy mutt's side over one of your own?" Graybeard sighs, his pride hurt in more ways than one.

"Don't do this, old man. Yer attackin' the wrong people."

"Wrong people?" Graybeard laughs. "Didn't seem they were the wrong people in the Neverglades, when you wet your axe with the blood of a dozen moondancers no more innocent than this cur you protect."

"That was different an' you know it," Pip defends. "Just cuz you lost a few digits in Nightfall doesn't mean the rest of us are scared of a lil snow. Where are yer balls, geezer? They fall off when Dane took yer spot? Eh?"

"Enough!" Dane shouts, the ice on the face of his mask forming a frown. "Tell me, Graybeard and Wasp, what difference does it make what direction we travel anyway? Look around you! We can't see more than fifty feet in any direction! What difference does it make if we follow Cur's smell over wandering aimlessly in hopes of finding shelter? If you know a surer path to guaranteed firewood, please, by all means, take the lead!"

Wasp and Graybeard look at each other as all those who've abstained from this argument watch intently for their response.

"No takers?" Dane asks as silence leaves us to listen to the whistling wind. "I didn't think so... Now get off your ass and fall in line, soldier. You've still got a few good fingers left—it'd be a shame to see you lose your ability to hold a sword, considering that's the only reason we brought you along in the first place."

9

APPLE ORCHARD

The sun has set, as it is so often prone to do. With its disappearance, the darkness sinks its freezing fangs into our ill-clothed bodies.

I can no longer feel any semblance of pain in my shoulder or back, nor in any inch of my body. The vicious cold has injected my limbs and joints with numbness. We Hunters move like tortoises through slippery mud.

I fantasize inwardly of summer, my mind no longer able to remember what it feels like to collapse with heat exhaustion. I would cut off and sell my left tit at this point just to feel the sun's kiss on my skin. Hell, I'd cut off and sell both tits for the chance to be burned by overexposure to daylight, something I once cursed in a past life as I lathered aloe to heal my stinging flesh.

I think about the feeling of a scalding bath and a warm bowl of broth. A thick quilt and fur pelts to wrap around my body.

My entirely too-thin thermal has frozen stiff atop my upper half, the sweat that soaked it from rowing now frozen solid like rigid cardboard. My face is burned by the wind's anger, and I'm forced to shift between inhaling through my nose and mouth, the bitter sting of the air making breathing unbearable.

Luckily, Graybeard and Wasp have stopped their complaining for some time now. Whether that's because of Dane's ridicule or because the winter has frozen their jaws shut, I'm unsure. We move in silence, everyone keeping their negative thoughts shoved deep inside their minds, no longer having the energy to protest every rusted step we take.

The snow drifts we trudge through have reached my waistline, meaning they nearly extend to Pip's neck. The dwarf grunts angrily as he fights against the tightly-packed snow. It would be easier for him to just walk behind someone taller, mooching off their progress. But Pip's pride is too great to profit off another's march, so he deliberately punches and kicks and tackles the snow out of his way like a beetle rolling an insurmountable boulder of dung.

"There," Cur wheezes, pointing in the distance. Steam rises from his shirtless figure. Quite a while ago, the Lycan tore his shirt from his body, insisting it was doing little more than trapping him in ice. A Lycan's average body temperature, I've gathered, is much warmer than a human's. Vapor lifts from Cur's skin as snow strikes him, melting almost instantly, then evaporating back into the hostile climate. Our tracker continues, "That is where Ghost's scent leads..."

Only a few dozen yards away, in the space where our vision becomes blocked by the blizzard is an odd landmark. Rising from the snow dunes as a perversion of nature are several trees made from nothing but ice. I try to swallow, but the saliva inside my mouth has long been too frozen to warm my throat. My heartbeat quickens as we approach the few dozen trees, only to see that it is actually an entire forest as the blizzard subsides.

"Drakini!" a voice calls to me from the forest's threshold. Hearing my true name spoken aloud ignites something inside me I forgot existed. I look around, only to realize my fellow Hunters have disappeared. So too has the snow vanished. I'm no longer standing in dunes of ice, and violent cyclones of hail no longer bombard me. Instead, I'm standing in a lush meadow as a gentle, midnight breeze kisses my neck.

"Where... I don't... Where am I?" I whisper to myself as I spin, searching for some trace of Cur, then Dane, then Pip. My companions have faded from existence it seems, leaving me to peer in confusion at the one who calls my name.

My heart sinks as my eyes lock on the man standing at the base of a beautiful, blossoming apple tree.

"Dad?"

10

COMFORTABLE LIES

"Oh, my precious daughter!" he shouts as a woman approaches his side, a woman I haven't seen since I was a little girl—my mother.

"Drakini," she sighs in relief, holding her arms out for me to join her.

"Mu-mom?" I stutter in disbelief.

What the hell is happening?

One moment, I'm freezing to death in the arctic tundra. The next, everyone I came to the Deadlands with melts away with the snowy landscape, replaced by two people from my past that I watched get murdered firsthand.

I stumble forward like a mouse who's spotted cheese in a place it shouldn't exist, likely knowing there's a spring-loaded trap ready to snap its neck if it bites down on the temptation.

I had nearly forgotten what my mother looked like, what her voice sounded like. But now that she's standing before me, memories of the woman flood my mind like she was alive only yesterday.

"Am I... Am I dead?" I ask, staring at the ghosts who await me eagerly on the apple orchard's tree line.

"Dead?" father repeats, chuckling as he wipes away tears of happiness. "Don't be silly, my sweet girl! Your mother and I have been waiting for you here... We can finally be together!"

"Nothing can separate us here, darling," mother says, smiling as her open arms beg me to come closer. I pause in my procession, looking around at my surroundings once more. It is still dark out, but it almost feels like summer here. The humid atmosphere makes my skin sweat. After hours of trudging through snow, this place feels like a slice of heaven on earth. But as with all things in life, if it seems too good to be true, it likely is.

"I... I watched you die," I say, staring at my father. "Knights from the Areopagus... They killed you..."

Father frowns as I say this, looking at me like I'm crazy for reciting facts I've accepted as truth.

"Drakini... Surely you don't believe that... Come to me, we can figure all this out..."

"No," I shudder, shaking my head as tears fall down my cheeks without my permission. "No... No, none of this is real!" I bend over and run my hand through the grass, then poke the soil with my finger. "It was snow," I whisper to myself, then scream, outraged, "Dane! Cur! Anyone!"

"Lower your voice, Drakini," mother cautions, her arms still open to receive my embrace.

"I'm sorry for calling you weak, darling," father says, triggering something in my brain to overload with emotions. This man, this imposter, shouldn't know about my final conversation with my father, the one where he refused to let me go to war because I was too weak. "I was wrong, Drakini... You're not weak... You're the strongest girl I know—stronger than your mother and I combined... Now please... Just come to us..."

"Drakini?" another voice calls, causing my heart to sink a second time. I know that voice, it's one I never would've expected to hear for the rest of my life. Nikolai cheers emphatically, "What are you doing back so soon from your mission? I've missed you!"

My vision is brimmed with tears as I stare at the Undead teenager, the same one I left behind in Areopagus to embark on this expedition. He looks exactly the same as when I saw him last. His silver hair sweeps over his brows, its jagged cut revealing his optimistic, amethyst eyes. His body is covered in the armor of a Black Knight; his arm cradles a knight helm under his armpit. "Are you just going to stand there? We've been waiting for you, me and Garmin both... Garmin!" Nikolai shouts, twisting around to peer into the orchard's darkness.

From the shade of the apple grove comes a man I haven't seen since shipping off for Skaar. He stares at me with disbelief, his eyes sparkling with joy to see me once again. Garmin Vaid whispers, "Long time no see, Drakini of Fyrefell."

My legs tremble as every ounce of my body resists the urge to reunite with the four people I miss most in this world. I have sailed across the known world and landed in an uncharted nation without the slightest hope of making it back to Areopagus alive. Seeing my loved ones gathered in a place I thought I would die is enough to make my heart explode with joy...

But this isn't right...

None of this is right...

My mother and father are dead...

Nikolai and Garmin are in the Areopagus, a world away from this hellish iceland.

Garmin reaches up toward one of the trees and plucks an apple, its red exterior shining in the moonlight like a piece of candy. "You look hungry,

Drakini of Fyrefell," he says, his voice making me swoon. He tosses the apple toward me, and I snatch it from the air before it can pass over me. I examine it, mesmerized by its glistening surface. I see my reflection on its face, and I'm shocked at what I see. Peering back at me along its glassy surface is not a broken down, half-frozen girl, but instead, a well-groomed, beautiful female with my likeness.

"Take a bite," Nikolai encourages. "This fruit can give you knowledge... It has the power to remove the lies of this world, leaving nothing but the truth."

"It grants eternal joy, Drakini,'" mom says, her mouth smiling with encouragement. Dad adds, "Eat of this fruit, and you will be cured of life's many sufferings... You'll never grow tired again, never go hungry, never age, never fear..."

"We can all live forever, Drakini of Fyrefell," Garmin whispers.

Their words send chills over my body as I lift the apple slowly toward my mouth. I don't know how—I don't know why—but it feels like I'm powerless to exercise my own discretion. In this moment, I've never felt more tired, more hungry, more fearful, and this apple has just been presented as a solution to every problem I've ever encountered. If I bite into this apple, I convince myself, all of this will make sense...

I'll gain understanding...

I'll know how my mother and father are able to be here despite me watching them die....

I'll be able to spend eternity with all those I love most...

I'll never have to suffer...

I won't have to seek the approval of others...

I'll finally be... complete...

Drop the apple, Huntress, a feral voice growls from the depths of the shadowy orchard. A set of yellow, unforgiving eyes glow in the darkness, and only then do I have the strength to release the fruit from my grip, shattering this hallucination as the distorted voices of my friends and parents scream out in eternal agony.

11

HARSH REALITY

The lush orchard and inhabitable landscape breaks like glass before my eyes—all that remains from my hallucination are those feral, glowing, yellow eyes.

"Wisteria," I whisper through chattering teeth. I fall to my knees, the dense snow dune crunching beneath my weight. "I never... You... I don't..."

You created me from necessity—so you could cope with the suffering of life... Well, child, this is a time you need me by your side more than ever, she purrs sympathetically, almost like a mother would. But unlike my mother, who stood on the threshold of the forest, insisting I come to her, Wisteria leaves the ice trees behind her, approaching my frost-bitten body. She nuzzles her furry head against my own, sitting before me as I kneel in defeat. Her lush tail flicks the snow behind her, then wraps around me comfortingly.

"It felt so real," I sob, cradling my head in my hands. The gravity of the moment sets in—I realize all at once that if it hadn't been for Wisteria... I would have bitten into that apple... And only the gods know what would have happened to me if I'd chosen to give in to that moment of desperate temptation.

You will have time to cry later, Wisteria says, nudging my head with her muzzle, imploring me to look her in the eye. I lift my head, the tears along my cheeks instantly freezing. Her amber eyes are merciless in the darkness of night; they peer into the fabric of my being, gutting any semblance of fear I feel in this moment. *Your fellow Hunters need you, Drakini... They are trapped in visions of their own minds as we speak.*

I look over her shoulder at the forest of ice. The trees are no longer the fertile, regular trunks of bark and wood, as they were when my parents stood before them. Instead, they are sculpted from ice, rising from the ground like unholy perversions of nature. From their jagged branches hang glowing spheres of frozen blood, orbs which look deceptively similar to polished apples blown from glass.

At the foot of these trees are my companions, the same ones I called out for when my hallucination arose.

Cur.

Dane.

Pip.

Calico.

Whistle.

Wasp.

Graybeard.

Katana.

Lullaby.

Each one of them kneels before the forest of ice, an orb of frozen blood cradled in their hands. Their eyes are glazed over, each one of them trapped inside their own mind, each one of them seeing a vision that begs them to bite into the fruit, each one of them seeing their deepest desires brought to life as if it could become reality.

My eyes flick between them, then settle on Dane. Of all these Hunters, he is the only one who raises the frozen fruit to his lips, the only one mentally weak enough to cave to his fictitious desires. Ironically, the only thing that stops him from sinking his teeth into the glassy sphere is his silver mask, which stands as a barricade between his mouth and the fruit.

I gasp as his zombie-like body presses the apple where his mouth should be. In his current state, he's too delirious to lift the mask before trying to consume the cursed object.

"Dane!" I shout, staggering to my feet. I instantly sink several feet through snow, falling back to my arse as I'm stripped of my balance. I don't know what will happen if Dane manages to bite into the glassy apple, but Wisteria's arrival is the only indicator I need to know it won't be good.

To say I run through the snow would be a gross misstatement of my procession. I kick, flail, thrash, and tackle my way through several snow-drifts to reach Dane's kneeling body. I dive as he lifts the bottom of his mask, slapping the bloody fruit from his palm as he opens his mouth to take a bite. His mask slips back in place as I crash to the ground, huffing and puffing from the exigent circumstances.

"Huntress," Dane gasps, his hallucination fading as reality comes crash-ing back. He mutters, disoriented, "I don't... Where... I was just..."

"On your feet, soldier!" I scream, wrestling with ice to find my feet. I grab him by his cloak's collar and rip him upward, our bodies pressing together as he leans on me for strength. There's no time to explain the danger we're in, so I shove him toward Pip while I slide in Cur's direction. I order, "Knock the fruit from their hands, now!"

Whether Dane understands the purpose of my demand or not, I'm un-sure, but he certainly understands the urgency in my tone. Simultaneously, we smack the blood-apples from Pip and Cur's grip, ripping them from their eternal fantasies at the same time.

Without taking time to explain, Dane and I move to our next targets—Calico and Lullaby. We successfully strip their hands of the forbidden fruit and watch their bodies collapse as reality sets in.

"Dane!" I scream, pointing to Graybeard, who kneels furthest from us both. "Stop him!" I shout, my heart sinking as the elderly man raises the apple to his frostbitten lips. Dane sprints to save the old man, but his feet move too fast for his balance to handle. His feet slip on the ice as he changes direction, then fly out from beneath him. I watch in horror as Dane crashes to his back, the impact knocking the wind from the masked man.

Graybeard opens his mouth as Dane unholsters a hand-cannon without hesitation. I hear the revolver's hammer click back. A loud boom shakes the icy forest overhead as a cartridge fires. Graybeard closes his mouth around the apple. In the split second it takes for my racing heart to pound a single time, the bullet reaches the bloody orb, piercing it.

The frozen sphere explodes in Graybeards grasp, its bloody contents splattering against his face and beard before his teeth can sink into its exterior. If Dane's body had been positioned a few feet to the left or right, his cartridge would have blown Graybeard's brains along the snow. It was the fate of the gods alone that saved this old man's life. The gods, and Dane's unfailing aim.

Graybeard falls flat on his face as Dane rests his head against the snow, his chest heaving with adrenaline as his revolver smokes beside him.

I shuffle cautiously across the ice to reach Whistle, then Wasp, and lastly Katana. The veil of their hallucinations lift, fracturing their brains in different ways as false paradises are replaced with bitter purgatories.

"Huntress," Cur exclaims as I take in the forest's surroundings. He stands to his feet and glides against the ice until he reaches me. Without explaining himself, he places his freezing fingers beneath my chin, examining my face. "Your eyes... They've... lost their color... They're not yellow anymore..."

I remove his hand and look to Wisteria, whose eyes have stolen the amber from my irises. She paces impatiently, no one from our party able to detect her presence. She is a figment of my imagination, born from necessity and circumstance. Truth be told, this whole party is safer now that she's arrived, though they don't even know she exists.

Without her, I would've bitten into that apple—we all would have bitten into that forbidden fruit.

Before her unexpected arrival, I was beginning to lose hope of surviving this night.

But now that she's here...

As odd as it may seem...

I suddenly have the strength to endure. Something which—

Drakini, duck! Wisteria shrieks.

Without questioning the hellcat, I grab hold of Cur and drag him to the ground with me. As we fall, I feel the air inches above my head vibrate as something flies over us. A lock of my hair is cut by the razor sharp object, falling atop Cur and I as we slide across the ice.

The ice cracks to my side as the projectile meant for my head impales a snowdrift. Its wooden handle quivers from impact. I don't even have time to identify the weapon before Dane shouts, "Spears! Take cover!"

The Hunters scatter around me as the icy forest shakes violently, icicles echoing as they shatter against the quaking earth.

"Dorin lanaré!" a foreign voice bellows as a monstrous beast emerges from the forest, a human rider saddled to its back.

Veska talan!" another man cheers, twirling a fishing net over his head as his beastly steed shatters a whole tree's trunk that stands in its way.

Nara veska amir!" a third announces, yipping and hollering as the bear he rides upon lets out a gut-wrenching roar.

Cur slides his body over to the spear these attackers so graciously gifted us, ripping it from the ice. He slides in front of me, placing himself between me and the nearest adversary. Suddenly, it feels like I barely know Cur as his body language changes into something entirely animalistic. Though he hasn't shifted into his Lycan form, Cur's throat lets out a menacing, guttural growl from his stomach as the nearest grizzly bear locks eyes with him.

The grizzly's rider, a man with blood painted across his face to form foreign runes, tightens his grip on the massive bear's reins, then lashes the grizzly's hindquarters with a whip, prompting him to charge. The grizzly lets out a feral roar. Cur howls demonically, spear pointed to kill.

I want more than anything to stop what's about to happen, but I can't conjure the strength to establish peace. My lungs are frozen solid in my chest. My body is so numb that I can't tell if my limbs still obey my brain. No matter how hard I flex my fingers, feeling won't avail itself. I am helpless, I realize. For the first time in a long time, I'm helpless. Without Cur, I would have no way of surviving this beast's lethal intent.

They charge one another as Dane's hand-cannons echo in the distance.

The grizzly's massive paw swats at Cur, breaking his spear in half, then sending his body flying.

Blood splatters in my eyes, blinding me.

I fall to my knees.

I fall to my knees, and for the first time in my life, I pray to the gods for help.

12

NAKED & AFRAID

O ur bodies hang upside down like pieces of jerky slow-roasting over a fire.

By the time I come to, my head is already pounding from the surplus of blood that floods my temples.

A warm draft washes over me, instantly making me aware of my naked-ness, which causes me to cover my chest with my bound hands.

We Hunters who've survived the attack sway in the open air, each one of us stripped of clothes and put on for display like dangling ornaments from the cave's ceiling. Below us are shimmering, aquamarine waters which exude steam like a freshly drawn bath. I don't know much about how or when we got here, but I'm able to piece together our surroundings.

This is the place Cur's nose was leading us; it is a cave of sorts, though it looks more like an underground kingdom than a naturally eroded burrow. I can make out a horizon far in the distance—an underground horizon which reveals great temples carved from preexisting stone. But closer, much closer, is an embankment where this natural spring meets a wall of stone elevated several feet above it, suggesting that those who fall in these waters will forever be trapped until their muscles yield and their lungs drown.

"Hunt...ress..." a voice moans from nearby. I twist my head and see Cur, bound by his feet much like myself. His upper torso is a ghastly mess of carved flesh and dried blood. The mere sight of it makes me nauseous, though my stomach has long run out of food to regurgitate. Tears well in my eyes as I examine his wounds—the grizzly bear's strike mauled his chest open from shoulder to opposite hip bone. Strands of severed muscle hang from him, revealing his sternum and ribcage. Flies the size of a swollen eyeball dance across his body, buzzing menacingly as they spread infection inch by inch over his wounds. His skin, once a dark shade of caramel, is ghastly white from blood loss.

"Cur," I sob, instantly choking on tears. I reach for his feverish body, cursing under my breath as my hand falls short of his comfort. I whisper to him, conjuring every ounce of bravery to dispel my fears, "Just hold on... You aren't going to die... Just stay with me..."

"Death..." he sighs, licking his scarred lips as he points toward the horizon. "I smell... death..."

I twist my body, forcing the rope that binds me to rotate toward his pointer finger's guidance. All hope of surviving this imprisonment drains from my body in a single, sob-interrupted sigh. I cover my mouth as I resist the urge to scream at what I see, inwardly whimpering at the injustice of the situation.

There, along the embankment, strung up and suspended by more than a dozen hooks, is Ghost, the Undead we risked our lives to find.

And find him we did... Or at least, found what little of him remains...

His head hangs low, unconscious with his greasy black bangs covering his face to conceal his glowing red eyes.

His back has been sculpted along his spinal cord; the flesh that once covered from his neck to tailbone is now torn and stretched to either side of him, several hooks fastened along the perimeter of canvas-tight skin. Each of his ribs, which once protected his internal organs, have been snapped outward, giving the appearance of featherless wings, almost as if the torture method has been designed to mock the Undead's ability to fly.

I choke on my tears as I see Ghost's lungs have been dragged out of his body, both of them quivering as they inflate, then deflate. Inflate, then deflate, slowly suffocating with each impossible breath.

Several dozen barbarians patrol the perimeter around the lifeless Undead, each one of them laying timber on the cavernous floor, as if they are erecting a pyre to light beneath the Undead.

You need to get out of this place, Drakini, a voice echoes from beneath me, then adds, *Your life depends on it, fearless child.*

I crane my neck toward the glowing waters below, expecting to see some semblance of my naked reflection in its surface. Instead, glimmering in the teal, glassy waters is a crimson knight, his outline distinct and undisturbed by the lake's ceiling. I moan, delirious, "Dyyyrraaannn?"

Staring into the waters is like gazing into a portal to the afterlife. Thousands, if not millions of unidentifiable souls swarm behind the crimson knight, all of them flailing—screaming as if they've been cursed to drown for all eternity, forever stuck in the split second before their lungs force them to inhale water.

"You died..." I stammer, blood pounding behind my eyes, forcing me to focus solely on my mentor's figure. "I watched you die, Dyran..."

I was killed by the Wendigo, and this is the place all souls travel once claimed by the Creator's executioner, he states, his helm's visor dark and hollow. *These natives who captured you... They worship the Wendigo—they prepare the way for its rise to power... But you, Drakini... You are the first human to ever break free of their mirage... None who've held the Arcadian Apple are able to see through its lies—its seduction. Those who hold it see paradise, and their minds become lost to their greatest desires. I didn't see the power you possess when I was living, but now, in the afterlife—I see the strings of fate which have chosen you, which have guided you to this foreign nation, which have instilled you with the ability to disobey this perverted nature.*

"Even if I understood what you're saying, which I don't," I whisper angrily under my breath, frustrated by my ignorance to his words. Not wanting the barbarians to hear me speaking to myself, I mutter in a low tone, "If I join you in those waters, something tells me I'll never leave them... And if I remain here hanging, something tells me I'll end up looking like Ghost."

We are in an enclosed cave, Drakini... Use your brain; where is this water coming from?

Pip grunts as he wakes, immediately cursing as the influx of blood in his head strikes him with a migraine. "Luna's lament, my head ain't ached like this since my ale was drugged in Varne! An' my jimmies! Those damn savages took my jimmies!"

"Quiet down," I warn, cutting the dwarf off before he can continue his complaining.

Pip's face is already blush from hanging upside down, but it grows several shades redder as he lays eyes on my naked body. "Well slap my fanny and call me Judy," he exclaims, his eyes lingering on me longer than I'd like. "Dane warned us Hunters what'd happen if we laid hands on our first Huntress recruit, but if I'd known you were toting around an ass like that all this time, I'da befriended you the night I laid eyes on ya."

"As flattering as that is, you're not my type," I spit angrily, unsure how the dwarf's mind can flirt at a time like this. "You're our medic, Pip... Take a look at Cur... If I can get us out of here, is there anything you can do to save him?"

Pip grunts as he swings his arms to slowly rotate his body in Cur's direction. I hear a harsh inhale as he lays eyes on the Lycan's wounds. Cur, who's barely holding on at this point, stares at Pip with the look of a dog that's been kicked. His dark eyes water, holding back a world of tears he's unwilling to release.

"The kid's ah Lycan, which means he's got healin' abilities us humans don't... But I ain't ever seen no Lycan incur wounds like that and walk away from them livin'. The boy needs a full moon if he's to heal... Needs to have himself a moondance... Either way, I can't treat wounds like that unless you gotta plan to get us outta here."

"The moon was nearly full when we were attacked... It'll be completely full in two, maybe three days. Can he last that long?"

"If the bastard's still alive now, I don't see why not. His healin' mechanisms are only gonna get faster the closer he gets to his moondance... Talkin' bout his survival is a waste ah breath if we can't get outta here, though, which from my assessin' seems impossible."

"No, it's not," I reply. "Look over there, toward the edge of the lake." I point toward an area where the water is particularly active, bubbling ever so slightly, which sends waves ebbing to disrupt the stillness of the spring. "I'm no expert in spelunking, but this water is coming from somewhere... Looks like those bubbles lead to some sort of blockage."

"A beauty with brains, whatta rarity," Pip cheers quietly. "Only issue I'm seein' is—whatever bloke goes down there to break up the dam is gonna get swept up in the riptide. I, for one, nominate that bloke to be Graybeard, after all the trouble he's caused us. Say, where is that old..." Pip rotates in a full circle, only to conclude that Graybeard is no longer with us. "Ah, curse that arthritis-infested scumbag—I reckon he dropped dead after taking a bite of that damn apple. Aye! Would you take a look at this! They've hung a stranger upside down among us! I wonder what this miserable bloke did to get wrangled up with us..."

I turn to see what Pip is spouting on about, then nearly jump out of my skin at the sight of the man who's most certainly not a stranger to me.

"That's no stranger," I say to myself as a dozen mysteries become solved in a split second. "That's Dane," I conclude, staring at the familiar face that belonged to Garmin Vaid in a past life.

13

GARMIN VAID

My selection for the Hunters was no mistake, I realize after months of searching.

To the Hunters, this man is well known as Dane, the fearless leader of our cohort.

But to me, now that I've seen the face he's hidden behind a mask, he's known as Garmin Vaid, the sympathetic Arms Master who silently cheered for my success in the king's draft.

The things Dane said in the boat about my recruitment were a lie...

This man did not follow me without my knowledge, watching me fight in the tournament or train against shadows in the night...

Nor did he sit in the stands as other military recruiters placed bets against me prevailing...

He was there, hiding in plain sight the entire time—posing as an unsuspecting Arms Master so he could be up close and personal with military candidates competing for elevated status in the draft.

More than that, he did not lurk in the darkness of night when I took on Ventur—this is the man responsible for me being caught by Ventur in the first place!

If not for him, I never would have snuck to the Northern Military Sector, nor would I have spied upon Undead candidates...

And even worse, Garmin Vaid had the ability to save me from Ventur's bloodlust the entire time, yet he sat by and watched me volunteer myself as tribute in a duel that could have ended in my demise...

He was testing me, I realize...

He could have stepped forward and saved me, yet he stood back and waited to see how I would respond...

Hell, he even tried to talk me out of taking on Ventur!

But despite the doubt he wanted to instill in me, I didn't back down, and I humiliated my Undead opponent.

My relationship with the Arms Master was never random, as I once considered it.

He's been watching me since the first time I got knocked in the dust, and he's been silently watching how I respond to adversity.

"All I'm saying is," Pip announces, having never seen Dane's true face before, "If my face looked like that, I sure as hell wouldn't be hiding it behind a mask my whole life."

14

LIBERATION BY LYCAN

"Something is coming," Cur moans, his voice indicating that he barely clings to this life. His nose twitches as he continues, "I smell it... a scent... a Wend... a Wendigo..."

Pip laughs, "You're about to kick the can, Cur, are you sure it isn't your upper lip you're smelling?"

Painfully, Cur grimaces, replying only with two words: "The... antler..."

Pip's laughter dies immediately, realizing what Cur alludes to. Before embarking on this mission, Dane petitioned King Silenius to retrieve a part of the fallen Wendigo's antler from Skaar—the same one Dyran managed to kill. Knowing that we would have a Lycan at our disposal for tracking Wendigos, Dane gave the antler to Cur before embarking on this journey. A target odor, Dane called it. Something for Cur to familiarize himself with so he would know what to search for when we got here.

"Uhhhh, guys..." Calico calls out, suddenly flailing in his restraints like a bat waking from a nightmare. "What the fuck is that?"

Barbarians in the distance begin stomping their feet in synchronization. Drums pound from some remote chamber, echoing off the walls, making the air itself tremble.

Garmin's eyes snap open, his mouth gasping for air.

The first thing he sees is me.

He touches his face with his bound hands, feeling for a mask that isn't there.

Mixed emotions swell in the air between us. I don't know if his lies should make me feel betrayed or honored. I thought I knew who this man was, but from the way he looks at me now, I'm not even sure *he* knows who he is. Sooner or later, a person with two faces forgets which is real.

Drakini, Dyran shouts from the waters below.

I look away from Garmin, knowing whatever negativity I feel can be dealt with later, after we survive this.

Dyran warns me, *If you don't get out of here now, you and your friends will never leave this place.*

"Torin valesh, mora elash zarin, fiir vel amir," the savages chant as a ring of fire is lit around Ghost.

"You used to live here," I whisper under my breath to Dyran, recalling how he fell in love with a Deadlands native in a past life. "Do you speak this language? Can you translate these words for me?"

It's a grimoire—one they use for summoning a Wendigo. They say, "From the depths where shadows writhe and blood runs cold..."

"Ena kala dorash, Velashar!"

"We call thee forth, ancient one," Dyran translates.

"Fel zanar, irak tora lishan taran," they scream, drums growing louder in the distance.

"Bound no longer, rise to feast upon the light..."

"Vel mora sharan tir dorim!"

"And bring darkness to this world," Dyran finishes as chills wash over me.

Ghost's head budges ever so slightly as the heat hits his flayed body. He isn't dead yet, but he sure as hell is close.

"Is that... Graybeard?" Calico asks, noticeably disturbed.

I instantly see what he's talking about as two savages drag a half-unconscious man toward the flaming circle. I squint my eyes, gasping slightly as I realize Calico is right. Though I can't make out his face from here, I recognize the mangy head of gray hair that trickles down into an uncomely, knotted beard. But this man is not the same as when I saw him last. His head bleeds profusely from the temples where a set of grotesque, gnarled horns have sprouted from his skull. His flesh, once wrinkled and loose, is now so tight around his bones that it tears at the seams. Bone and fur spurt forth from the lacerations, reminding me of the same monster I encountered on Skaar, the one Dyran forfeited his life to overcome.

"Wendigo," Cur whispers, his eyes closed while his nose twitches uncontrollably.

"Wendigo," the barbarians chant in perfect harmony with the thundering drums.

"Wendigo... Wendigo... Wendigo..." Over and over their voices repeat, each time growing louder and louder. Though I don't speak their language, I don't need Dyran to translate this word for me. Its syllables have been burned into the surface of my brain. Since the first time I heard it spoken, my eardrums have associated its utterance with a natural response—fear.

"No," Dane says, seeing Graybeard at the same time as me. "It can't be... I shot the apple from his hand..."

His shot shattered the apple, sending a fraction of it into the man's open mouth, Dyran says, dismissing Dane's words. *His mind is forever lost in Arcadia, and his body is ripe for Steppenwolf's army.*

I can see several bloody stains in Graybeard's snowy beard from where the Arcadian Apple exploded. It isn't entirely impossible part of the apple flew into his mouth, completing the bite he desperately yearned to take.

Either way, Dyran is right. Between Graybeard's animalistic appearance and the demonic chorus of incantations the savages scream, I can feel the weight of something horrible about to happen.

They throw Graybeard to the ground only inches from the fire, then back away from him immediately, like he's a bundle of black powder with a lit fuse.

"Say, what's the cur doing?" Pip asks, pulling me away from the ritual, just as Graybeard's body starts convulsing.

"No... time..." Cur grunts, forcing the words from his throat as my eyes lock onto his bloody hand. From his bleeding fingertips grow a set of obsidian claws.

"Don't do it," I cry out, knowing his intentions before he can carry them out. "Don't you dare do it!"

"It's... going to... be okay," he reassures as I panic, repeating the same words he spoke to me after pulling me from the ocean's merciless riptide. He lifts up a chunk of hair, my hair, and holds it under his nose, smelling it. For a moment I'm confused, but I suddenly remember when the Deadland savages launched their attack above-ground. Their spear cut a strand of my hair loose, and somehow, Cur has managed to hang onto it this whole time. Now he smells it, familiarizing himself with my natural scent, committing it to memory. He continues, "I will... find you... after this..."

He lifts his thumb up to his mouth and bites down on the claw that grows from its tip. Slowly, agonizingly, he uses his canines to rip the sharpened nail free. Blood gushes as his teeth remove it from his thumb, and he lets out a muffled groan as he spits it into his bloody palm.

"Pip... Catch..." Cur warns, tossing the nail through the air toward the upside down dwarf. Pip tracks it through the air with feverish eyes, realizing this projectile is our ticket out of these restraints. He claps his hands like a man trying to kill a gnat, cutting his palms open as he clasps the claw safely.

Cur uses every ounce of willpower remaining to sit up, his torn abdomen flexing as he manages to reach the rope that binds his feet together.

"Don't!" I scream at him manically as Graybeard rises from the ground in the distance, no longer a human, but instead, something diabolical.

My heart breaks as Cur's claws effortlessly slice through the rope.

He flashes a forced smile in my direction as his body falls.

The drums beat fast in the distance.

The barbarians scream on the embankment.

A Wendigo rises, taking over Graybeard's body.

Ghost's red eyes shed tears of blood.

The water splashes beneath us, shattering the image of Dyran and replacing it with one of Cur diving into the lake's depths.

Time slows as I scream at Pip, "The claw! Give me the claw!"

"No," Garmin orders Pip, overriding my authority. "The tracker has sacrificed himself so we may live. I won't lose another Hunter, especially not to save a Lycan."

"He's a human!" I scream. "He will die if he breaks that dam!"

Pip's eyes flick back and forth between me and Dane, his face conflicted on who to listen to. Whether the dwarf wants to admit it or not, he's grown a soft spot for the Lycan, and I can tell it pains him to see Cur sacrifice himself for our survival.

"You don't get to decide who lives and who dies, Huntress," Garmin replies, his face emotionless.

"Neither do you!" I growl, tears falling down my forehead. They fall through the air and become one with the lake.

The drums and chanting cease simultaneously as the Wendigo crouches by the fire, touching it with its skeletal fingers. Silence echoes as the flames freeze, instantly turning from spires of blazing orange to raging stalagmites of ice.

Ghost's suspended body shudders as the heat in the air freezes around him, trapping him in a vacuum of inescapable cold.

The Wendigo gingerly steps over the ring of ice it's defied nature to create, closing the gap between him and Ghost.

The bubbles in the water increase as Cur pummels the blockage.

The Wendigo places its spindly finger beneath Ghost's chin, lifting his ruby-red eyes to take in the monster before him. He's playing with his prey, I realize.

A geyser of water erupts suddenly, jetting from the lake's mouth like projectile vomit. The cave's infrastructure shakes as a plume of rain showers the embankment of bowing savages.

The exploding shower causes the Wendigo to look at the lake, exposing his demonic face for me to examine. The rain turns to hail in the presence of the Wendigo, creating a blizzard as the monster quickly realizes what's happening. With the speed of a cheetah, the Wendigo leaps over the ring of ice and sprints to the rising lake as it floods over the side of the embankment.

The Wendigo kneels, placing its fingers in the rushing waters in an attempt to freeze the tsunami, but it's too late.

The water the Wendigo touches turns to ice, spreading several feet across the lake's raging surface, but the roaring waters rise too fast and too violently to be stilled by the beast's black magic.

The water level rises slowly, then all at once.

A giant wave surges, feeding on the endless flood from the broken dam. A mist sprays me as the wave climbs, almost reaching high enough for my fingers to touch. Then, just as the lake begins to freeze over from the Wendigo's touch, the wave breaks, crashing over the embankment to consume everything in its wake.

The tide decimates everything in its path, and we watch from the safety of the cave's ceiling as it pummels the savages and their summoned monster, sucking them into its frothy maw to drown in its oxygen-deprived gullet.

My heart aches as I search the waters desperately for some sight of Cur's body, hoping to see him break free from the rapids and gasp for air.

No such thing happens though, and so I silently hold my breath, waiting to see how long I can make it before I can go no longer, convincing myself that if I can hold my breath long enough, it will allow him to do so too.

What foolish things we tell ourselves in order to find hope in hopeless situations.

I gasp as my lungs beg for air, silently cursing myself for not being stronger.

He has been underwater three times longer than the duration I held my breath, meaning if there was a chance of him surfacing, he would've done so minutes ago.

Crude barbarians scream in the distance as the flood fills every nook and cranny of their vast burrow. Their great city is downslope from this lake, so it is quickly submerged like the fabled city Atlantis, though none will survive this watery hellhole.

Slowly but surely, the exploding geyser runs out of steam, but not before the screams of savages are drown out completely. After only a few minutes, their entire city is underwater, and we Hunters are left to stare at the still waters below us, silently realizing it was our bondage that saved us.

Only now does Pip begin sawing at his restraints with Cur's torn claw, and just before his rope begins to unravel thread by thread, he passes the obsidian dagger to me. Pip's restraints snap, and he plummets into the ocean.

I stare at my reflection in the bloody claw, then look directly at Dane, silently hoping he sees the hatred in my eyes.

Whether irrational or not, my heart blames him for Cur's death.

Dane is not the man I thought he was, and there is now a part of me that wishes it was him who sacrificed himself to save us.

I cut the rope and throw the claw to Calico as I fall.

In my mind, Dane could use some more time hung up on his decisions.

PART TWO

Wisteria

15

TEN YEARS LATER

"Tonight is the night we've trained for," I say, my voice somewhere between a whisper and a growl. The endless winter winds carry it to my audience of battle-hardened warriors. I continue, speaking the language of Deadland natives that the Ka-El so graciously taught me over the past ten years, "The night we've prayed for, the night we've spent years designing, the night our enemy will come to dread..."

Chains rattle in my grip as I slide my fingers across my chain dart, looking to my closest companions as wolves howl in the distance. Dane's expressionless mask is solemn; Pip's lips curl in a maddening smile; Katana's face is smitten with euphoria; Calico's different colored eyes brew a storm that demands destruction...

We Hunters have been through so much in such little time.

These lands have taken everything from us, but they've given us much in return.

"Soren Kael, we are forever indebted to you and your people... If not for the Ka-El, this hostile world would have frozen the blood in our veins and blackened our skin with frost. It was your people who showed us warmth in a place it cannot exist. You taught us how to live off a land destined for death, and so we Hunters vow to use this second chance to liberate your people from Steppenwolf and his Wendigos!"

My eyes follow a dark shadow stalking through the crowd—a dark shadow with bright, yellow eyes that glow brighter than the sunset on the horizon. Ten faithful years Wisteria has been by my side, each day daring me to adapt and evolve. In the Areopagan draft, she turned me into a warrior in a matter of days. In the course of a decade, though, she's turned me into a legend.

I am the only person present who can't count the Wendigos I've killed with two hands. It is this achievement alone that places me on this pedestal, leading both the Hunters and Ka-El.

This tribe is not one who follows weak leaders.

Their loyalty is earned through action alone, and my actions have spoken loudest amidst many nights of silence.

But these men and women who look up at me with hope in their eyes don't know my secret...

They have no idea the creatures I see, the ones that don't really exist.

If they knew about Wisteria, or Dyran, or Havik, or Grite, or Lu Bu, or Osprey... Would they still think me fit to lead?

Or would they think me some delusional lunatic, a woman who relies on figments of her imagination to prevail in battle?

Wisteria approaches the front line of soldiers, sitting beside Dane as her eyes urge me to continue my speech. The night will come soon, and then the time for words and bravery will have expired.

"Listen to the wolves howling in the distance, descendants of Ka-El... Soon, your howls will join them as we hunt that which hunts us... When that sun fades, the light of the full moon will be the last light our enemy sees before fangs and fur surrounds them!"

The massive natives let out several howls and jeers, hyping themselves up for what's coming. It wasn't until I met a member of Ka-El that I realized how large men can truly be, and how small Pip actually is. Even the women here are several heads taller than me, even though I'm above-average height for a woman my age. More than that, the men are sculpted with little more than muscle—not an ounce of fat is detectable from head to toe. They've been raised on little more than elk meat and water in this land where potatoes and barley refuse to grow.

"You are Lycans," I say, smiling as I stare at the wild savages. Their bodies are painted with runic war patterns, and even us Hunters mimic their rituals. Etched lines of blood-red paint are lathered across Pip's face, as with Ghost and Calico. Even Dane's mask has been decorated for battle, as is custom among the Ka-El.

The lower half of my face is covered with a ventilator mask, so I have opted for a simpler design—three vertical lines of blood draped on my forehead, symbolic of the Hunter Creed. The first line is for the protection of innocence; the second, vengeance toward evil; and the third, sacrifice of self.

"Lycans—the same beasts the Creator wishes to eradicate, alongside the Undead... But the Creator is incapable of destroying that which he creates, so he sent a devil to do his dirty work... Tonight, we will teach the Creator a lesson, Lycans! Tonight, we will send him a message... We will not go without a fight, we will rage against the dying of the light! We will not go gentle into that good night! We will rage! Rage against the dying of the light!"

Lycans all around scream and howl as bloodlust consumes them, each of them stripping their thick pelts as they prepare themselves for a moondance.

They shout their creed, one line after another, its words a battle cry to the indifferent gods above.

"When the moon is bright,
Wendigos beware!
The Creator can't save you,
By a mortal prayer!"

Osprey descends from the sky, landing on a branch overhead.

Steppenwolf's forces are less than a click away, Drakini, she whispers.

Imaginary soldiers shoulder their way through the snowy forest, each one of them returning to report on their scouting expeditions. Havik and Grite are led by Dyran, the crimson knight who has even more experience slaying these beasts than me.

Ooooo, I can't wait to get my hands on the moccasins you're about to make! Mongreloid moccasins! Grite shouts excitedly.

Smol gorl need make big mookaskins for Havik! Havik bellows, rubbing his abs with all four hands.

It is an acquired skill, being able to hear these voices without reacting to them externally. I turn to face them, pretending that I am peering through the woods. I look to Dyran, urging him to report on what he's seen.

They await your party among a grove of Arcadian Apples, Dyran informs curtly. *They will rely on their blood magic to save them, just as we foresaw. They will trap as many of you in visions as possible, seeking to turn the tides of war by turning you humans into Wendigos.*

"And Steppenwolf?" I ask, whispering under my breath so none from my army can hear me.

If he's here, the Wendigo leader is doing a good job concealing himself. Not one of us managed to spot him, and believe me, he's a difficult individual to miss.

I figured as much. The infamous Steppenwolf has evaded me all these years, silently watching from the shadows as I dispense of his soldiers one after the other. But how many soldiers can he stand to lose before facing me himself? That is the true question, and tonight I will find the answer.

A breeze shakes the surrounding forest, sending a chill coursing through me. I reach into a pouch at my hip and retrieve two ignisberries, then lift my ventilator and place them on my tongue. I grind them between my molars, puckering my lips as a spicy, fiery juice is released. I swallow the fire, then feel it ignite my blood. In a matter of seconds, their warmth spreads to my fingertips and toes, turning my body into a furnace incapable of feeling cold.

If not for Soren Kael and his clan of Lycans, we Hunters never would've survived long enough to discover these berries. Thanks to them, though, we have a way to feel warmth on the coldest of nights. Another gift they've given us added to the impossibly long list of lessons they've taught.

We owe the Ka-El our lives, then some.

The Wendigos exist to hunt their species extinct, and we Hunters are all that stand in their way. In their wolfish state, a Lycan cannot kill a Wendigo.

Killing a Wendigo requires killing it twice—and to do that, a rational, human mind is required.

The Creator gifted these monsters with the ability to cast illusions—illusions of perfection, ones designed to trap the mind in an eternal state so the Wendigo can inhabit their body. Once a mind becomes trapped in this false reality, it is impossible for a human to free themself... But, there is a way to slay the demonic spirit that inhabits their body.

To kill a Wendigo, one must first destroy their illusion.

Then, and only then, will their body be susceptible to death.

Try to slay them before that and their body will regenerate, heal, and return with a vengeance.

Shattering an illusion, though, is easier said than done.

There is a reason I am the only human present who's killed more Wendigos than I can count. Without Wisteria, I'd have no way of knowing truth from falsity. She, for some ironic reason, is the anchor that grounds me to reality. Without her appearing in these illusions, I'd surely choose a Wendigo's comfortable lies over life's harsh truths.

Defying the Wendigo's manipulation doesn't come without its own consequences, though. Those who fall victim to their mirages suffer from distorted reality for hours, sometimes days after falling prey to their promise of paradise. Dissociation sickness, the Ka-El call it. Poor Pip was stuck in a coma for a full week the last time he encountered one of the demons. Since then, the dwarf with a once infallible pride has shrunken away every time their name's uttered.

I look back to my fellow Hunters, searching each of their eyes for whatever fears they may hide.

There's Katana, a man I knew next to nothing about by the time we arrived in these hostile lands. Named aptly after his weapon of choice, the katana, this warrior descends from some ancient order of fighters known as the Samurai. Before meeting him, I had never heard of such a sect of warriors, but Katana's prowess in battle is the only proof I need to know that they not only exist, but they wield swords like a blacksmith wields a hammer. Before Katana, I had never met a man whose words were so soft-spoken yet took action that spoke volumes itself.

Calico, named aptly for his mismatched irises, has become a close friend through the years. In so many ways, he reminds me of a fox. Clever and cunning with unmatched guile, but he's more than that. Where most men fight with weapons, Calico's sword and shield are words. Pip's told me stories about him over the course of ten years that have left me speechless. Whenever the Hunters are assigned to a particularly complex mission, they send Calico in to prepare the way, because only a man of his talent can gain intel while making an enemy feel like a friend. It's said that Calico's words can make a banker donate to charity, force a warrior to sheathe their sword, and lead a lifelong sinner to repentance. Without his charm, there's no telling how long it would've taken to win over the Ka-El, and without his intelligence, it would've taken twice as long to learn their native language.

Lullaby rarely speaks, but when he does, it's softly spoken whispers in the ears of his dying prey. I've witnessed it a handful of times, saw him cradle a cannibal's corpse and lull him to the afterlife with inaudible slurs. Pip says his lips are poisonous and his tongue is a scorpion's tail. Dane told me that the Hunters found Lullaby as a child—the boy's village had sewn his mouth shut with thread so he could no longer utter his curses. The locals said the boy's own parents locked him away because whenever he spoke, death followed. There were so many stitches in his lips that it took Pip the better part of a day to remove them, but where Lullaby's village feared his curse, the Hunters found a way to make it a force for good.

Then there's Wasp, the Hunters' chief poisoner. Whenever a target needs to be dealt with swiftly and inconspicuously, the Hunters send Wasp. Unlike me with my chains or Pip with his axe or Dane with his revolvers, Wasp does not fight fair battles. A blow dart and needle is all the shifty man needs to accomplish his goals, and it's said he's killed more men and women in secret than all other Hunters combined, though Wasp would never confirm or deny such a statistic.

As I look upon the faces of my fellow Hunters, I'm reminded of those sacrificed by these lands. Their absence is entirely too tangible on a night like this, where we near completion of our mission. Ghost, whose body was never recovered from the tsunami's wreckage. Whistle, whose mind was consumed entirely by a Wendigo years ago. All those who died the night Sun Treader went down, and Seance, who died before ever knowing his life was in danger.

"Are you ready, my love?" Dane whispers from beside me. His left hand touches my shoulder gently, further igniting the ignisberries' warmth through my body. Tied to his ring finger is a braided cord of silver coils. They are the same silver coils that wrap around my own ring finger, signifying the oath we took in marriage several years ago beside the heat of a burning hearth. *Dai selas, ena vir*—Two hearts, one flesh, the Ka-El say. When the Ka-El imprint, they indicate it by sacrificing an elk, then making vows beside the burnt offerings produced from its corpse. Because Lycans cannot touch silver, the Ka-El thread coils of gold around their ring fingers. But we Hunters are different, Soren Kael explained, and so our matrimony was designed to be set apart from their traditional customs.

Silver, Soren Kael said, symbolized our union. Although the precious metal can kill a Lycan, it can just as easily be used to protect them, when placed in the right hands. We were, Soren Kael announced, the right hands to wear such a lethal weapon, thus solidifying our truce between Hunters and Ka-El.

I run my hand across Dane's mask. Though it blocks his face from my view, his likeness has been etched across my closed eyelids. Though I am now his leader, I would not be the woman I am today without this man by my side.

In a land where cold nights want nothing more than to freeze your heart, Dane is the furnace keeping numbness at bay.

We've had our differences, but what couple hasn't? It wasn't until we escaped the Ra-El that I was able to put aside my feelings of betrayal. Though I thought he lied to me under the alias Garmin Vaid, I later understood he kept his identity from me as an act of love—to let me find my way in this world and earn respect from other Hunters without them thinking his feelings for me swayed his judgment.

"I have no choice but to be ready," I reply, my voice distorted by the mask Dane forged for me. Though I lost the helm Garmin Vaid made when the Sun Treader went down, he's followed me to these lands and made another. And thanks to its woolen interior, my nose and mouth are forever safe against frostbite. I continue, "But our enemy knows we are coming, and I've felt Steppenwolf's eyes on me all these years."

"You've broken their illusions and killed them more times than I can count, Drakini," he whispers comfortingly. "Since the moment I laid eyes on you, I've seen that the content of your soul is different. It's unbridled, like a wild stallion... If you cannot overcome Steppenwolf, I promise you there is no Sylvian, Lycan, or Undead in existence that can stop this monster in his goals."

"What if his illusions are stronger than those of his minions?"

"I don't care if he shows you the Creator himself; I know you, and I know your will is mightier than his. Even if he promises you the world in your palm, I expect you to crush it in your grasp."

16

GODDESS OF THE HUNT

The heatless sun is setting. The Ka-El will soon lose liberty to their beasts within, and this whole plan revolves around trusting them to exercise enough restraint to attack that which attacks us Hunters.

I retreat to a glistening grove of ignisberry bushes, their frozen, orange facade glimmering in the dull sunlight. In this isolated grove, I'm surrounded by Wisteria and her shadow soldiers. It has become common practice for me to pray with Wisteria before every battle, and my fellow Hunters and members of Ka-El know to leave me alone in these moments.

We huddle together as I kneel and press my forehead against Wisteria's. Dyran, Havik, Grite, and Lu Bu huddle around us, placing their hands on one another's shoulders. Osprey fans her tremendous wings and encloses us, blocking out any noise from Ka-El's camp.

To an outside looker, they'd see only me—kneeling in the snow whispering to myself. But to me, these individuals around me are as real as the sun that sets in the distance.

Before coming to these lands, I never considered myself a religious individual. In my youth, I could count on one hand the number of times I prayed to the gods... But in this circle of those I trust, we pray not to the gods, but instead, to the spirit inside me.

Wisteria purrs, *To the almighty Huntress that resides inside...*

Lu Bu continues, rhyming, always rhyming, *We ask for the serenity to accept that which we must abide...*

Havik adds, *Give small gorl courage to fight...*

Grite recites, eager to deliver his line, *Make it hurt whenever she bite!*

Osprey chirps, *Let her see through the enemy's lies...*

Dyran finishes, *Give her the strength to bring about his demise.*

"Amen," I whisper.

17

STEPPENWOLF

"Something's wrong," I whisper, ordering my unit to halt in their steps. "No, this is all wrong..."

We lurk in the forest's early evening shadows, looking outward toward the open expanse.

"I'd say so," Pip remarks grimly. "Where'd all the fekking Arcadian trees go?"

We've scouted this land for several months, strategically selecting it for tonight's battle. We've examined it countless times, then mapped it, then memorized it. I could close my eyes and picture this battlefield inch by inch, but the stretch of land before us now looks nothing like what we've scouted.

Pip is right... We chose this plot first and foremost because it had the largest Arcadian orchard we've ever seen. It's commonly known that where there are Arcadian Apples, Wendigos are never far.

The ice trees grow over Ra-El burrows—Mora velan, mora falen, the Ka-El say, translating loosely to "As above, so below." In other words, the blood sacrifices they make underground directly fuel the Arcadian trees. The Ra-El worship the Wendigo, practicing dark arts like blood magic to advance Steppenwolf's goals. In every Arcadian Apple is the soul of a Wendigo's host, forever preserved in ice while their body is eternally controlled by some parasitic spirit. Without the Ra-El, there would be no Arcadian Apples to spread Steppenwolf's legions... Even after all these years, I maintain my ignorance in blood magic, but I know there is a direct correlation between the dark art and Steppenwolf's power as strong as the correlation between the cold and snow.

The natives call this place Teufelshörner, better known in my mind as Devil's Horns. Rising on either side of the Arcadian orchard are two mountainous spires that curl into pointed arches, giving the appearance of... well, a devil's horns.

But the trees of ice have vanished, along with the Arcadian Apples which hung from their sharp, hostile branches.

It's like an army of trolls marched through this landscape, obliterating everything in their path and crushing it into the densely-packed snow until any trace of its existence was lost in history.

More than that, I sent Dyran, Grite, Havik, and Lu Bu to patrol this area only minutes ago, and they all returned with no reports of abnormalities. *They await your party among a grove of Arcadian Apples*, Dyran said upon returning from his scouting mission. But as I stare at the desolate wasteland before us, there is no grove, and there are no Wendigos.

There are only those cruel horns pointing to the full moon which rises on the horizon, causing shivers to run down my spine as darkness settles and wolves howl in the distance.

"Are you ready, my love?" Dane whispers in my ear. It's the same question he asked before we left, the same question I've already answered. It's an odd thing to ask in a moment like this. I turn to face him, starting to speak until I see there's no one standing behind me.

"... Dane?" I call out into the shadows, pivoting madly as I realize my fellow Hunters have vanished in the blink of an eye.

I don't understand... He was just there... And Pip... Pip was also there...

It's begun, Wisteria purrs from the shadows, her yellow eyes illuminating the snowy forest behind me. *You've entered an illusion, Drakini.*

"That's impossible," I whisper, turning to take in my surroundings. "No, this isn't how their illusions manifest... This is no paradise..."

It's always paradise...

The Wendigos always cast illusions of grandeur to convince their victims to forfeit their souls.

But this is the same icy hell I've traversed the past decade.

This is the same miserable reality I faced moments ago... The only difference is, I'm alone now.

The howls of Lycans slowly fade.

There is no longer a moon above.

There aren't even the dull glimmer of Arcadian Apples to break up the darkness.

I grip my chains tighter as the Kunai dart's spearhead sways beside me. A tightness builds in my chest as thunder rumbles overhead. The sky sparks, releasing a violent bolt of lightning. It strikes the ground right in the center of the craggy horns. I stagger back as the light reveals—for the briefest of moments—a backlit figure walking toward me. Its demonic image sears my irises, forcing my eyes to linger on its ghastly memory as darkness settles.

Thunder roars and lightning strikes a second time, illuminating the same space, yet this time there is no monstrous silhouette to be seen.

My heart races as I whisper beneath my breath, "This isn't right... Something's wrong..."

To which a voice replies from the darkness, "Do you feel that?"

The voice is ethereal, echoing in the atmosphere like the thunder before it. Its malevolent tone smothers me, suffocating me from calling out for help.

"That's fear," the voice continues, circling my head from all directions. "Suck it in... Linger in it... Let it undo your soul."

It's him, Wisteria growls, stalking past me. She stands in front of me, my sole protector from the abyss. *It's Steppenwolf*, she purrs, confirming the paralyzing fear I already felt deep in my mind.

The chains I hold are the same ones I've used in battle for nearly a decade. Their whistle on the wind is a song stuck in my mind; they've slain more foes than the number of links that make up their entirety and saved my life almost as many times as Wisteria. I know them better than I know myself, which is exactly why my heart skips a beat. Something is wrong, I think to myself for the hundredth time as the chains pulse in my hands. Their texture changes abruptly, turning from cold metal to wet, slimy... scales?

The chains slither in my hands, causing me to shrink back in fear as I look down. There in my frozen hands is a python, its spearhead-shaped skull lifting against all odds to occupy the space in front of my face. Its slitted eyes gaze deeply into my soul as its forked tongue licks the air between us. I want to scream, I want to run, I want to die as it slowly wraps itself around my neck, constricting its body around my own.

Every inch of me is paralyzed. The breath has been sucked from my lungs. I'm helpless to do anything but stand here and accept my fate as the same weapon I carried moments ago betrays me.

Drakini, snap out of it! Wisteria shouts, looking back at me as lightning strikes once more. This time, the violent light reveals a scene that shatters my soul. The Arcadian orchard has reappeared, only now there are bodies suspended from their frozen branches, each one hanging from their noose-tied necks. They are my fellow Hunters, the closest of which is Dane's unmistakable face, now stripped of its mask.

"It's... not... real..." I spit, trying to convince myself that this is all an illusion.

"I wouldn't be so sure of that," Steppenwolf asserts, the voice no louder than a gust of wind, a mere whisper echoing amongst snow. The massive snake continues to contract. It squeezes the life from me, causing pressure to build behind my eyes. Steppenwolf continues, his voice sinister, "I've been watching you for quite some time... You are the one they call Huntress... The one the Ka-El put all their hope in... The one the child king sent to be my undoing... The one who's defeated my soldiers time and time again..."

Damn you, get up! Wisteria howls as a figure approaches from the transient veil of darkness. *It isn't real, Drakini! You need to look past his lies!*

"Well, well, who do we have here?" the monster calls, revealing himself for the first time. But it is not a monster who leaves behind the bleak doom, but instead, an angel of light. In all my years, I have never seen a man of such perfection. He makes even Dane look ugly, though Dane makes most maidens swoon from a single glance. He has dark brown hair, dark like the bark of some ancient pine, starkly contrasted by his electric blue eyes that almost look as if bolts of lightning explode behind their glassy surface. His jawline is so sharp that it could cut my lips if I were to kiss it—his Adam's apple, my tongue upon a single lick. There is a wild quality about his face, an admirable look of comfort, as if this world of darkness is his, and I am safe so long as I reside with him by my side.

The strange man kneels before Wisteria as the hair upon her back stands, a feral growl vibrating in her throat. He leaves a gap between himself and my hellcat, wisely keeping his distance as he examines her. He laughs charmingly, "Ahhh, so this is how you've withstood my minions all this time... It's been quite some time since I've found a Seer."

My head is swimming, but not so much that his words don't cause me to panic. All these years, I have been the only person able to see Wisteria, to acknowledge her existence. She is, and always has been, a figment of my imagination... It is not possible for others to see her, and yet this peculiar man stares directly at her, almost as if he is studying her.

I drop to my knees as the python's hold becomes impossible to overcome. I can't tell if the arctic tundra has disappeared or if the surrounding darkness is merely my narrowing vision. It's like I've been teleported into some different dimension from my worst nightmares, and I am now kneeling before this alien world's ruler, completely restrained by his relentless will.

I hear the string of a bow twang from behind me, then hear the unforgettable scream of Havik and Grite as they storm forward from my imagination into existence. With the speed of a metaphysical god, the stranger's hand closes around a projectile meant for his head, plucking Lu Bu's arrow from thin air as he stands to face his attackers. His lips rise in a crooked sneer as Grite and Havik leap toward him. Unfortunately for Grite and Havik, Wisteria is not the only imaginary friend of mine that this man can see.

Grite and Havik freeze in midair, suspended several feet off the ground as this stranger examines them as they struggle.

"Truly fascinating," he remarks as Grite screams like a raccoon caught in a trap and Havik bellows like a bull evaded by a matador. Only now does this stranger look at me as I fade from consciousness on the ground before him, my head feeling as if it is seconds from exploding.

Lightning strikes behind the lone man, revealing his true form for a split second, so fast that if I had blinked, I would have missed it. But I didn't miss it, and the lightning bolt burns his true image into my mind, causing my blood to freeze within. Though the light vanishes as fast as it emerged, allowing the stranger to project this false version of himself, I now know with certainty this man, this thing, is Steppenwolf.

In that moment of illumination, I saw this devil for who he really is... His face was a symmetrical mask of sculpted bone, two horns pointed to the sky like the craggy rocks behind him. He had venomous, sardonically white eyes capable of burning my body with frost from a momentary glance. Draped down the back of his head was the mane of a lion, cutting off at his scarred shoulders, which extended into long, vascular arms that were grey with permafrost. His claws were so long and sharp that they cast shadows taller than the mountains in the distance.

Let Havik down! Havik's voice booms, his four arms writhing in the open air like a child learning to swim for the first time.

I'll break those fucking horns off your head and use them as toothpicks! Grite shrieks like a rabid eagle. *Keep sneering, we'll see who's smiling when I rip your prick off and stuff it so far down your throat you'll be vomiting piss!*

"These are quite the friends you've made," Steppenwolf says, finally speaking to me directly. It isn't until this moment that Osprey swoops down from the sky, diving with her talons ready to shred this monster to pieces. Almost as if on cue, Dyran and Lu Bu launch themselves from the darkness, Dyran's sword raised and Lu Bu's bow drawn. Steppenwolf utters a mere two words, "That's enough," and all three of them freeze in their advances, joining Grite and Havik in suspended disbelief.

Break the spell, Drakini, Wisteria commands. *He can only hold us here so long as you believe his lies! Break the illusion! Break it now!*

"Watch closely, Drakini," Steppenwolf commands, lifting my body telepathically with the slightest flick of his fingers.

Drakini! Wisteria cries aloud, panic in her voice. Since the day I met her, I have never heard her sound so frightened, so powerless. *Break the—*

A loud snap sounds as Steppenwolf rings her neck before my eyes, snapping it before she has time to finish her sentence.

"No!" I scream, a fury unknown to even the Creator erupting inside me. Wisteria's lifeless body falls to the ground, instantly absorbed by the darkness. It vanishes from my sight like a plume of smoke. Suddenly, an inexorable rage overwhelms me. I shoulder my ventilator mask aside, allowing me to bite down on the snake's scaly exterior beneath my chin. Jolts of pain shoot through my jaw as I do so, several teeth breaking as they bite down on cold, metallic chains. I scream out in pain, my gums bleeding profusely, which only adds to my anger.

"Like I said, I've been watching you for some time, notorious Huntress... I get the impression pain is something you enjoy," Steppenwolf says. "I can tell from looking at you that you've always gotten back up when life's knocked you down... So allow me to show you what true pain feels like—then we will see how mighty your will truly is."

Using only his fingers to manipulate my imaginary soldiers, Steppenwolf rotates Lu Bu's body, then forces her to release her arrow. The shaft flies straight, then buries itself in Dyran's visor, killing him before he has time to even register his death.

"If you want a toothpick so bad, I'll give you a toothpick," Steppenwolf tells Grite, thrusting the arrow he previously caught straight into Grite's mouth as he screams several inaudible slurs.

Save us, smol gorl! Havik pleads, screaming for help for the first time since his inception. Tears cascade down my cheeks as Havik's eyes beg for me to shatter the illusion, something I'm utterly unable to do.

"Small girl can't save you from me, big fella," Steppenwolf mocks. The earth cracks beneath him, splitting in two to reveal a dark chasm. Whatever force held Havik suspended disappears, and the ground swallows him whole. Despite my body's shrill sobs, I can hear his bellow echo for several seconds as he falls into an eternal abyss. I want to focus on the internal agony that swells inside me, but the explosion of feathers overhead scatters my thoughts. I look up and see Osprey is no longer hovering frozen in the air—instead, bloody feathers float peacefully around us like impure, animalistic snowflakes.

Lu Bu screams, taking my attention away from Osprey's raining corpse. Even as she dies, she manages to make her final words rhyme: *You may have won the battle tonight, but Huntress will be your end, Wight!* The remaining arrows in her quiver lift, levitating up and over her shoulder, rotating midair so their sharpened heads point at their former wielder. I squeeze my eyes shut, clenching my teeth as they thud into their target, silencing Lu Bu's furious scream.

When I open my eyes, my dead companions have disappeared, each one of them sufficiently wiped from existence, even if their existence had only been known to me before this night.

When I open my eyes, it is just me and this monster, and I have been defeated before so much as raising a finger.

18

LIBERATION BY LYCAN (PT. 2)

T he snake that constricts me melts from existence. Chains fall to the ground, leaving me free to breathe as I collapse against the cold, dark earth. My tear-soaked face kisses the snow beneath me, preserving the tears as icicles which cling to my cheeks.

I look up, my head so light that I fear I'll pass out if I move even a centimeter. I stare up at the stranger, sobbing, "You are him! You are Steppenwolf!"

"What gave it away?" he cackles, his distorted voice both godlike and sinister. "You know, you really aren't the enemy I thought you were... Given the fight you've put up against my Wendigos, I thought you'd give me a run for my money... I mean come on, did you really think defeating me would be as easy as distracting me and my forces so your Ka-El hellhounds could move in for the kill? Look around you, pathetic woman!"

The illusion he projects temporarily fades, revealing the reality I should be seeing. The darkness cracks open like a parting curtain, revealing behind it the corpses of several dozen Lycans lying lifeless in the snow beneath a tremendous grove of Arcadian trees, their blood staining the snow a dull red several shades darker than the apples that twinkle above them.

The illusion isn't lifted long enough for me to count their bodies, but it is pierced long enough for me to know this is the entire Ka-El army that lays slain under the light of the full moon.

It was my job to defeat Steppenwolf's illusion by the time they arrived, leaving his body vulnerable to their wrath.

But I failed this mission before I could even start, I realize, leaving those who trusted me most at the mercy of Steppenwolf's demented demons.

The veil of darkness closes, leaving me in solitude to reflect on my failures.

I sob, hating myself for how weak my voice sounds, "If you're going to kill me, get it over with, demon spawn! Let me join my companions in the afterlife!"

"Kill you?" Steppenwolf repeats whimsically, as if he didn't hear me right. "Why on earth would I do that? A woman with your powers would serve much better under my rule than dead. You are a Seer, the first I've encountered in many years. I'm already unstoppable, but with you as my servant, my Master's plan will take less time than I anticipated."

"I'd sooner be cursed by Damon than serve you, devil," I spit, my voice cracking as I subconsciously mourn all I've ever loved.

"Mmmm, I'm sure you believe that, but there's much the Creator can offer for your services, Huntress... Or should I call you... Drakini..." He peers at me sympathetically, almost as if he cares for me. He is a devil posing as an angel of light. A deceptive serpent, a ravenous lion on the prowl seeking unsuspecting prey to devour.

"We Wendigos are humanity's final reckoning, Drakini... There is nothing the Creator won't do to right his wrongs... I mean, imagine being an all-powerful god, graced with the power to create all we know and love on this earth, yet cursed with the inability to destroy any of it. That is where I come along, Huntress... You see, the Creator has spent eons staring at this majestic world, forced to watch humanity fuck everything up... First, there was Luna and Solis's insubordination... Then, to fix it, the Creator cursed their offspring—Dagon and Damon—to teach humanity a valuable lesson. But instead of learning from their mistakes, they chose to lean into them and multiplied, spreading their scourge across the face of the earth.

"That didn't make my Master happy, I assure you. In his benevolence, though he lacked the power to destroy this world, there was an alternative... The Creator cannot destroy, but he *can* create—and so he created me, the one destined to destroy it all."

Lightning flashes as thunder booms, changing his appearance once and for all. The fleshy facade is torn away as my eyes become temporarily blinded by the light. When my night vision returns, I see Steppenwolf for who he truly is—a projection of the malevolence the Creator wants to express but is incapable of—a form of absolute evil which stands undiluted by any force of light forged against it—the ultimate embodiment of hunger and greed and decay—the final evolution of humanity indeed, the evolution that will run our race, and every other race, to the brink of extinction.

"I am pestilence," the Wendigo growls, his voice no longer nonchalant, but immortal once more. "I am famine... I am true evil... I am Steppenwolf... Only through me will the Creator's goals be accomplished... A fresh start for creation—a blank canvas."

"I came here to kill you," I mutter, my mouth a tea kettle reaching a fever-pitch. "If you think I'd join you in destroying my own species, you're more delusional than the imaginary soldiers you just killed!"

"Imaginary?" Steppenwolf asks, intrigued. "Ten years you've seen those creatures, and you still believe them to be imaginary?"

"They're no realer than this false domain of darkness you cast, Skinwalker!"

"Tell you what," Steppenwolf says, dismissing my hostility. He raises his claws and points beside me. Again, the veil of darkness splits in two, like double doors thrown open to reveal reality. The full moon above spills light on the scene, showing once more the carnage of war. All around us are the dead bodies of the Ka-El, steam rising from their lifeless corpses. But in my immediate vicinity, close by my side, are my fellow Hunters, each one of them kneeling beside me. They are positioned in a straight line placed shoulder to shoulder. In each of their hands is an Arcadian Apple, once again reminding me of the first time we stumbled across an Arcadian grove. Each one of them stares down at the shimmering globe of frozen blood in their palms. Their minds no longer occupy thoughts of their own—they have each been transported away from this world to one where comfortable lies reign supreme.

Directly to my right is Dane, my husband, his silver mask reflecting the glow of the forbidden fruit he holds. I lunge to slap it from his palm, but the second I move even an inch, the double doors of darkness slam shut, causing my companions to vanish from sight. I fall face first against the ground, my hand assaulting the empty air where Dane's hands were a split second ago.

"The terms of my agreement are simple," Steppenwolf asserts, his ghoulish body looming over me as I wallow in defeat. "Your service for their lives, Drakini. I will let them leave these lands and report back to their child king on the things they've learned, and I will teach you how to use your powers. It's a win win win... The ones you love most will survive, you will become more powerful than you could possibly imagine, and I will move one step closer to reaching my Master's goal..."

It is in this moment that something inside me breaks, but not in the way I've been broken in the past. Ten years ago, it was my *mind* that shattered, causing my brain to birth figures capable of protecting me from the things I couldn't protect myself from. But now... Now it's my heart that shatters... This monster has taken EVERYTHING from me... Wisteria is dead. Dane is well on his way. The Ka-El. Pip. Havik. Grite. Cur.

Cur...

The name sparks something in me...

Suddenly, the cracks in my heart align perfectly with the splinters in my brain...

My head throbs as my heart races...

I wince in pain. A sharp jolt shoots directly from my heart to my head.

A howl sounds in the distance, reverberating off the walls of Steppenwolf's domain.

At first, I think it's a mere hallucination, another way my mind plays tricks on me in moments I feel too weak to continue fighting.

But Steppenwolf looks up as the dome of shadows quakes around us from the furious howl. I watch him intently from the ground, realizing from his perplexed expression that something like this has never happened—realizing that the howl most certainly was not a hallucination.

Steppenwolf averts his eyes from the trembling sky, staring at me venomously. I have no reason for it, but in the heat of my delirium as my brain feels as if it will explode and my heart feels like it will turn to a black hole, I sneer. This is Steppenwolf's world, a place where he controls everything inside its domain. And yet, somehow, this guttural feeling of rage and agony I feel manages to strip him of his control.

"What are you—" he starts, cut off as a slashing noise sounds from behind me. A gust of wind rolls past me, bringing with it fresh snowflakes. I tilt my head, trying to see what was capable of stopping the Wendigo mid-sentence. There, floating in the transparent darkness as if there is some sort of invisible wall, stands a set of claw marks. The winds of reality rush into Steppenwolf's projected illusion, causing the curtains of darkness to flap as a set of eyes glimmer like stars emerging from behind an overcast sky.

Slowly, a set of humanoid fingers covered in black fur and tipped with ghastly claws grab hold of the torn veil. Then, just as Steppenwolf lunges to grab hold of me, the Lycan swiftly rips open the wall of shadows like a piece of fabric torn in two.

Once the partition is severed, the entire dome pops like a bubble, allowing the full moon to shed light on the demented wolf as he crouches, spreads his arms, and lets out a blood-curdling howl. Steppenwolf tries to grab hold of me but is thwarted, cut short as the Lycan tackles him without warning.

I try to stand, try to grab hold of my chains, try to do anything other than lay here like a pathetic damsel in distress, but the world around me spins so fast that I fear I may vomit. I am suffering from dissociation sickness, a common symptom that follows a Wendigos illusions. In this moment, I can't tell what's real and what's not. Everything is blurred—objects faze in and out around me—shadows move in my peripheral—my senses succumb to overstimulation.

I can't trust anything...

I can't even know if this Lycan is real, or just another figment of my imagination.

I see the sparkling light of several Arcadian Apples, still held in the palms of my fellow Hunters as their minds are consumed by its fallacies. I stagger toward Dane, or who I think is Dane, determined to bring him back to me from whatever falsity preys upon him. There's a distinct ringing in my ears that drowns out the feral fight in the distance.

I reach out for Dane but my depth perception is all wrong. One moment, I feel as if I'm standing right next to him. The next, my vision zooms out and I see he's several yards away from me. Back and forth, back and forth, my tunnel vision zooms in and out, bobbing side to side as my stifled breathing sends clouds of frost from my ventilator. At one point, I'm on my knees. Then, by some miracle, I'm staggering on my feet. But I blink my eyes once and I'm back on the ground crawling through snow, unsure if I ever truly stood moments ago.

Time cycles in loops. I pull my body across the slick ice, only to shrink several feet back and realize I never truly moved forward.

I have felt the effects of dissociation sickness before, but never with such maddening potency.

Suddenly, I'm hoisted in the air and Dane's body is fading in the distance. My vision bobs up and down as I'm carried through time and space. I see Steppenwolf standing on the battlefield, blood spilling from his decaying, monstrous body. He is perfectly centered between two craggy mountains that look like devil's horns, and I hear him scream violently, "You cannot run from destiny, Drakini! You have my terms—you know where to find me when you've come to accept them!"

I lower my head and catch wind of a familiar scent. I whisper, "Cur..." just before my mind goes dark.

19

CUR (PT. 2)

I have been married to Dane for eight years.

I have known him for ten.

He has warmed my bed more times than I can count.

I have confided things in him no one will ever know—my doubts and insecurities, my traumatic past and future desires.

He has been my champion in a world that wishes to see me fail.

If not for him, only the gods know where I'd be now... Out of everyone that entered Silenius's draft, I am the one he chose for the Hunters.

There is no one in this world I love more than Dane...

And yet...

When I awoke from my feverish delirium...

It was not Dane's name I called out for...

Nor was it Garmin's...

When I awoke, my subconscious mind desired only one name.

When I awoke, Cur is the only name my lips called for.

20

DISSOCIATION SICKNESS

"Cur!" I scream, shooting upright as I'm ripped from my feverish nightmares. I pant uncontrollably; my hands shoot to my throat, fighting to remove a python that is no longer there.

Fight-or-flight instincts kick in, and flight immediately takes a back seat as I jump to my feet, clenching my fists as I survey my surroundings. I have no way of knowing what, if anything, is real. My night terrors have been filled with scenario after false scenario, each one more unrealistic than the last. Visions of Wisteria dying, then me ruling by Steppenwolf's side, then Dane's bloodied body in my trembling hands. My lungs are hyperventilating as I fight the panic rising in my chest—a sense of impending doom constricts my frame, feeling like the rocky walls around me are quickly closing in. Vertigo takes hold of my vision, making the ground shake. I'm forced to stagger my feet and spread my arms for balance. Though I stand still, my eyes zoom in and out on the campfire beside me.

A ghost from my past emerges from the shadows of this cave, causing me to question everything I thought I knew.

"Huntress," he whispers, his face compassionate, like he knows the pain and confusion that flow through my body. I haven't seen Cur in ten years, yet his dark eyes haven't changed a bit since the moment I stared at them last. He is shirtless, just like he was the last time we were together, only his body has been changed drastically by the Deadlands. His abdomen is impossibly lean—his abs look like individually balled fists punching the outside world from his diaphragm—his obliques are so sharp that they look like fish gills, like a Lycan has slit open his sides with their claws. He quickly closes the gap between us, not giving me time to react. His arms wrap around me, putting an end to my swaying. Heat radiates from his tired body, swaddling me in a blanket of comfort, filling my nostrils with his familiar scent, unlocking memories in my head I previously thought were long gone. "You're safe," he whispers as I close my eyes to lessen the nauseating vertigo.

"This isn't real," I tell myself, knowing the truth in my heart. "It's just an illusion... You died... Ten years ago, you died..."

"Shhhh," he hushes, rubbing my back.

"I need to shatter the illusion," I say, convincing myself this is just another part of Steppenwolf's plans. I need to break free of this vision... I must shatter it... Only then can I slay Steppenwolf and save my fellow Hunters. "This is just some hell designed to distract me..."

"This is not hell," he counters, pressing his body into mine. "Hell is where I dreamt of you and woke up alone... Hell is ten years of solitude, forced to watch you from a distance, living as a lone wolf while you married another man, while your reputation echoes through these lands without me by your side..."

I push him away, nearly falling on my ass from lack of balance. Emotional and physical pain throbs through me. I can't even ascertain what actually happened when I faced Steppenwolf, much less discern whether I'm still under his influence. This cave, this fire, this long-lost flame I feel—all of it could be a setup—a way to distract me from dealing a killing blow against the Creator's hellish spawn.

I pant, leaning against the cave wall to balance myself, "Prove to me you're real... What are the odds you died ten years ago, only to reemerge when I lose everything that matters most!"

"I understand you're confused," Cur says, raising his hands defensively, an innocent look in his eyes. "I can explain my absence, just give me a chance... Please, all I need is a chance..."

There is a wild look on Cur's face. His face twitches; his bottom lip quivers as he fights the urge to dump ten years of torment onto my already fatigued and disillusioned mind.

My knees buckle and I slowly slide down the rocky cave wall, wrapping my arms around my legs as tears fall from my eyes once more. I curse inwardly, pissed at my inability to repress my emotions to the same degree Cur does.

"Tell me everything," I mutter, utterly defeated as I put my head between my knees. I repeat, mumbling through my legs, "Tell me everything, and I swear to the gods, if I think you're lying, I'll slit your stomach open and hang you from your own entrails."

21

Blood Moon Hex

"It's called a Blood Moon Hex," Cur explains, the firelight dancing along his face as he sits opposite from me across the campfire. "You've allied yourself with the Ka-El, so I'm sure you know exactly what I'm talking about..."

He's right, I do. The Blood Moon Hex is the most feared grimoire among the Ka-El—a hex that all Lycans fear more than the full moon. It is a spell used by the Ra-El to effectively turn off a Lycan's humanity, allowing their inner beast to take complete control of their body—not only when the moon is full, rather, every second of every day. The way it was explained to me by the Ka-El made sense at the time... Lycans cannot be trapped in Arcadia, but their human counterpart can. When the moon is full, the beast within takes control of their bodies, making it impossible for their minds to be consumed by delusions of grandeur.

But just as a human can be enticed to give over their body to a Wendigo spirit with an illusion of paradise, the Ra-El have discovered a way to trap a

Lycan's human spirit in their mind, essentially allowing the beast within to come forward while their soul unknowingly submits itself. To the Ra-El, this is the next best thing besides clearing the way for a Wendigo to seize a mortal body.

"I have no memory from that time in my life," Cur admits. "I came out of it even more confused than you are now... All I remember is cutting myself free from the cave ceiling... I remember falling into the water, then breaking open the dam so you Hunters could escape the Ra-El... I remember running out of air, and I remember an overwhelming sense of peace washing over me... And then, darkness... But through that darkness, it was your hand that grabbed hold of me, just as I saved you from the shipwreck. You pulled me from the waters, and with Pip's help, you nursed me back to life...

"We lived an entire life together, though I knew none of it was false. I don't say any of this to make you pity me—that's not what I want... But you and I... We... We married, Drakini... I came to love you more than I've ever loved anything on this earth... Not only that... We had a child together—a sweet baby girl... I know it sounds crazy, but I still remember holding her crying body in my arms... It felt so real, realer than even this moment... It changed who I was as a man, fundamentally... It made me learn to live for someone other than myself, and I was so goddamn grateful to raise her by your side.

"We started planning our escape from these Deadlands, in order to bring our daughter to safety. We split our time three ways—during the daytime, I tracked and surveyed the Ra-El and the Wendigos they worshipped. But during the night, in the concealment of darkness, you and your Hunters worked on building a ship that could get us the hell out of here. But regardless of our hunting and building, our full-time job, together, always remained raising our daughter.

"But as our daughter grew older and learned how to speak, she became increasingly wiser than her years... She had your yellow eyes... The same ones you had when we came to these lands. She always had this serious look on her face, and she always asked so many questions about the world... At first, I just thought it was a phase—ya know, how children are never satisfied with the answers you give them so they always ask a series of follow-up questions. She'd go on and on and on if you let her... She'd ask, 'Why is it always so cold?' to which I'd reply, 'Because that's how it is during the winter.' She'd ask, 'What is winter?' and I'd answer, 'It's the season where everything gets cold, where the sky's rain freezes into snow.'

'When will the sky rain without freezing?'" Cur asks, inflecting his voice to mimic our nonexistent daughter's voice. Tears brim along his bottom eyelids, causing me to realize something devastating. I've just lost everything—Wisteria, Dane, my Hunters, my shadow soldiers... But I'm not alone in this pain. Cur, too, has lost everything, living an entire life without realizing it was a dream all along.

He continues, wiping the tears in his eyes, "It wasn't until we prepared our attack against Steppenwolf that her questions began to dismantle the life I thought I knew and loved... She increasingly became more and more skeptical... When she learned what Arcadia was, she asked me how I knew I wasn't currently under the Wendigo's influence. I assured her a Lycan like me couldn't be deceived by a Wendigo, but she pressed on... She asked why the same stars were always visible in the night sky... Why she'd pick an ignisberry bush clean of its fruit one day, then return the next day and see it was laden with berries once more... Why everything was going our way in a hostile land designed to break us down... Progressively, the questions got harder and harder to answer, and soon, she stopped asking them altogether.

"'This world isn't real, dad,' she told me one day, her amber eyes almost glowing as she spoke the words. Naturally, I didn't want to believe her... But her assertion was only a confirmation of something I'd known for a long time... For years, she'd been sowing seeds of doubt in my mind, and by the time she took her stand, I knew without a shadow of doubt she was right. I stared in her eyes and watched as they slowly morphed into a single, great light too bright to stare at... And that, Drakini, is when I awoke from my dream, staring at the sun in the sky as I laid in chains outside the Ra-El's burrow...

"It took months for me to learn what had happened—I was so dissociated from the hallucination that I wanted to die when I was forced to see reality."

I cut him off, urged to ask a question that burns at the back of my tongue, "Our daughter... You said she had my eyes... What was her name?"

He looks at me, partly intrigued that this is the question I'd choose to ask, partly saddened to speak her name aloud for the first time in this cold world of reality. "You named her Wisteria," Cur says, a single tear spilling down his cheek as he confronts her memory.

Utterance of the name ignites suspicions in my mind that cannot be explained away by mere coincidence. These past ten years, I have not told a single soul about Wisteria or her imaginary companions, not even Dane. The fact that Cur not only had this vision, but that our daughter was miraculously named Wisteria and had the hellcat's yellow eyes... It's almost like... No, it can't be... Could Wisteria, a figment of my own imagination, appear to Cur to break him from the Blood Moon Hex, just as she's shattered Arcadian visions every time I've encountered a Wendigo?

I bite my tongue, wanting to stab him with questions until he bleeds out, but I don't want to influence the story he tells. There will be plenty of time for questions later, but something tells me Cur just needs to talk, after years of solitary confinement.

"A single raven came to me as I wallowed in delirium," Cur continues. "At first, I thought it was a damn mirage because the bird could talk... Turns out, apparently all ravens are able to speak, though they're quite stubborn in which words they use. Her name was Netherwing, and she came to me while my brain and heart mourned the loss of one life and adapted to the rise of another. She pecked at my chains where they were bolted to the mountainside until I was freed from their hold. Somehow, while my head felt as if it had been drugged, I stumbled after Netherwing for what felt like days, though it could have been only minutes, I'm still unsure to this day. But this is where she brought me, and this is where I've remained for years."

Cur stands and grabs hold of a torch whose end rests in the campfire. It illuminates the walls behind him with its dancing flames. Across the craggy surface of the cave, previously hidden by shadows, is a vast series of tally marks so wide that the flame cannot illuminate where they start or end. He picks up a rock from the ground and sets it against the wall, scratching another tally like a raindrop adding to an ocean of water.

"Nearly six years, that's how long I've held refuge in this cave. I've marked a tally for every night that's passed... And you say I died ten years ago... That means I was a prisoner of the Ra-El for four years, living in a false world while they used my Lycan form for gods-know-what. If it wasn't for Netherwing, I would have died during my dissociation sickness..."

"Nether!" a voice squawks, causing me to jump. Wings flap, casting a massive shadow across the torchlit wall, like some great eagle materializing from darkness. I instinctively grab hold of a rock beside me, ready to go out fighting if I must. But Cur doesn't flinch in the slightest, and my fears are quickly proven to be misplaced as a raven no larger than a common pigeon lands on Cur's shoulder, eyeing me with its beady black eyes. Cur smiles, raising his hand to stroke the bird's raised neck feathers.

"She brought me food while I was sick, even packed snow in a bowl so I would have drinking water once it melted... She's a smart bird," Cur says.

"Smart!" Netherwing echoes, cocking her head to the side as she analyzes me, ever-suspicious of my presence.

"She'll warm up to you—just isn't used to having company is all."

"She's... Quite the companion," I say, smiling as I meet her eyes. I don't know why, but it makes me happy to see Cur hasn't been completely alone all these years. Life in the Deadlands is too hard to sojourn alone. The raven reminds me of Wisteria in many ways, Cur's own dark guardian constantly looking out for him, protecting him when he doesn't have the strength to protect himself.

"That she is," he confirms, then continues, "I scratch her back, she scratches mine... These last six years would've been impossible without her, that's for sure."

"If the things you say are true, if you really were trapped by the Blood Moon Hex for four years, why didn't you come find me once you were freed?" I ask, not wanting to change the subject, but silently yearning for the answer. "Your last words to me... You said you would come find me," I say, choking on tears building in my throat.

"That's the thing," Cur whispers, shifting uncomfortably in the shadows as he lowers his torch. "I did find you... After the dissociation sickness lifted, however many months that took, I was hellbent on finding you... And I did," he says, lifting his wrist for me to see. Tied loosely to his forearm is a bracelet of woven... hair?

"This is the hair you lost when we were first attacked by the Ra-El all those years ago. I've held onto it all these years, knowing it would lead me back to you... And it did, but by the time I found you... It was too late..."

"What do you mean it was too late?" I don't mean to scream, but the question is forced from my diaphragm by several violent sobs. Tears fall without remorse now, soaking my face.

"I... When I..." Cur stutters, ashamed of the words he wants to speak. He starts over and tries again, "You have to understand, Drakini... I lived an entire life with you as my wife, even if that life was only an illusion... The coldest day of my life was the day I found you... It was snowing, hard... I know you don't know this, because you don't have my sense of smell, but it's difficult to track a scent in a blizzard... It's like following footprints in the sand, except a hundred waves have washed over them by the time you find them... But you, Drakini... You have a scent I could never forget... I could track it through the sleet and snow... I smell it in my dreams, when my mind revisits that version of my life that never was... And so, with Netherwing's help, I found you in a matter of days after setting my mind to it..."

"And?" I ask, sniffling snot so it doesn't leak from my nose.

"And I... I was too late," he answers innocently, a broken smile on his face and a quiver in his voice. "You married Dane, and when I saw that, I wasn't strong enough to make myself known to you. I stumbled on you two in the midst of a fresh snowstorm, and before I could so much as call out your name... You... Well, you leaned in to give him a kiss... It sounds fucked up to say, but it's almost like the Fates knew I was watching... But before I could feel sorry for myself, I saw the reason you two were alone in the woods... You were burying a... There's no easy way for me to say it..."

"Burying our unborn child," I whisper, saying the words he's too afraid to utter.

"Yeah," he sighs, ashamed of himself for bringing it up.

"It's okay, I whisper reassuringly. "The Ka-El call it a blighted birth—when the child dies before reaching full term... They say it's these cursed lands and the wicked spirits that walk them... Said the baby never stood a chance in the first place, though I'm not sure if I believe them."

"How, erm... How old was it when you... ya know..."

"A few months... My belly had only just grown rounded when I woke up one night with a pain in my abdomen."

"I'm sorry, Dra—"

"Don't be," I say, cutting him off. "It was years ago. I've had my time to mourn."

"No," he replies, shaking his head. "You don't understand... I feel so fucking selfish, so fucking guilty... All these years, I've felt terrible, but... When I saw you burying your child I... Fuck..." Cur slides down the rocky wall behind him, cradling his head in his arms as he breaks down. Netherwing leaps from his shoulder and shouts, "Selfish!"

"What is it? What's wrong, Cur?" I ask, wanting to close the gap between us. I think better of it as I anticipate the words he holds back, words that I know will knot my stomach.

He looks up at me, tears streaming down his defeated, hollow cheeks. "I was fucking happy when I saw it! In some dark, twisted way, I was glad the gods had conspired against your union with Dane! It's so fucked up; it's so selfish; it's so goddamned pathetic! But that curse—the Blood Moon Hex—it changed me... It stole the innocence from my eyes... The peace from my mind... The light in my life... I lived in the dark so long that it became a part of me... You were the only thing that got me through, Drakini, and when I saw you in love with another man... It shattered me whole!"

"How dare you," I say, rage boiling in my veins. I stand, no longer feeling the fatigue or sadness or pain. He looks up at me, his face red with embarrassment. But my next words are the ones that make him turn white as a ghost. "You had no right to withhold yourself from me just because

I married Dane! I loved you, you idiot! Fuck that, I didn't just love you; I needed you!"

"Needed you!" Netherwing echoes violently, ruffling her feathers as my aggression builds.

"I mean, what the fuck is wrong with you? You can sacrifice your life three times for me, but you aren't fucking brave enough to sacrifice your pride? And while we're talking about saving me, how the fuck were you able to find me and break through Steppenwolf's illusion, on a full moon no less? You expect me to believe that was some sort of coincidence?"

"You wouldn't believe me if I told you," he says, staring at me like a dog who's disappointed its owner. That is Cur's greatest weakness, I've gathered. He sees himself as no human's equal. Whether he wants to admit it or not, humanity has convinced him he's no better than a stray dog. Though he stands up for himself when others call him horrid names, the confidence he portrays is no realer than Steppenwolf's illusions. This world has told him he isn't good enough so many times that he's convinced himself it must be true.

"Try me," I dare, gritting my teeth.

He sighs, not wanting to talk, yet not wanting to upset me any further. "Since the Blood Moon Hex was lifted, things went back to how they always were. I was human any night the moon wasn't full, but on the nights Luna showed her face, the beast within emerged for its moondance... Us Lycans, we... I... You can't remember what happens when you shift... It's like one moment, you feel an indescribable agony come over you, then everything fades to black, like you're sleeping... That's how it's always been since the Curse of Dagon claimed me, and that's how it was when our daughter freed me from the hex... But last night, everything changed Drakini. I saw her again... After six long years of misery, I saw her... Our daughter... Wisteria... She came to me when I shifted. There was still that split second of pain as my body shifted, and darkness followed once more... But in the darkness, I wasn't alone... I saw her yellow eyes in the distance, crazy as that may sound..."

"It doesn't sound crazy," I say, my anger fading like smoke from an extinguished candle. I can't even begin to explain how far from crazy it sounds. If anything, it sounds like the most sane thing I've ever heard after ten years of guidance from the hellcat's amber eyes. If anything, his testimony only proves his sincerity. But could it be possible? After all these years, did Wisteria truly reveal herself to another? Though she was spawned from the cracks in my mind, perhaps it isn't impossible to believe she came to Cur, not to save him from the full moon, but instead to lead him back to me...

"I didn't understand why she came back," Cur admits. "I mean, I hadn't seen her since the hex was lifted... I thought she was gone forever, a figment of my imagination I'd never see again. But last night, she called to me from the darkness, Drakini. She called to me, and I followed her voice. She was screaming so frantically—trying to tell me mommy was in trouble... I ran like hell to get to her, faster than I've ever run in my life. But when I reached her... There was some sort of invisible barrier cast, like a wall of glass. I ran straight into it, and she pounded her little fist against it from the other side, crying out for me to save mommy—to save you... In that moment, there wasn't a thing in this world I wasn't willing to do to save her. It was like the entire six year period I spent coming to terms with her absence vanished in an instant, and suddenly I was willing to sell my soul itself to get her back. I channeled every negative emotion these Deadlands have cursed me with in that moment, and somehow, in a split second, I felt more human than ever before.

"I shattered the glass that kept me from her, Drakini... But as the glass fell, I felt... Dread... I don't know how to describe it, no matter how bad

I want to. It was like I was struck by a lightning bolt made entirely of concentrated fear, as if I'd just sacrificed my soul to the devil... It felt like some omnipotent set of eyes were watching me from the darkness above. I was no longer alone in the darkness, but not in a good way. I was so afraid that it was hard to breathe, like I was suffocating on the dread in my chest. I didn't know what to do, but I knew I needed to get our daughter far away from the evil descending on us... I put her over my shoulder and ran even faster than before. I ran, and I didn't look back... When I awoke, I was here, and I wasn't alone... Except it wasn't my daughter who laid by my side... It was you."

22

SILVER PROMISE

"A Wendigo's curse doesn't end when you shatter the illusion," Cur mutters, picking himself up off the ground, then closing the gap between us. He is so close to me that I can feel his every exhale warm my neck. "In fact, when you shatter the illusion, I'd argue that's when the curse begins... The curse isn't living in paradise... It's getting to live in paradise, then having to return to a reality—one that falls so short of paradise that it feels as if you've been sent to hell... When I lost you and our daughter, the world lost its color, and I lost my purpose. But when I awoke from last night's moondance and saw you by my side... I swear to the gods it's the happiest I've felt since breaking free of the Blood Moon Hex."

"Don't swear to the gods," I say, so many emotions swirling in my stomach. "Swear to me," I command, raising my hand to caress his cheek. As my palm makes contact, Cur gasps, then flinches away violently. He covers his cheek where I touched him, cursing under his breath. When he lowers his fingers, I see a burn wound seared near his sideburn, as if someone has branded him with some shapeless symbol. I inhale quickly, the butterflies in my stomach instantly fluttering away to take refuge in someone less problematic than me. As I stare at my hand, sorrow pierces my heart. There, nestled neatly on my ring finger, is the braided silver band I've worn since exchanging vows with Dane. I've worn it so long that I forgot it was there, and my careless act caused silver to come in contact with Cur's face, burning him as a consequence.

I can see the hurt in Cur's eyes as he stares at the silver ring, touching his cheek once more. In this moment, my heart is torn in two between two men, though only one of them is here to receive my love. This ring I wear is symbolic of the forbidden love I feel... It is no coincidence that the only thing standing between me acting on my desires in this moment is a wedding ring cast from a metal that is lethal to Cur. Even when Dane is not here, the promises I made to him make themselves known...

When I married him, I vowed to love him in sickness and in health... In life and in death... Truth be told, I don't even know if he is alive anymore, nor do I know if he's joined the ghosts of these Deadlands. But I do know one thing for certain...

When I married him, when I made those vows... I had no idea Cur was alive.

If I had, I wouldn't have stopped until I found him—until I repaid the life-debt I owed him—until I could look him in the eye and tell him how I truly felt about him.

"Drakini, it's okay," he whispers, shrinking back from me. "You don't have to—"

His words fall short as I slowly remove the ring with my right hand, lifting it into the air so his eyes can follow it. Without saying a word, I let it fall into the crackling fire. I reply, my body yearning for his, "I know I don't have to. But this is something I've wanted for longer than words can describe."

I watch his Adam's apple quiver as I pull on my leather jerkin's strings, loosening its grip on my upper torso. A chill washes over me as my clothes fall to the ground one after the other, but the warmth of the fire kisses my flesh ever so delicately. Cur's face reddens as he takes in my nudity. The last time he saw me this naked, our lives were on the line. Without thinking twice, he selflessly sacrificed himself so I may live.

It wasn't Dane who saved me. Not Pip. Not Katana. Certainly not Calico.

It was this man—this hero.

Tomorrow isn't promised in these lands, so tonight, I will leave no emotion unspoken. Tonight, I will tell Cur how I feel about him. But I won't do it with words... Tonight, my body will prove my love with action.

23

BROKEN PROMISE

I've had sex with Dane more times than I can count.

But tonight, I learn what it feels like to make love.

24

Cold World

I nuzzle my head against Cur's chest, breathing in his musk like it's a drug I can't get enough of. In this concealed cave, there's no telling how long the two of us have slept, but after last night, I wouldn't be surprised if we slept the day away. My body aches in ways I didn't know were possible, and my heart flutters in ways that make me fear it might break. Yet somehow I still find myself drawn to the pain.

After Steppenwolf's mirage, I feared Cur was just some extension of my sanity slipping.

But after last night, I know for certain he is real.

I run my hand along his bare chest, then down his stomach, whispering in his ear, "You know, I still don't know your real name."

He stirs from his sleep, laughing and yawning at the same time. "It's a bit late for that, don't you think?"

I laugh with him for a moment but double down on the statement. "I'm serious," I say, sitting up slightly so I can look him in his dreamy eyes. "I mean, what if it's something lame? What if I just cheated on my husband with a Theodore or Kristoff? Or worse, what if you're a Bartholomew?"

"Very funny," he groans, stretching his limbs as his body wakes slowly. "I'll have you know my name is one of a kind, thank you very much."

"Then tell it to me," I plead, placing my chin on his sternum. Even from this angle, looking up at him from below, he is the most attractive man I've ever seen. We were both kids when we came to this hostile land, but the snow and ice have made Cur a man unlike any other.

"Maybe some other time," he replies. "Now bundle up, there's something I want to show you."

Just like that, he stands from our makeshift bed of grizzly pelts and starts dressing, expecting me to do the same. I look at his mysteriously tan skin, wondering how he's able to avoid paleness in a region the sun hardly shines. I bite my lip, realizing I want him again, even though I overdosed on him last night.

Hell is where I dreamt of you and woke up alone. That's what he said to me yesterday, and his words are etched on my heart like some fiery scripture, impossible to forget and painful to carry. I've encountered Arcadia more times than I can count, but I always had Wisteria to anchor me to reality. I can't imagine what it would be like to live a whole life, only to realize it was a dream all along. The worst part is, there's no way of knowing if my current reality is a vision of similar sorts. For Cur, there was never any indicator that signaled where one life ended and another started. I no longer have Wisteria to ground me, so Cur could be a ghost inside some invisible domain Steppenwolf cast inside my fractured mind.

"Show me what?" I ask, still devouring his half-naked body with my lustful eyes. I stand, letting the pelts fall to my feet so Cur can see my body once more. When he turns to look at me, I see the hesitation he battles. He clenches his jaws as I lick my lips. Between us floats a tension so palpable that I feel I can't even take a step forward without disturbing it.

"Don't look at me like that," he warns, trying to avert his eyes but struggling with some unspeakable desire.

"Or what?" I ask, taunting him like a child expressing a crush they can't communicate.

"Don't," he says, doubling down. "Last night was a mistake. You're a married woman, Drakini."

I instinctively hold up my left hand, showing off my naked ring finger.

Replying without words, he points to the burn mark on his cheek.

"That's a worse wound than any Dane has ever taken on my behalf," I remark.

"Then why marry him?" Cur asks, his voice sheltering his emotional pain.

"This world is cold, Cur. Do you blame me for trying to find happiness in your absence?"

"I blame you for finding happiness in a place you knew you'd never find it."

"But I've found it here, with you... Would you choose to deprive me of it further?"

"Don't make me the bad guy here, Drakini. You aren't the victim."

"You owe me this."

"Do I?" he scoffs. "How do you figure?"

"Because I was the only one that treated you with kindness," I reply, closing the gap between us. My hand grips the grizzly pelt draped over his untied jerkin. I give it the slightest pull. He does nothing to prevent it from falling. I can tell from the way he looks at me that he wants this as much as I do, but his willpower is stronger than mine. He stands at the edge of a cliff, ready to jump after me. I need only jump first and he will follow me into the abyss.

I remove the jerkin from his shoulders, knowing fully well that whatever he wanted to show me can wait.

The glowing embers of the fire die out, but Cur's feverish body replaces its heat so fast that I don't even notice.

25

MOON TREADER

"My gods," I exclaim, staring up at the massive ark that stands half-built between two leaning trees. "How did you... When did you... I don't..."

I'm at a complete loss for words as I stare up at the boat, its bulky frame nearly the same size as the Sun Treader which brought us here. But it's distinctly different from the Sun Treader... It's... It's like a piece of art almost... Though it isn't finished, it's beautiful... I don't know anything about boats, and I've never used my hands to build something of this proportion... But I don't need to be a builder to know this ship is the ticket out of this hellish place.

"What do you think?" Cur asks, running his hand across the bow. The main beam that curves along the front is covered in chiseled sheets of rock, almost as if Cur bent boulders to make them conform to the curvature of the boat. I don't even have to ask what the rocky battering ram is for—I lived through the Sun Treader's demise... Cur has fortified the ship's bow with rock as a way to withstand sheets of ice and lurking glaciers. It's an idea so genius that I can't even begin to wrap my head around how he came up with it.

"What do I think?" I stammer, marveling at the creation. The mast casts a shadow over me, blotting out the sun's freezing rays. "I don't even know what to say... You did this? All by yourself?"

"Not necessarily," he replies, then chuckles, "Netherwing helped where she could."

Netherwing shouts from his shoulder, "Moon Treader! Moon Treader!"

"Come on," Cur groans. "I wanted to be the one to reveal the name, feathered menace."

I run my hand along the hull, walking toward its stern. Only half of the hull is finished. My hand reaches the space where the wooden planks die off, allowing me to peer inside the ship's skeletal structure. It isn't as big as the Sun Treader was, but what it lacks in size it makes up for in its unique shape and unconventional materials.

Moon Treader looks as if it will only carry half the passengers Sun Treader could, which seems appropriate considering we've lost three-fourths of those we came here with. Where Sun Treader was long and oblong, Moon Treader is shaped like a bullet made to be fired from Dane's hand cannons. It is sharp in the front and carries little resistance on its sleek siding; its body is made from white oak, teak, and ashwood.

"Where in the hell did you learn how to do this?" I gasp, unable to look away from the galley. I look at Cur, who waves his hand nonchalantly, as if he built nothing more than a snowman. I continue, "I thought you were from the desert? How does a sand-junkie know how to make a boat?"

"I told you," he says, pushing a hand against a single plank, as if he means to test its structural integrity. "In those four years I was a prisoner to my own mind, you Hunters built a boat to get us out of here. Even if it wasn't real, the things I learned from it was. I'm just glad I paid attention when your people built it."

"You mean to tell me... You learned how to build... THIS," I say, waving my hands violently at the barge, "From OBSERVING?"

"Something like that," he says dismissively, not seeing this skiff for the miracle it is. He continues, "Don't get too excited yet. It's not even finished... We don't even know if it will float yet."

"Your humility never ceases to amaze me," I whisper, my heart racing. Never in a million years did I think we'd find a way off this hellish continent, and yet all this time, Cur has been using his free time to build an answer to my prayers.

"I was planning on finding you again when I finished it, you know."

"I sure as hell hope you were," I laugh. "I mean come on, you know no one out there can row like me."

26

GHOST OF GUILT

"What was he like?" I ask, laying beside Cur as my chest heaves for air. The more we make love, the longer and more intense the sessions become. It's exhausting, yet there's nothing in this world that has brought me such pleasure. I wipe the sweat from my forehead as a wave of euphoria glides from my toes to my fingertips.

"Who?"

I'm not alone in my exhaustion. Cur pants so fast that I fear he might hyperventilate. His upper body is slick with blood and sweat. I let myself get carried away, and my nails cut his skin open in several places. How else am I supposed to express feelings that cannot be spoken?

"Dane," I exhale. "In the visions you saw... From the Blood Moon Hex... What was Dane like?"

"You want the truth?"

"I'd expect nothing less."

Cur sighs, not wanting to be the one chosen to speak these words, but I leave him no option. "At first, he was cold... Distant... This place changed him... Made him dwell on his failures as a leader... Before long, he let these thoughts start to consume him. All he could think about was where he went wrong and how he could get back at Steppenwolf. You and he soon stood at odds over what was best for the group. You criticized him for not putting the needs of the Hunters first, and he lambasted you for losing sight of the enemy. He even... He... I'm unsure how to put this nicely, so I'm just going to say it... He publicly demoted you when you became pregnant with Wisteria. He wanted to exile you from the Hunters completely, but the others came to your defense... But still, he wasn't happy. He said the baby was proof your head wasn't on the mission at hand—said this wasn't the place to bring a baby into the world."

"Do you think he was like that because of your subconscious feelings toward him?" I ask, unable to see how my husband could be capable of such defamation.

"I suppose there's no way of knowing. All I know is, it only got worse from there. He stopped speaking with you, then started going on scouting missions alone. Then, one day, he left and never came back. Naturally, we sent search parties after him, but it was ultimately him who found us."

"What do you mean? He came back?"

"Yes and no... I don't know what happened exactly, but when he returned, he was no longer Dane. Natives say the Wendigo is the ultimate symbol of selfishness—a being unwilling to put the needs of others before their own desires. After disappearing into the wilderness, whether battling internally with himself, or externally with another, Dane lost. When he returned, he did so as one of them—a Wendigo. So maybe, just maybe, it was a blessing you chose him over me in this life... Who knows what would've happened to him if my vision was reality... Maybe, just maybe, in a world where he loses you to another, that loss is enough to turn him into a monster."

I lay here, my face nuzzled into Cur's side, mulling over these words. Silently, they torment me, causing me to feel the first shred of guilt since removing my wedding ring. Dane may not be perfect, but he has trusted me with his heart, and I have stabbed him in the back while he's held as a prisoner of war, or worse, as he watches over me in real time as a ghost. He deserves better from a wife than me. In a way, I have been more selfish than even a Wendigo these past days, caving to every desire that enters my heart, then justifying it with pathetic excuses of not knowing what my future holds.

Silently, as Cur falls asleep, I loathe myself inwardly. What a horrible mess I've made... And worse yet, something tells me the webs I've spun will soon be the same ones that lead to my downfall.

What would Wisteria think, if she were here?

No, I tell myself, biting the inside of my cheek to drown out the memory with physical pain. She's dead. There's no use concerning myself with opinions of the dead. Despite the love I feel for Wisteria, she wasn't strong enough to save me from Steppenwolf.

But I lay beside the man who was, and that alone is what gives me the comfort to close my eyes, silence my thoughts, and go to sleep once more.

27

SKELETONS IN THE CLOSET

"What are you talking about?" I ask, frustrated by Cur's chosen topic of discussion.

"You've changed, Drakini," he asserts, his accusation immediately causing me to get combative.

"You went ten years without seeing me," I shout. My voice causes snow to fall from the frozen branches overhead as Cur drops a piece of lumber. "Of course I've changed! I'm not a little girl anymore!"

"No," he defends, moving away from the boat so he can prepare himself for this inevitable argument. "You misunderstand. It's been half a month since I saved you from your encounter with Steppenwolf, and you haven't so much as mentioned a plan to get back at him... The Drakini I knew ten years ago would have immediately dropped everything to make a plan of attack! It's almost like... that fire you had inside you... the one that made you so different... it's gone... Whether he's the one that took it from you or it's something else, I don't know. But when I knew you ten years ago, you weren't even willing to concede to Pip in a battle of rowing. And you damn near led us into hell itself for a chance to save Ghost—an Undead you didn't even care about. But what now? You lost a fight against Steppenwolf and you're just going to give up? That isn't you, Drakini..."

"What do you want me to say?" I gasp, clenching my fists. "That monster took everything from me, Cur. He killed the whole pack of Ka-El as a result of my failure! He took the remaining Hunters, my husband included, as prisoners! Hell, there's no way of knowing if they're even alive anymore! They may even be Wendigos themselves for all I know! I lost, Cur. I took on my enemy and gave it everything I had, for what? I prepared for that encounter for ten years and lost, so what makes you think I'd ever reconsider taking him on a second time?"

My voice is venomous, but not because Cur is wrong. His words are like knives pressing into emotional wounds that haven't had a chance to heal. He is judging me based off impressions I made when I was only a kid—a naive girl of sixteen, no less. And even worse, I had Wisteria these past ten years to make up for my many weaknesses. Now that she's gone, I can't communicate to Cur how sorely outmatched we are, which is why we stand in this makeshift shipyard working on Cur's galley—because the only option we have to win the coming war is to get the hell off this foreign land and inform Silenius of the threat we've encountered. Whether Cur wants to accept it or not, this boat is the only practical answer we have. If we can't get out of here, everything we've uncovered will die with us and be covered by snow alongside our corpses.

"Drakini," he sighs with a tone of disappointment. "This isn't you and you know it. The past two weeks, the only interests you've expressed are fucking, hunting, and building this damn boat... If I knew seeing it would distract you from seeking vengeance, I would've never showed you it in the first place. And don't get me wrong, your safety is my priority, so I'm not saying I want you to take on Steppenwolf again... But the girl I knew would have moved heaven and hell for a chance to save her soldiers and pay Steppenwolf back in blood for his misdeeds."

"Well I'm not the girl you knew, Cur!" I scream, "What do you want me to say? Huh? That I'm scared? That facing Steppenwolf was the most afraid I've ever been in my entire life? Because if that's what you want me to say then I'll say it! He didn't just defeat me, he destroyed every part of me that made me who I am, damnit! There are things about me you don't know, Cur! Things about me that no one knows!"

"Well what the hell is stopping you from telling me?" Cur asks, holding his hands to his sides as he looks around. "If you haven't noticed, we have all the time in the world out here... Just tell me—tell me everything... Speak now or forever hold your peace!"

He's right. But just because I'm in the wrong doesn't make me feel any less crazy. I want more than anything to tell him about the skeletons in my closet—to tell him about Wisteria the hellcat and her brigade of fanatic, masochistic followers. Grite and Havik and Lu Bu and Osprey. I want to tell him about Dyran's ghost; I want to tell him how these imaginary beings are the only reason I'm alive today—how they've been guiding every decision I've made for the past ten years. I want to tell him how Steppenwolf killed them—want to tell him how I'm nothing without them...

But once I admit to these things, I'll never get these words back. I'll be left at the mercy of Cur's judgment, and I can't stand the thought of the man I love most thinking I'm some delusional, broken woman. More than that, I don't want to admit the guilt I feel, nor for him to know I gambled hundreds of lives away over false confidence given to me from some make-believe, fictional character with yellow eyes.

Tears build in my throat as this conversation reaches its precipice. I choke on the words as they bounce up and down in my throat, each second bringing them one inch closer to leaving my mouth. I swallow them down, but they surge back up just as fast. For ten years this has been my greatest secret. I've held it close to my chest, hiding it away from the world for fear of the reactions I'll receive.

Finally, without thinking, my mouth opens without my permission, and words fall out whether I want them to or not. "I... I see things," I begin, not daring to look Cur in his eyes for fear of his condemnation. "Things... People... Spirits... I've never really been sure what to call them... All I know is, no one else can see them."

"Like Arcadia?"

"No," I answer. "Arcadia is a hallucination—a mirage... But these things I see, they are real to me. They appear in real time, unaffected by reality but distinctly real in their own way... They walk and talk and do everything me and you do, only they aren't... real... It's nearly impossible to explain, Cur, but I swear to you it's the truth. At first, there was only one of them... A hellcat—something that looks like the crossing of a lynx and panther—named Wisteria. She came to me randomly one day at a time I needed saving. It sounds insane to say, but if it wasn't for her, I wouldn't be here today... You've saved my life three times, Cur, but this hellcat... She's saved me more times than I can count..."

"Wisteria," Cur mutters in amazement, looking at me sympathetically, almost as if he understands. "What are the odds that this hellcat is something only you know about, yet I was able to discern her name while under control of the Blood Moon Hex!"

"I had those very thoughts when you spoke of our daughter," I admit, finally brave enough to look at him after hearing the excitement in his voice. Where I expected to see disappointment on his face, I instead see...

understanding. Patience. Sympathy, even. "But it isn't just her, Cur. Somewhere, from the cracks in my brain, she's summoned others. A four-armed behemoth named Havik, a moccasin-crazed goblin named Grite, an archer who doesn't miss and feels the need to rhyme every sentence, a gigantic falcon, and even the ghost belonging to a knight I once knew... I see all of them, hear all of them, I was even trained by all of them! Everything I am, everything I've become, is a lie! And after Steppenwolf..." The words choke in my throat. I fall to my knees, crunching the snow beneath me as I break down.

But by the time my knees touch down, Cur is there, his hands planted on my shoulders as he sinks to the ground in front of me. I don't dare look up at him, but I don't have to. He wraps me in his embrace so the world can't see me cry, and finally, after two weeks of repressing the pain, I mourn my fallen friends fully.

"What happened after Steppenwolf?" he asks in a low whisper, rubbing my back slowly.

"I thought..." I say, sobbing the words inaudibly into his chest, afraid to speak them aloud for fear of acknowledging their truth. "I thought only I could see them... But... Steppenwolf... He saw them too... He... He... killed them..."

The first flurries of a coming storm fall from the overcast sky. The clouds in the distance darken. I've just revealed to Cur my greatest secret, and he receives it with open arms, kissing my head as I cry into his shoulder.

I don't know what I've done to deserve such love, but as I place all my emotional weight on Cur, I find he's been preparing all these years to help carry the burden I've shouldered alone all this time.

28

EYES OF PISS

"Packing?" I repeat Cur's answer with confusion. "Packing for what?"

Cur scurries across the cave I've come to accept as my new home, grabbing miscellaneous items and stuffing them into a knapsack made from worn leather. We've only just returned from a taxing day working on the boat, and without a word spoken, Cur's urgency suggests he's made plans for some mysterious expedition.

"There's someone you need to meet, Drakini. We only have two weeks until the moon is full again, and the journey is long. I need to get you there safely before my next moondance. I can explain more when we're on the way, but for now, grab whatever you need for the road and put it in this," he says, tossing me a bag of my own. I catch it, then stare at it like it's some alien object I've never seen before. This doesn't make any sense. I just spilled my guts to Cur and revealed the reason behind my sulking, and now he bustles around like a madman. It's almost like my insanity is some infectious disease that's spread to his brain.

"Is this about what I told you? About Wisteria? Because if so, I'd rather not be kept in the dark on whatever scheme you've cooked up."

Cur stops in his tracks, perhaps realizing his manic behavior is unsettling to me. He looks at me intensely, a glimmer of excitement in his eyes. "I know you thought I'd think you're crazy when you told me about the things you see, but they made more sense to me than anything I've ever heard, Drakini. If anything, they made me realize the boat isn't our way off these lands... It's you, Drakini. You're the key to defeating the Wendigos, I'm certain of it! Everything makes sense, dating back to that ice demon that drowned Seance within minutes of our arrival... He called you a Seer, I remember it like it was yesterday. Back then, I didn't know what he was talking about... But now, after everything I've been through, combined with what you've told me... I think I understand!"

"Maybe you can explain it to me then," I laugh nervously, fumbling with the bag in my hands. "Because right now, I'm more confused than the day knights showed up to my town announcing the King's draft."

"There is a man I've encountered in the wilderness—a Lycan like myself. I met him quite some time ago, not long after the Blood Moon Hex was lifted from me. Maybe it was fate, or maybe it was pure luck that brought him across my path as I sought supplies for the boat. His name is Fenric 'Daybane' Draven, better known in these parts as 'The Wolf Who Howls at the Sun.'"

"Gods, Cur," I groan, instantly siding against this moronic idea. "I'm well aware of Daybane—the Ka-El spoke of him like he was some deranged lunatic. Where his name is mentioned, laughter follows. He's like a king's jester, garnering disrespect wherever his reputation is brought up. Surely this man is not the one you've gotten yourself all worked up over."

"I am well aware of Draven's reputation, Drakini, but you need to hear me out, because you two are not so dissimilar."

"Are you calling me crazy?"

"Not in the slightest, but other than you, he is the only person in this land who's rumored to have faced Steppenwolf head on and lived to tell the tale! That's why he's so snotting crazy! His encounter with Steppenwolf shattered his mind—left him in a state where he howls at the sun and can no longer tell his left from his right, among many other quirks, I'll warn you. But after your own encounter, I'd think you'd have sympathy for a man who's been through precisely the same struggle as yourself."

"How do you know he's faced Steppenwolf? How do you know his mother didn't just drop him on his head a dozen times when he was a babe?"

"Because unlike you, I've met him in person, so I've formed my own opinion on him instead of listening to what others have to say about him."

"Draven!" Netherwing shouts proudly, casting shadows as she flaps through the air. She parrots, "Crazy! Crazy! Crazy!"

"See what I mean?" I ask, laughing at Netherwing's choice of words.

"You need to trust me on this, Drakini. I'm not saying he isn't off his rocker, but I do think he is the only one on this side of the world that can help you. When I met him, he smelled your scent on me, even though it had been years since I'd seen you! But not only that, he identified your scent as one belonging to a 'Seer,' just like that snow demon. Without even meeting you in person, he knew exactly what you were! He was rambling, but he called you 'The Worthy One—the one with eyes of piss.'"

"How flattering," I mutter.

"Eyes of piss!" Netherwing squawks unflatteringly.

"I think that's just his own twisted way of saying you have yellow eyes," Cur defends, "But that's not the point. The point is, he knows who you are, Drakini! He knows *what* you are. Almost as if he's seen you before, without ever really seeing you. I wrote it off in the moment as a coincidence, but coincidences be damned. I have seen Wisteria without knowing the role she played in your life, and he has seen you without ever laying eyes on you. There's something here, Drakini. A way through, if my gut instinct can be trusted. Maybe he can help you rediscover yourself, or maybe he knows how to defeat Steppenwolf... I don't know what answers we will find, but we will never know if we don't try..."

"I appreciate you, Cur. More than you know," I say, dropping the bag he's given me so I can touch his shoulder tenderly. I look him in his eyes as I speak my next words. "You've helped me mourn my lost ones, and you didn't question my sanity for a second... But you still don't understand what this has done to me... I am nothing without Wisteria, Cur. I can't face Steppenwolf without her—I couldn't even prevail when she *was* by my side! I wasn't strong enough then, and I don't know if I will ever have the strength to face him a second time..."

"Then let me help you find it," Cur says, brushing my hand off his shoulder, then bending down to pick up the bag I've dropped. He hands it to me once more. "Wisteria saved me from the Blood Moon Hex. I don't know if I would've ever woken from that curse without her, and I never would have been able to save you from Steppenwolf without her. I know how indispensable she's been in your life, because I've witnessed it myself. To you, she was a guardian angel. To me, a daughter. If she's truly dead, I feel the same dread you do... But if I know Wisteria, I know she'd be disgusted by your moping around and she'd blame me for letting you play the victim. Even if she is dead, she's still with us, Drakini. And maybe, just maybe, Daybane knows a way to help you see her once more."

"Fuck," I whisper, gripping the bag tightly. I hate a lot of things in life, but there are few things I hate more than admitting I'm in the wrong. I have a lot to think about, but something tells me from the outcome of this conversation, I'll have plenty of time to think about it along the journey ahead.

"What did you do with my mask and chain?" I ask, causing Cur to look at me with a glimmer of whimsical suspicion in his eyes. I add, "I'll go with you to meet this lunatic Lycan, but I'm not going without a chain in my hands and a dagger fixed to its final link."

29

DRAVEN DAYBANE

"What do you think your brother is doing right now?" I ask Cur as we dig our way through shoulder-high snowdrifts, partly because I want to lighten the mood of our journey, but also so I can have a break from this back-breaking labor. I've been through a lot in my life, but in this moment nothing seems worse than this journey we've embarked upon. It's a silly notion, I know. I've been stabbed, dropped from the sky, hung upside down, raped, and had my brains bashed in more times than I can count—but as I look up at this pile of tightly-packed snow that we've pummeled through for hours, I'm made to feel that this is an all-time low.

We've been on the road for days with little confidence in the direction we travel and no finish line in sight. Meanwhile, the snowfall hasn't slowed and the temperatures only seem to plummet the farther we go. I feel like a rat trapped in a maze, only instead of being surrounded by walls, I've been dropped in the antarctic and told to find the first budding flowers of spring.

Maybe Cur's right, I think to myself, though I'd never admit it aloud. My encounter with Steppenwolf changed me somehow... The Drakini I knew weeks ago wouldn't be caught dead complaining over inclement conditions like I currently am. Hell, if my sixteen year old self was here, she'd be sprinting across this winter wasteland with reckless abandon, marking her path with snow angels on the ground so she could find her way home.

But I'm not the girl I was at sixteen, and I'm not the woman I was weeks ago. Sure, I've faced enemies stronger than me in the past. Hell, the enemies I've made have been *exclusively* stronger than me, if I'm being honest with myself. But Steppenwolf isn't just stronger than me, and the war he wages is not one that can be won by physical prowess or strategic advantage. His war is one of the mind, and gods know my brain has been broken too many times to hold his parasitic visions at bay.

"Huh?" Cur asks, panting as he retreats from the wall of snow before us. His knuckles are covered with frozen blood from punching the ice. Split skin frozen over, then split again just as the bleeding dies down.

"I asked what you think your brother is doing right now," I repeat, then add, "You told me about him, remember? After the Sun Treader went down and it was just us—you told me you accepted responsibility for the murder he committed... Do you ever think about what he's doing on the other side of the world? Do you think he is making the most of the freedom you bought him?"

"Not a day goes by that I don't think about him and my parents," he sighs, slumping against the wall of snow opposite from me. "I have no way of knowing what happened to them after Silenius recruited me. They could be dead, for all I know. When we came to these lands ten years ago and fell prey to Arcadia, right before you saved me from the apple's false visions, I saw him. He was standing at the edge of the orchard calling to me. He didn't look a day older than when I left him. He had this dumb smile on his face and a head of hair that looked like he'd just rolled out of bed."

"Was he cursed by Dagon as well? Was he a Lycan?"

"Not that I know of," he says. "Those cursed by Dagon don't often discover their curse right away. Most live most of their childhood thinking they're just another normal kid—only to be sorely mistaken some random night when Luna is full. From my understanding, Lycanthropy passes only through hereditary genes, but not all those with a Lycan parent are guaranteed to be cursed by Dagon. Neither of my parents are Lycan, but my mother's father was. He married a human, though, and so my mother was lucky that his curse didn't pass to her. I suppose she thought the curse was eliminated—thought she was safe to have children free from this monstrous disease. But somehow, when my parents conceived, the gods saw fit to resurrect Dagon's Curse in me. On the other hand, the gods withheld this burden from my brother, and I'm glad they did. I'd happily shoulder this painful life if it means he gets to live a normal one."

"You're a good man, Cur," I say, arousal igniting in my chest. My connection with this man is more than physical. I find him attractive, sure, but it's so much more than that. His chivalry reminds me of Dyran, but there's so much more to him. Cur is a masochist the way he puts himself in danger's way to protect the ones he loves. Every heroic thing I've done has been for selfish reasons—self-gratification, insecurity, arrogance. It stems from my incessant need to prove myself. But Cur does not act out of self-doubt; he is secure in his own skin.

Cur is a hero not because he wants to be, but because his decisions define him as such. He is everything I want to be, everything I set out to be before coming to this land of the dead. Somewhere along the way, I lost sight of what was most important. I earned the respect I desired and grew arrogant as no enemy I faced was capable of defeating me. I stopped standing up for what was right, not because I was morally blind, but because right and wrong no longer mattered to me.

Maybe, just maybe, the gods weren't wrong for making this my destiny. They have stripped me of all in life I find near and dear to my heart. My pride, my ego, my many victories. It's all meaningless now. In its place is the here and now, and with Cur by my side, I'm simply made a better person just for knowing him.

"You don't have to call me that anymore," Cur laughs, tearing me from my thoughts. "I'd say you've earned the right to know my name."

Excitement flutters in my chest. I speak eagerly, "Well it's about damn time. I was beginning to think I would die before learning—"

My voice dies off. I quickly clamp my hands over my mouth. Warm vomit burns the length of my throat. It surges upward and outward. It takes every part of me to hold it at bay, but I fight a losing battle. I rip my ventilator off frantically, and not a moment too soon. A wave of nausea overwhelms me as I let the torrent of stomach acid torpedo from my mouth onto the tops of my boots. I'm suddenly queasy, just as I was years ago when the waves rocked Sun Treader incessantly on our voyage here.

"Drakini," Cur says, hurrying to my side. He's caught off guard almost as much as I am. One moment I felt fine, the next, bile is melting the snow at my feet. It's almost as if the prospect of learning Cur's name was too much for my gut to bear. He gasps, "What's wrong?"

I wipe my mouth with the back of my hand, embarrassed. I want to set my companion at ease but fear the nausea will take advantage of my open mouth once more. All I can manage to say is, "Fine... I'm fine." The infamous words of any upset lover unwilling to speak their mind. Translation: I'm not fine; in fact, I have no idea why I'm vomiting without provocation—I've never once thrown up in all my life without there being a reason—but thinking about it will only make me more anxious, so I hope he takes my words for their surface value and moves on. Cur is many things, but a simpleton is not one of them. He sees right through my response and readies himself for war with my dismissive nature.

But a strange voice interrupts him.

"Late! You're terribly late!" a man shrieks from above in a tone so shrill that I'm convinced it's Netherwing for a moment. Cur and I lift our heads at the same time and see the strange man standing above us. He stands atop the edge of the snow dune we've spent hours trudging through. His legs are staggered wide, fists on his hips like he's some savior waiting patiently to be announced. But if this is who the gods sent to save us, we are truly doomed.

In his hand is a sundial—a primitive device used by natives to measure the time of day. The Ka-El didn't use these instruments, considering Solis hardly ever shows his face in these hostile lands. No sun, no light to cast shadows. Using a sundial in the Deadlands to measure time is like using a boat to travel across the desert.

"Late, so terribly late," the strange man says once more, now looking down at the sundial in his palm. He looks at it curiously, twisting his head in confusion, then tapping its needle with a finger. The needle spins like a compass pressed against a magnet, then settles once more. "Ah, damn thing seems to be an hour ahead! Forgive me, it seems like you're right on time! Only jesting, this thing's been broken for years," he laughs, tossing it in the snow like it's no more than a biodegradable banana peel.

"Who the hell are you?" I ask, the taste of vomit lingering on my tongue. I clasp my mask back in its place over my nose and mouth, my face feeling naked when the winter wind bites my lips.

"Daybane," Cur exhales with a tinge of regret in his voice.

"Name's Draven, but my friends call me Draven. You can call me the latter because I have a feeling we'll get along smashingly! Say, how 'bout a riddle? Fee-Fo-Fi-Fum, what's one thing all people are running from?"

Without giving me time to think, the man leaps from the edge and hits the ground. It's the most ungraceful landing I've ever seen. Upon impact, his feet slip out from under him and the thud of his ass on ice echoes. He howls gleefully, almost as if someone's just handed him a cart full of golden shekels. Instead of popping up on his feet, the old man lays down on his back and tucks his hands behind his head, staring up at the overcast sky. It's like he's forgotten Cur and I are even here, much less that he asked us a question moments ago.

"A shadow," I answer in a low tone. "Every person is running from their shadow."

The man's eyes slowly light up, followed by a sly smile. I don't know what to think about this man. He looks both young and old at the same time—if he told me he was eighty, I'd believe him, but I'd just as easily go along with it if he said he was forty-five. Living in this hostile environment has aged him significantly, yet it's preserved him at the same time. Draven is like a dry-aged steak. Back in Fyrefell, such a meat was a delicacy. It takes foresight and planning to make one—the butcher bathes a slab of ribeye in salt and lets it age sixty to eighty days, resulting in a foul-looking, mold-covered monster. But after trimming the outside and carving away the imperfections, you're left with a cut of meat unparalleled in flavor and texture.

Only problem is, no one wants to touch an ugly piece of meat with a ten foot pole.

"I've been waiting for you, Piss Eyes," Draven sighs happily. His wide smile reveals his gleaming white teeth, something I wasn't expecting to see. Most men with erotic behaviors like him are lucky if they even have a single tooth remaining, but dental hygiene doesn't seem to be something Draven struggles with.

His eyes are blue. Not like the ocean, nor like the sky on a sunny day. They are like frozen glass, so light in their pigment that it almost seems like he's blind. I wouldn't be surprised if he told me he spends his days staring at the sun, burning his irises until they see nothing more than a permanent blotch of white light in the distance. And similar to his teeth, the hair atop his head is white as snow, not to be mistaken with a Celestial's silver locks. Despite his wrinkled face and blotchy skin, there's something charming about him. He's like an ugly old mutt you find rummaging through your garbage. The kind you decide to take in at first but tell yourself it will never sleep in your bed or eat table scraps, only to find yourself going back on those vows several days later.

"My name isn't Piss Eyes, it's Drakini, and my eyes aren't yellow, they're shit brown," I reply in a hostile tone.

"Ah, but they were yellow once, and you can bet your bippy they'll be yellow again," he sighs.

"How did you find us?" Cur interrupts. "I wasn't even sure we were going in the right direction. I only knew to go this way because a snow owl told my raven you lived in these parts."

"All who seek will find," Draven grunts, answering Cur's question without actually answering Cur's question. "Truth is, I've been watching you for two nights. Just wanted to see how strong your resolve was, so I let you keep digging. It's a life lesson, first o' many. Gotta dig till you can dig no more, then keep digging. It's when people wanna turn around that they miss out. Put down their pickaxes when they're only two swings away from findin' diamonds, I tell you."

"You certainly don't look like a diamond," I mock.

"Diamond in the rough, maybe. But hells, at least I stopped running from my shadow by the time I was your age," he rebuts.

"The hell's that supposed to mean?" I ask defensively, understanding I've been slighted but not quite sure how.

Draven rolls onto his side and stares at my vomit-covered boots, laughing to himself as he whispers under his breath something that sounds like, "I often have that effect on people." He looks up at me, still content where he lays in the snow. There's an innocent look in his eyes, one that tells me he's here to help, though I have no way of knowing how or why. "So you've come to Draven to find your oomph—get back your mojo—is that it?"

"Are you really as crazy as the Ka-El say?" I ask, not answering his question because mine seems more important.

"Crazier, probably," Draven says, undisturbed by the admission.

"Well how did you know I once had yellow eyes if you've never met me?"

"That's for me to know and you to find out, isn't it? I wouldn't be much help if I just gave you the answers to your questions. Much more fun to teach you how to discover them yourself. I've never been one to spoon-feed; hell, I don't even own a spoon. I eat with my fingers and that's never steered me wrong."

"I don't have time to discover them; Steppenwolf—"

"Has your friends? Your husband?"

"How did you—"

"Crazy has its advantages, Piss Eyes. You oughta stop caring so much what others think of you. Only then will the magic happen! Besides, if I know ole Steppenwolf, and you can bet your bippy I do, he won't harm a hair on your husband's chinny-chin-chin. Ever heard of security interest? The ole fart needs them so you come back. I call it a classic bait-and-stitch."

"Can you teach me?" I ask, jumping to the question that's led Cur and I across this bitter wasteland. "Can you teach me how to defeat Steppenwolf?"

"Well that depends," he answers.

"On what?"

"Why of course, on whether you're willing to learn."

30

THE WOLF WHO HOWLS AT THE SUN

"What is a hermit crab without its shell?" Draven asks, introducing us to his makeshift camp.

"A crab?" I guess, almost as unsure in my answer as I am placing trust in this man.

"So close, but no! A hermit!" Draven cheers. "I am a hermit! I live off these Deadlands, which is a paradox in and of itself!" He leaps into the air and crashes onto a snow-covered hammock pitched between two unreliable trees. The shock of his bodyweight causes more snow to fall atop him, but he doesn't seem to mind the cold exposure.

The man's home is almost exactly what I would expect from a man of his nature. The whole setup looks as if it could be broken down and packed away in a knapsack before a fleck of snow can fall from a cloud above to the ground below. The crazed man's belongings consist of little more than his hammock, a tarp, a few trinkets, and a glass filled with... orange juice?

I look to Cur, hoping desperately I'm not the only one who's having doubts. He averts his eyes quickly and hides his face, scratching his head in embarrassment. "Er, Draven," he calls out uncomfortably.

"That's my name, but please for the love of the gods, don't wear it out!"

"What... Uh... What exactly are we doing out here?"

"And how are you going to teach me to beat Steppenwolf?"

"Ah, two fantastic questions!" Draven shouts, hopping up from his hammock like it's burned his buttocks. "Come, come, gather around my most beloved possession!" Draven shuffles frantically through the snow, ushering us toward the glass of orange juice that sits motionless atop a snow-covered rock. Draven plops down to his ass, sitting criss-cross-apple-sauce. He places his hands around the glass like a frigid camper trying to warm their fingers before a fire. Cur and I eye each other once more, each of us hovering over the pedestal but not willing to sit on the frozen ground.

"And where, exactly, did you find oranges in this hell forsaken land?" I ask, knowing fully well that such fruits only grow in tropical regions. A citrus sapling would die in this land before a planter manages to dig a hole in the permafrost-infested soil.

Draven disregards my question completely, asking in return, "You believe you walk on solid ground, but it's all strings—tugged from the sound. A choice, they say, between what you know and knew... but choose you do not, for I chose it for you. What am I?"

"Welp, that just about does it for me," I sigh, looking to Cur for confirmation. "I've seen all I need to, are you ready to go?"

Cur bites his lip in contemplation, not nearly as dismissive as I am of our manic host. Draven's eyes look at us both at the same time, splitting apart and looking in different directions like they have minds of their own. "Are you predestination?" Cur asks, uncertain with is answer.

"No, I'm Draven, dear boy! I thought we've been over this!"

"Come on Cur, this man is just wasting our time," I say, scowling at our host, though he doesn't seem to take offense. When I look in the man's crossed eyes, it looks as if there isn't an ounce of brain activity inside his skull—the lights are on but nobody is home, my father used to say. I grab Cur's arm but he pulls away, angered by the hermit's answer.

"Listen here, you crazy old coot!" Cur growls, closing in on Draven so he has no option but to yield to my companion. "Every Lycan in a hundred mile radius does nothing more than laugh when they hear your name, and here we are, seeking you out for help, and this is how you act? The fate of the world rests on this woman's shoulders, and you're acting like this is some game! So if there is any time for you to be serious, it's here and now."

Every ounce of emotion drains from Draven's face in a second, almost as if Cur's words have ripped some fake mask from his head and forced us to take in his true appearance. In the blink of an eye, Draven's expression becomes more serious than even my own, which is terrifying in a way I've never experienced. He is like a clown whose makeup has been washed away, only to reveal to his audience that he was never truly smiling, rather, it was the flamboyant lipstick that made us think he was.

He stands without using his hands to assist him, rising from his cross-legged squat effortlessly, as if he is floating. An overhead tree casts a shadow over his stark face as he addresses me, and me alone, "Do you ever think you lost to Steppenwolf not because you weren't prepared, but because you're too damn serious? In a world that wants to make a joke out of you, where the Creator himself laughs at your existence, maybe, just maybe, you are the crazy one for expecting a different outcome. Ever think of that? Listen good, my friends, because I'll only say this once. You've both lived a lot, and yet you haven't been here a long time. You want to know how 'ole Daybane squeezed a glass of orange juice out of a frozen wasteland? The answer is both simple and complex—probably the latter for you both, seeing you lack faith. This orange juice is the reason I howl at the sun, good friends, because this sweet nectar you see is the only reason I'm still kickin'.

"I used to be all serious like you two in a past life. Hells, if you twisted my arm and pinched my nipple, I'd admit I was *more* serious than you and you combined. Used to run with the Ka-El back in the day, was a real rapscallion too if I say so myself. But that all changed when I came face to face with Steppenwolf. Used to howl at the moon before I met that joker, and he bent my mind so crooked I thought for sure I'd carry out my days as a pretzel. But that right there," Draven says, pointing up in the cloudy sky to a point where the sun barely peaks through, "That's what saved me, and I howl my praise to it every damn day I walk this earth. See, you don't fight a monster like Steppenwolf with your body. You don't fight him with your heart either. The only weapon that can beat the Antler King is this one," he says, tapping his forehead.

"And that's exactly what I did, and my eyes ain't even the color of piss, homegirl. Steppenwolf wants you to think the things you see are real, impatient woman. He feeds off dread and fear—gains power from the powerless. But you know as well as I do, not all that glitters is gold, ya hear? So when he was on the brink of breaking me, I looked up at the sun with all my might, and I stared at it for what felt like hours. I molded it in my mind, forcing it to submit to my will, so by the time I reached my hand in the air and grasped for the sun..." Draven pauses, a sly smile growing across his cheeks. "Sun wasn't there no more, my friends, and I pulled an orange from the sky in its place. Just like that, the demon's domain was shattered, and your good pal Draven was set free with an orange to prove it."

"That's ridiculous," I scoff. "Even with Wisteria, I—"

"Who are you talking to?" a man asks from behind me. I look at Draven suspiciously, then turn to face the man responsible for interrupting me.

My breath catches in my throat as I turn, coming to realize Draven is the one who stands behind me. His figure shimmers like a mirage in a mirror. I quickly look back over my shoulder, peering at the place Draven was less than a second ago, only to find he is no longer there.

"How did you..." My voice trails off as I look back to the place he just was, only to find that he's vanished yet again.

Cur, who's looked back and forth the same as me, exhales, "What in the world..."

"Who's the crazy one now?" Draven shouts, cackling.

By the time I turn to face Draven again, I'm forced to swallow my pride immediately. It is no longer Draven who plays with my delusional brain, but instead, nearly one hundred Dravens—each of them identical and indistinguishable from one another. The spectacle is just as surprising to Netherwing, who squawks, "Crazy! Crazy! Crazy!"

Standing together in a dirty, flea-ridden crowd, the mob simultaneously speaks, "We'll forgive you for not knowing what you don't know. We'd be impatient too if we were that serious. You've lived a lot of life in only a little time, Seer. You won't catch me begging you to stay, but perhaps you ain't as wise as you think, hmm?"

"How are you doing this? You're... just a Lycan... I thought only Wendigos could distort reality..."

"Thought peed his pants and thought he was sweating, my Pa always said! Thought-shmaut—thinking will get you killed deader 'an a raisin out here, deary! I've shown you what I have to offer, what I can teach you. The ball's in your court, if you're pickin' up what I'm puttin' down. So, before you make up yer mind, I'll leave you with a riddle," the crowd of Dravens state in perfect harmony. "I gift you a golden crown, but your head must fall. I swear to you the stars, yet you never stand tall. I offer the world, then take it away—what am I today?"

My mind is too shrouded in confusion to focus on the riddle. I've spent ten years seeing imaginary beings, and yet I'm once again forced to question everything I thought I knew. This man, a mere Lycan, has managed to alter my reality without the assistance of an Arcadian Apple, without his own Wisteria, without any noticeable powers outside his own insanity.

"A false promise," Cur answers. Netherwing screams at the top of her lungs, "False promise!"

Suddenly, upon utterance of the answer, the army of Dravens assembled before us explodes into a blizzard of ice and snow, each of their bodies turning into poorly shaped snowmen that collapse instantly. What they leave behind is a single man, the true Draven, who releases his control over the icy mirage. He has a wild look in his eyes, something I can only assume to be pride. The hair on his arms stands as goosebumps litter his skin. He dry heaves a moment, looking like he is going to vomit the contents of his guts onto the ground. But instead of yakking, his throat pulses as he lifts his head to the overcast sky and lets out a wild howl. The high-pitched moan tears apart the atmosphere, parting the clouds above to reveal the sun for the first time in several days.

I look to the pedestal where the glass of orange juice previously rested, but it has vanished from sight, as if it never existed in the first place.

Deranged as he may be, this man is the only chance I have at defeating Steppenwolf, I realize.

Beggars can't be choosers, my father used to say. Desperate times call for desperate measures, and I am riddled with desperation.

"I submit myself to your teachings," I announce with hesitation as Draven's howl echoes all around us.

31

DREAMVEIL

"I just don't... understand how... this is supposed to... help me," I gasp through burning lungs, leaning over with my hands on my knees. The mere thought of having to stand straight feels unbearable. I've been at this for hours. I've yakked more times than I can count. My head is light and my stomach is in knots. If this was the Areopagus, I'd be covered in sweat. But these are the Deadlands, so my sweat has frozen to my face and caused every inch of me to go numb.

Cur and Draven have gone away from this place, intent on locking themselves away for the night of the full moon. A short ways away from camp is a poorly-constructed drawbridge which spans a quarter mile expanse. Draven informed me it's the place he travels every full moon to sequester himself, cranking the rusted wheel on the opposite side to pull half the bridge up so his inner beast can't find its way back to the mainlands. Across the bridge, he explained, is a forested area large enough for his Lycan counterpart to roam, but the land reaches a treacherous drop-off Draven calls "No Man's Land," a valley of ice no living creature has ever dared to explore. No one knows how far the valley's bottom lays; its midsection is covered with a consistent veil of icy smog. All Draven knows is, those who scale down the side of the cliff never come back, and even Draven isn't insane enough to wonder where they've went.

In their absence, I've been given a single objective: Climb to the top of Grimspire Peak and locate Dreamveil, a wild mushroom native to this region that grows only at extreme elevations where the air is thinnest. Though I've lived here long enough to become accustomed to native culture, I've never met a single person who has knowledge of this herb until meeting Draven, go figure. All I know is, the key to immortality could grow from the top of Grimspire Peak and this climb alone would deter most from making the journey.

"Some answers can only be found amongst the clouds. That's where the gods stash away their secrets, after all," Draven said upon sharing this mission. At the time, the quest seemed simple enough. The hero's journey, an old storyteller in Fyrefell used to call it. Every few years he'd pass through Fyrefell as he migrated east or west—apparently he was an important person, the grownups used to say. A playwright, father called him, though father never said anything nice about him. Us children of the village would gather around the man when he sat in town square and listen to his tales, never really knowing which were rooted in truth and which were "tales taller than giants," as my father used to say. "Any hero worth their salt has to get lost in order to find themselves," the storyteller used to say—his name started with an A—Abracadabra or Alabast or Alakazam—I was too young at the time to remember it.

I don't remember his name, but I *do* remember his stories. Sometimes, he'd ask us children what the hero should do next once faced with a dilemma, letting us shape the story how we saw fit. He'd pull a seven-sided die from his cloak and take seven suggestions from the crowd, then roll it to determine which path the main character would take. Seven, the number of completion, he called it. I can only imagine what he would decide to do if he was the one writing my story. "No one wants to root for a character who's without afflictions," he said, though I didn't understand what he meant at the time. "A hero without tribulations is like Cardone without ghosts." I don't know why, but that quote always stuck with me.

The die that controls my life is not currently seven-sided, though. I have two options: I can continue to climb this mountain in search of some fabled herb or quit and go back to Draven's camp. It would be easy enough to quit, I admit to myself. I could just tell Draven I reached the top of the peak only to find that Dreamveil doesn't exist, because at the end of the day, half the things Draven speaks about don't exist. This mystical herb could very well be another spawn of the madman's lunacy.

But that isn't who I am.

Steppenwolf has defeated me, but Draven has dared me to rediscover myself. Like my life before Wisteria appeared, I have the option to get back up after being knocked down. It's been so long since I've been belli-whopped by an opponent that I've forgotten what it feels like to doubt my abilities, but I'm finally able to bask in my infirmities. Without Wisteria, and without Havik and Grite and Dyran to guide me. Just me, myself, and I.

I curse inwardly, forcing myself to stand up straight and control my breathing.

I stare up at the long road ahead of me.

Climbing a mountain is like running a marathon vertically. The peak of Grimspire is concealed by the mist of clouds—my eyes cannot see how far or close it rests. I could be several hours or several days from reaching the first hint of Dreamveil. The wind assaults me, ripping through the thick layers of grizzly pelts I've bundled myself in. Thank the gods for my mask, which is the only reason my nose and lips haven't fallen from my face, I'm sure.

One foot in front of the other, I tell myself. Don't focus on the finish line, focus on each step. That is the only way I'll reach the end of this impossible mission.

32

A BLAST FROM THE PAST

I locate what I assume is Dreamveil exactly where Draven said I would find it—growing in the craggy fissures lining Grimspire Peak. "Fuck," I whisper under straining breaths. This whole time, thoughts of proving Draven's madness were all that carried me forward. But as I spot the icy mushrooms which bloom from the cliff's infertile rock, I stand to be corrected.

I am not well-versed in the world of horticulture, but I do know the existence of such an herb should be impossible. I am thousands of feet above sea level in the coldest climate this earth knows. There is no soil here—no sun to feed these crystalline spores. Everything a plant needs for prosperity does not exist in this environment. And yet, I lean against the mountainside to collect myself and stare at the glowing yellow mushrooms like a woman who's just found water in the desert.

I kneel, partly to closely examine the amber spores, partly to relieve my feet of the weight they've dutifully carried all this way. The mushrooms have the appearance of the same poisonous caps that grew outside of Fyrefell, except they're entirely different at the same time. The shape is the same, sure, but the mushroom itself appears to be made from... rock. Its umbrella-shaped cap is a mixture of calcified condensation and shards of gravel. Dripping from its surface is a phlegm-like mucus the color of amber sap. I touch it with my fingers, then watch how it sticks between my index finger and thumb like freshly sneezed snot. Out of curiosity, I bring the sap close to my face and smell it, surprised to pick up on notes of citrus taffy.

"Drakini," a man says from the shadows of a nearby alcove. My heart jumps in my chest, knowing almost instantly that this is some form of auditory hallucination. After seeing figments of my imagination for an entire decade, I've developed ways to separate real from fake. Up here, after climbing a mountain for several hours, the possibility of running into someone who knows me by name is less likely than the existence of these mushrooms.

I lower my sticky fingers and look up at the man, squinting as a gust of snow conceals his identity from me. He is not someone I recognize, yet there's something oddly familiar about his appearance all the same.

"It's me," he says, his voice a whisper that carries across the mountainous expanse. "Myre, from Fyrefell," he explains. I squint harder, trying to parse through the information. It takes a moment for me to understand; first, because he speaks in my native tongue, which I rarely speak anymore, and second, because I haven't heard that name since departing the Areopagus.

"Myre," I repeat the name aloud, letting its weight rest on my tongue. All at once, memories come flooding in, reigniting a past life I'd nearly forgotten. Myre! Yes, I remember, the little boy from my village I protected from bullies as if he was my own brother. Silenius's draft separated us, but I found him on Skaar, a prisoner to the Undead candidates. It was Dyran who saved him, and he was later drafted into the Ranger Corps, never to be seen again.

"My gods, Myre," I gasp, realizing it's been over ten years since I've seen him. "Of all the people for my mind to conjure in this moment, I find it odd you are the one who's been channeled."

He steps forward from the shadows, revealing himself for me to analyze. Just as I hardly recognized him after the draft, he is now a man who's aged a decade. He is no longer the little boy who needs protection from others, I gather, looking at his lean, athletic physique. Though he was shy and timid as a boy, Myre has grown into quite a warrior himself. Whatever regimen the Rangers implemented in his training, it's given him hard, masculine features. He's nearly twice his boyish height and has stormy grey eyes that encapsulate thunder. His hair is braided tight against his scalp and his red beard manages to collect snowflakes despite his existence being questionable at best.

"Are you... dead?" I ask. "Is that why you're here? You died in real life and so now you're here to haunt me like the rest of my shadow soldiers?"

He laughs stoically, which catches me off guard. In my mind, I still associated him with the high-pitched, girlish tone he had as a boy. "You're a Seer, not a Necromancer, Drakini."

"Everyone keeps throwing that word around. Back in Fyrefell, they called you looney if you saw things that don't exist, but in the Deadlands, you're suddenly a Seer. But that doesn't answer my question. Why you, and why now?"

"The subconscious mind has a funny way of working. You should know that better than most. Your mind is no different. Wisteria no doubt explained that you birth us from necessity, and I just so happen to be the person you need most right now."

I scoff, "Let me stop you right there, Myre. There's a lot of people who could be helpful to me in a moment like this. I need Wisteria's wisdom. Lu Bu's arrows. Havik's brute force. Grite's savagery. Osprey's insight. Dane's leadership. Cur's love. Hell, even a head doctor would be enlightening. But you? No offense Myre, I'm sure you've come a long way from childhood, but you're not exactly a compass of courage."

"Which makes me the perfect candidate to show you how to handle fear."

"Fear? I'm not... Listen, I didn't lose to Steppenwolf because I was afraid, okay? I lost because he was stronger—plain and simple. I lost because—"

"You lost because you let him win, Drakini," Myre says. "Your battle with him was not one of might; it was a battle of confidence. Whether you want to admit it or not, he killed your shadow soldiers because you let him. I think deep down you know I'm right. Wisteria doesn't exist—she never has; therefore, she is not something that *can* be killed. But you let Steppenwolf get in your head, and now she is dead all the same."

"I couldn't stop him!" I scream in defense. "It's like fighting a god, Myre! He can alter the fabric of reality; he can turn your own mind into a prison!"

"Then make a goddamn key to free yourself!" Just as I think Myre is getting ready to snap and let me have it, he lets out a long exhale, then sighs, "You know what, let me show you something." He snaps his fingers, and reality vanishes.

33

Boys, Boys, Boys

"**G**ive it back!" Myre shrieks, running back and forth between Fromm and Ziggy frantically. The bullies, each substantially bigger than Myre, take turns throwing a bronze sterling through the air. To some, a single shekel is chump change—but to Myre, that coin represented an entire week's worth of groceries for his family. Tasked with going to the local market, Myre's parents entrusted him with buying food while they picked up extra work at the town mill.

Buying groceries is a simple enough task for most, but for those easily preyed upon such as Myre, it presented additional problems.

"Or what, chicken neck?" Ziggy laughs, catching the shekel thrown to him. He balls his fist and places the coin atop his thumb, jeering, "Tell ya what! We'll flip for it... Heads, you get your coin back! Tails, and we belliwhop you till you beg us to take it!"

Myre frantically looks back and forth between his two tormenters, knowing from previous interactions that they aren't joking in the slightest. His face is flush with anxiety, not only for his wellbeing, but for the prospect of losing his parent's hard-earned money. Every species of animal has what's commonly referred to as a runt. It is the puppy too small to suckle its mother's teat; it is the gosling abandoned by its mother because it was not strong enough to migrate; it is the pig unworthy of slaughter because it is far too scrawny to produce meat. One look at Myre is enough to determine he is humanity's iteration of a runt, and life will forever be unfair to him for it. His hair is greasy, his buckteeth are two sizes too big, his face is sickly pale. So, after being given two options by Fromm and Ziggy, one of which will lead to his body getting beaten to a pulp, Myre has little recourse but to stand there stammering.

Just as Ziggy gets ready flick the coin, a voice shouts out, "How about option three: I belliwhop you both until you pee yourselves, then tell your friends you got beat up by a girl!" A girl not much larger than Myre enters the scene, clothed in indigent rags that hang loosely from her skinny frame. Despite the dirt and dust caked on her cheeks and under her fingernails, her smile suggests she doesn't fear these bullies in the slightest.

"Should've known this little swamp rat would come to your aid yet again, Myre," Fromm chuckles. "Go back to your hole, Drakini. Let us boys be boys."

"Boys, boys, boys... You never seem to learn your lesson, do you?" Drakini says, flexing her fists at her sides. She cracks her neck twice, once to each side, then starts bouncing on the balls of her feet.

"Drakini," Myre calls out, partly relieved to see her, partly ashamed he can't fight his own battles. His initial embarrassment fades as his face looks at Fromm, then Ziggy. He scowls, instantly angered. "Give them hell, Drakini," he sneers.

The coin falls from Ziggy's grip as Drakini tackles him, using every ounce of her momentum to knock the wind from his lungs. The two fall to the ground and kick up a shroud of dust as they roll, each one of them throwing fists and elbows. Fromm remains distanced for a second, but as the dust settles, he sees it's Drakini who has Ziggy pinned to the ground, throwing hammer fists into his face like cannons launched against a castle.

"Say uncle!" Drakini screams as the blows continue to rain, but even if Ziggy wanted to yield, her punches don't allow him the chance to speak.

Ziggy lets out a shrill scream as his nose cracks, and only then does Fromm throw himself into the fray of battle. He tackles Drakini off his companion's body, pinning her to the ground for a taste of her own medicine. He gets in a few good punches, blackening her eye and bruising her jaw, but this is not the first time Drakini has been on the receiving end of a boy's feeble blows. In an attempt to repair Ziggy's reputation, Fromm cries out, "Say uncle, bitch!"

The next punch he throws is his last. Though it's initially aimed for Drakini's nose, her head moves at the last second, and Fromm's knuckles crash into the hard clay beneath her, sending a jolt of pain up his forearm and into his shoulder. In his moment of unexpected pain, Drakini throttles her forehead into his own, injuring herself in order to inflict maximum agony on her opponent. The noise of their skulls clacking echoes, and Fromm unwillingly falls to her side, writhing with his throbbing head in his bloody hands.

Blood trickles from Drakini's forehead and nose as she rises with an eerie smile on her lips. She scoops the bronze sterling and approaches Myre, extending her arm to return it to its rightful owner. Myre smiles as he accepts it, and as the coin transfers ownership, Myre transforms into a man grown once more. Suddenly we are back on Grimspire Peak, and I am standing an arm's length away from Myre as he lifts a bronze sterling in the air for me to examine. It is no longer the little, fragile boy who stands before me. Instead, it is a man hardened by a life of trials and tribulations, but somewhere in his face, I can still see the boy too weak to fight his own battles.

"You asked why it is me who appeared to you, Drakini. I know what it's like to be afraid better than most, and I know what it's like to lose a protector. When Silenius initiated the draft, you were no longer there to fight my battles for me. You were my Wisteria, but I couldn't rely on you once I was sent to the Eastern military sector. For the first time in my life, I was alone, forced to face life's many evils with nothing more than my own meager abilities. In a matter of weeks, I had to evolve, Drakini, the same as you. The candidates in my military sector were savages, much worse than anything Fromm and Ziggy were capable of. It was kill or be killed, just as it was on Skaar when the Undead flayed open my back. You saved me back then, so let me save you now... Not because you are as weak as I was, but because you can be so much more, and I can help you unlock your true potential..."

"The student becomes the teacher," I laugh through chattering teeth. After hearing what Myre's had to say, I realize he is the perfect person to help me through the problems I face. "I'm sorry for being so dismissive, Myre... I just..."

"No apologies needed, Drakini. I'd be skeptical too if I was you. But I'm not the boy you knew. I've been a Ranger for ten years, and I've fought my own battles just as long. Now, how about we flip for it?" he jokes, showing me both sides of the coin. "Heads, you let me train you alongside Draven; tails, you tell me to fuck off and I leave you alone."

A chill shudders through me as he rotates the coin, revealing that both sides of the coin have a head inscribed on its surface. It's the first time Myre's ever said a joke to me, but I'm struggling to find laughter.

Do not trust the man with the double-headed coin... The words flash in my mind from some past life, though I can't remember where or when. This man is not the same as my other shadow soldiers. Before today, Dyran is the only spirit I've known to follow me after death, and after this interaction, I have no way of even knowing if Myre is dead or alive in real time.

There's an uncanny glimmer in his eyes that seek to win me over. Sure, he isn't the boy I knew in Fyrefell, but Myre was never known for his encouragement or optimism. If anything, the man before me now is Myre's antithesis—a cheap knockoff that ignores the few things I admired about my childhood friend.

I'll tell Draven about this encounter and seek his council. Until then, Myre flips the coin, and my fate is sealed.

Just like that, my hellcat mentor is replaced by a scaredy-cat.

34

OUT OF BODY EXPERIENCE

"Consume the Dreamveil, Drakini," Myre says, completely catching me off-guard.

I'm weary of Myre for reasons I can't explain. The coin has vanished from his grasp, but I can't escape the nagging feeling that some premonition of the past has come full circle. Perhaps I'm overthinking it, but I can't get over his charming smile. Is it possible for a man to change this much in ten years? I am not the girl I was at sixteen, so maybe this gut feeling inside me is my mind playing tricks on me.

"Excuse me?"

"There are things about your powers you don't know—things you can't know—until you've transcended this reality."

"Again, excuse me?" I say, laughing nervously, staring once more at the calcified, frozen mushrooms beside us.

"It would take me hours to tell you what your powers as a Seer are, Drakini. But will take only a few minutes for me to *show* you. Dreamveil has psychedelic properties, ways to shed this reality and transport to another dimension. Imagine it like this—right now, you are a force to be reckoned with, like a lioness in a zoo. But imagine if you could leave the zoo. Imagine if you could see what lurks beyond your artificial habitat. Until you leave this world, you will never truly understand the powers you're capable of—the powers that have been inside you all along."

"Erm, I see things that don't exist, Myre. That's not exactly a power…"

"It's all linked, Drakini. Can't you see that? You have the power to alter your reality! It's the reason no Wendigo could defeat you! They, too, can alter a person's reality, but you were always able to see through it… It is a rare ability for a human to possess, and yet you have it! Steppenwolf, the Wendigos, Arcadia, Wisteria and your abilities, it's all linked, Drakini. But your finite mind prevents you from seeing the web that connects the dots. Dreamveil can lift the haze though. Draven was right to send you here… After his mind was touched by Steppenwolf, it left him with a fraction of the powers you possess… He has Seer Sight, but you… You have the potential to be the most powerful Seer that's ever walked this earth."

The corner's of Myre's lips twitch ever so slightly. For the briefest moment, I'm slightly disturbed by his eagerness. Maybe I've grown used to Wisteria's calm indifference, but I've never seen Myre this excited about anything. But this isn't the real Myre, I tell myself, it's my mind's recreation of a boy I no longer know. I have no other option but to trust that there's a method to my mind's madness.

"I just don't see how… Ugh," I say, filled with skepticism. I've finally reached the point where the things I know are heavily outweighed by the things I don't. I need answers, and if this mushroom truly is the way to find them, then bon appétit, I think to myself as I bring my sap-covered fingers to my lips, licking the taffy-flavored liquid before fear can cause me to hesitate.

Instantly, my mouth is set on fire, causing me to salivate. My jaw tingles, sending shudders down my body. In a split second, my vision zooms out through a tunnel of light. My body is shot from a cannon through the atmosphere. Everything distorts. Light throbs all around me. Stars shoot past me. Every color of light known to man, and many that aren't, strobe all around me. Reality explodes. I want to scream but I'm in some place where oxygen doesn't exist. The walls of the world fall like peeling wallpaper, exposing a kaleidoscope spectrum of breathing hues. Suddenly, I can see sounds and hear sights. My body is propelled through a swirling vortex at the speed of light. And then, when I'm convinced I will become consumed by the cosmos—my conscience collected by some greater, omnipotent being—I emerge on the other side.

35

?

N o configuration of words exists to describe what I see.

36

NINE MONTHS

My body convulses as I wake, my mind consumed by matters of the infinite.

I let out a scream, though I'm not in pain. Overwhelmed is an understatement. I am a fish who's been lifted from the ocean to see the world beyond water; I experience a different kind of dissociation sickness. Unlike the days following Steppenwolf's illusions, where I could not tell what was real and what was fake, I look at the dark sky above and see now that everything is fake. This whole world—a simulation. A creation made by the Creator for us to exist—words on a piece of papyrus breathed to life; the second dimension transcended to the third. And yet, there is a vast universe outside this domain.

Domains within domains. Lies and truths folded into one another until neither can be separated.

Constantly shifting shapes.

Perfect symmetry.

An imperfect algorithm.

There were faces all around me.

A high-pitched growl, followed by the low hum of a cackle.

The end of the world—death and decay.

Creation anew—brilliant dismay.

No individuality, all-consuming gray.

A single eye staring—millions pray.

Chains around them—sins weigh.

I'm crying, I realize. Nothing makes sense anymore, yet everything made perfect sense when I stared at the vision. My eyelids were peeled back; a third eye opened from my forehead, and it saw more than my two mortal eyes ever have. A portal opened between my brain and the secrets of the cosmos. But now that I'm awake, the secrets flee my mind faster than I can hold onto them, like steam dissipating into the environment never to be seen again.

"Drakini!" Myre calls from some distant world. Everything about this world is suddenly underwhelming, now that sounds can only be heard, as opposed to seen or felt or tasted. He is snapping his fingers in front of my face to anchor me back to this false reality. I open my eyes and stare at him, looking up with indifference. He isn't real; I know that with certainty now. But then again, none of this is. I've seen the order of the universe; I've seen the words written by the Creator which orchestrate all of this. We are characters written on a page—actors and actresses tasked with putting on the best goddamn show this world has ever seen. We have an audience of one—the all-seeing eye—the Creator who peers down on us with amusement and wrath.

"Quickly, Drakini," Myre says urgently. "Tell me everything you saw... Speaking these things is the only way to commit them to memory... Say it all as fast as you can, even if it doesn't make sense."

I comply, partly because I'm too disoriented to argue, but also because I desperately want to remember the things I've seen.

"A shattered world... No, a shattered brain... A brain the size of a world... The Creator's brain, and on its surface is our world... There was a pantheon of... Demigods... No, they were... Nine Harbingers... Nine Harbingers to mark the end of the world, each one of them warring against another... The Wolf... The Bat... The Wolf with Wings... The Sun... The Moon... The Enchantress... The Death-Defeater... The Huntress... And lastly... The Reaper..."

"Keep going Drakini... Keep digging! Say as much as you can before it's forgotten!"

"Their war broke the earth—broke the Creator... It was... It was awful... Nine nations divided inside an endless abyss... A queen with silver hair and purples eyes... She wore an upside down crown and raised an army of the dead... They called themselves the Fallen... And the Reaper opposed them... And the Death-Defeater opposed them both... War within wars... So much death and destruction..."

"And who won?" Myre asks.

I look up at him with tears in my eyes, choking on my words as I speak. "There... There was no winner, Myre."

"And the Huntress? Do you see now that you play a part in all of this?"

"I... The Huntress... There was a whole army of shadow soldiers," I reflect coldly. "And they were visible to the entire world—she could bring them into reality, or bring others into her domain... I'm unsure... Wait... I remember something... Yes, it's coming back to me! The Huntress was able to unite several of the Nine... Children of Dagon and Damon, the Wolf and the Bat; the Wolf with Wings, he was a One-Eyed Wolf—a descendant of Sylvian the First; and the Reaper, the one known as Skathen... I can't remember... I could see it all so clear moments ago, but it's all so foggy now... Myre," I gasp, "I need to take the Dreamveil again—I have to! I need to remember how to use my powers! Wisteria was there! She was by the Huntress's side! I have the power to resurrect her! I need more answers... I need more—"

"Slow down Drakini," Myre orders, moving his body so he stands between me and the Dreamveil mushrooms. Suddenly, the spores' yellow lights call to me with an undeniable allure. I need more. I must have more. Their psychoactive abilities are the only way for me to transcend my humanity and become one of the Nine. Without them, I am only Drakini. But with them, I will be a god in my own right.

"Your mind cannot handle more right now, Drakini. Use your restraint. If you take this drug without self-control, you will lose your mind and everything you saw will be for naught."

"You don't understand, Myre... I need..."

"You need to meditate on what you've seen, that's what you need. There are Nine Harbingers, and you will come to this mountain peak nine times before you face Steppenwolf again. Each moondance Draven and Cur take, you will journey to see me once more. That leaves eight trips to the top of Grimspire Peak to consume Dreamveil—each separated by a month to reflect on what you've seen. After nine months, you will be ready to face your foe, and you will have a new army of shadow soldiers to accompany you."

"How do you know these things?" I ask, then think of an even better question to ask, "And why nine months?"

"I know these things because I've been born from your brain, and I know things your body does not," he says ambiguously. "Nine months because you are pregnant with child, Drakini of Fyrefell... Let me be the first to offer my congratulations, old friend."

PART THREE

37

MONTH ONE

M y head spins as I make the journey back to camp.

Pregnant?

I can't be pregnant, I tell myself.

But no matter how many times I tell myself that, I know the revelation is true.

After my encounter with Steppenwolf, I slept with Cur more times than I can count. If anything, I made a lifetime worth of love with him, as if it was him I chose to marry and made vows to... But he isn't... That man is Dane, yet I removed my wedding ring in favor of cheating on him, and now my adultery has materialized in the form of flesh and blood.

I feel sick to my stomach, knowing that my unfaithful decision will now haunt me the rest of my life. I secretly hate myself for betraying my husband, yet at the same time, a silent part of me is antagonistically happy this baby belongs to Cur. I made a decision I'm not proud of, and yet the thought of raising a child by Cur's side is one that brings me immense joy.

I vomit multiple times on my trek back to Draven's camp—partly from anxiety but mostly from morning sickness.

Do I tell Cur?

No... Absolutely not...

If Cur found out I grow his seed of love in my womb, he will oppose any notion of me facing Steppenwolf once more. He spent multiple years in a world where I was his wife and provided him a daughter. If I tell him about this epiphany, he will do everything in his power to ensure that illusion becomes reality.

It will be easy enough to hide from him. When I was pregnant years ago with Dane's child, my stomach hardly showed evidence of such until several months in. With enough concealment, I can carry this child to term without him ever knowing, and I can face Steppenwolf once more without him standing in my way.

Still though, I can't defeat the nagging thought in the back of my mind that Dane is still out there, held hostage by Steppenwolf until my return. I don't know what I'll do if I have to face him and admit my treachery; nor do I know what he will do if he learns I've birthed a child to the same Lycan we brought to these lands to be our tracker. Dane is a kind man, but I've seen what he's capable of once pushed to his wit's end. I don't want harm to come to Cur for my own mistakes, but I fear Dane will not take this news lightly...

It is a problem I must face another day. Worrying now will only harm the child's health.

"I am with child again," I whisper under my breath, feeling glee for the first time since receiving the news. I tell myself, no longer in a whisper, "I am allowed to be happy... I have another opportunity to bring life to these Deadlands... Against all odds, I have been blessed with the chance to be a mother once more..."

I grit my teeth as my lips smile. I failed to bring my child to term my last pregnancy. I will not fail again, I tell myself.

Draven was right about traveling to Grimspire Peak.

On its mountaintop, I discovered more than just my future potential. The things I saw and the things I learned lit a fire within me. I no longer have any other choice but to defeat Steppenwolf. Not only for myself, not only for this world, but now, for my future child.

38

Month Two

"Cur, over here," I call out in a hushed tone. I crouch in the snow, bringing my hand close to the massive print etched in the ice. It is twice the size of my palm, and its tracks are recent.

"What is it?" he asks in a whisper, planting his spear in the snow as he crouches beside me.

I point at the track, then lift my finger to show the trail of bear prints that lead into the forest. We have been hunting since dawn, battling the elements for a chance to secure several day's worth of meat. The elk in this region are sparse. Hours ago, I came to accept we may return to Draven's camp with little more than a few snow hares and arctic foxes. But whatever bear left this track is big enough to feed us for several weeks!

"What are you pointing at?" Cur asks, analyzing the snow closer.

I look at him skeptically, unsure if he's joking with me or not. I point back at the ground, saying, "A bear print, it's right here..." My voice trails off as I stare back at the ground, surprised to see the tracks have disappeared entirely. I touch the snow in an attempt to prove myself right, but my palm is the only print that remains in the snow when I test my theory.

"It was right... I don't..."

For a moment I feel as though I'm going crazy, then think better of it. A thought dawns on me, causing me to smile. Since my use of Dreamveil nearly a month ago, things have been different. Reality is not the same as it was. Though my third eye has closed, it is no longer sealed shut with stone. I have seen queer things of late. Things I shouldn't be seeing. When I meditate with Draven, I'm able to sometimes gaze briefly into the world beyond this one. It's strengthened my instincts and senses, allowing me to trust in my insanity, as Draven instructed me to.

I stand once more and reach for the chain around my chest. When my rope dart isn't in use, I've grown accustomed to wrapping it diagonally over my shoulder, across my midsection, and around my opposite hip. Slowly, I unravel it, not wanting to make more noise than I have to. I close my eyes and meditate, focusing on the midpoint of my forehead in an attempt to bring the next dimension into my own.

At first, all I see is the blackness of my eyelids. But as I breathe deeply through my nose, pause, then exhale with control, I start to see a white pattern emerge among the darkness. I focus on the pattern intently. They are little specks of white, similar to what happens when I stare at a flame too long, then close my eyes and am still able to see the outline of its silhouette from behind my eyelids.

I focus. I breathe. I focus. I breathe.

The specks of white become more defined with each passing second, and after a few minutes of meditating, I'm able to see them for what they are—bear prints. From the blackness of my closed eyes, the same trail that led away from me moments ago is now clear, bleeding white energy in my mind clear enough for me to see what Cur cannot. I feel a tugging in my stomach. I've worked on making my delusions a reality for several weeks under Draven's instruction. It takes an immense amount of intention, paired with an innate ability to trust in myself.

I see the paw prints and believe in their existence, then open my eyes once more.

There, paved along the snow like footprints in wet cement, are the bear's prints once more.

Cur inhales sharply, looking at the ground before us as I drag the prints into reality for him to see.

"Holy fuck," he gasps, staggering back. "I see them Drakini! I couldn't see them, but now I can!" He's smiling stupidly at me, realizing I'm progressing in my powers. He closes the gap between us and places his arms on my shoulders, looking at me with amazement, as if he's proud of me. It makes my stomach flutter. I touch the side of my abdomen, knowing this man's child grows inside. This thought alone causes it to flutter even more.

Snowflakes land on my eyelashes as I look at him, smiling back. I'm speechless. This is the first time I've been able to cast my hallucinations for others to see.

But my happiness can only last so long.

Dread fills my stomach as a primal roar sounds from nearby. It is the exhale of an infuriated animal, and its voice cracks with several high-pitched trumpets, like the sound fingernails make on a blackboard. To my surprise, Cur's ears twitch. His hands tighten on my shoulders, turning instantly from an intimate touch to a protective vise. Before I can protest, he pulls me behind him as he turns to face the bear tracks.

A shroud of ice crystals fills the air around us like a cloud that's fallen to earth, camouflaging the demon I'm responsible for summoning. Its roar persists, sending shudders down my skin as I grip the chain in my hands tighter. Cur's head swivels defensively as he brings his hunting spear in close, squatting slightly in anticipation of an attack that can come from any direction.

He defended me from a bear before and it nearly led to his death. I won't lose him to one a second time.

"No," I say to him, placing my hand on his shoulder. I have to force myself to be calm. This thing is a figment of my imagination, and I am the one that brought it into this dimension. I am its creator, and I alone have the power to control its actions. Cur will gain nothing from plunging his spear into it—I can't even be sure such a wound would kill it. Everything I know about my shadow soldiers leads me to believe physical weapons cannot harm them, just as the wounds they inflict on me are illusory. "He isn't our enemy."

"Does he know that? Because he sounds pretty damn mad from what I can hear!"

"Come out, shadow soldier," I command. The frost from my words part the cloud of condensation down the middle. My eyes follow the bear's tracks to the path's end, then see the roaring beast in all his glory. There, only a few dozen yards from us, is a bear unlike any grizzly I've seen in this region of the world. Unlike the average grizzly, whose fur is brown and size is monstrous, the bear that left these tracks is as white as the snow around us. For a moment, I question whether my eyes are playing tricks on me, wondering whether or not the bear's fur is caked with so much snow and ice that it only seems white. Upon further examination though, that theory is disproven. The winter wind blows the creature's free-flowing hair, and it moves unobstructed.

"Is that... an albino grizzly?" Cur asks, whispering his words as if the bear will understand him.

"No," I answer, studying the creature more. "Its nose is black, not pink... And it is leaner than a grizzly; look how narrow its muzzle is... The Ka-El spoke of a bear like this once... They called it..." I rack my brain for the memory, not letting my eyes leave the shadow soldier for a second. Surely, I tell myself, if my mind was creative enough to imagine this creature, I can recall from my subconscious what it's called.

Polar bear, the beast grunts as its agitated roars subside.

"Yes," I confirm, smiling at the specimen. "Polar bear... He's a polar bear... The Ka-El said they're a sign of good fortune, though most believed they didn't actually exist. Their tribe told tales that the polar bear is a guardian—one that only makes itself known to those with winter in their blood."

"Can you... talk to it?" Cur asks, unsure how my abilities work.

"He's already spoken to me," I answer, causing Cur to look at the beast with bewilderment in his eyes.

"What is your name, polar bear?" I ask.

The bear takes several lumbering steps toward us. His heavy paws crush the ice beneath him. A cloud of smoke exits his mouth with each belabored breath he exhales. The bear's paws are big enough to kill a man with one swipe; his eyes are black and merciless. I psychoanalyze every inch of him, afraid that if I look away for even a split second, he'll disappear. With Draven's help I've become more confident in my abilities, but this is the first time I've ever dragged a creature from my own imagination into this world.

I am Behemoth, the bear grunts, though Cur likely only hears a growl. I don't know the ins and outs of what other people can perceive from my hallucinations.

"Behemoth," I repeat so Cur can know. "And why are you here?"

To warn you, he replies, shifting his weight as his eyes scan the surrounding forest.

"Warn us of what?" I ask hesitantly.

Suddenly, just as the words leave my mouth, the forest erupts around us. Plumes of snow explode as bodies rise from concealment.

Hollering and screaming erupts. Several spears fly, their sharpened tips aimed not for the beast, but instead, for me. Cur lunges for me as Behemoth lets out a mighty roar, causing the snow-laden leaves above to shake. Behemoth's mouth clamps down on a spear shaft, then snaps it in half as he flexes his jaw. I hit the ground in confusion as Cur covers me.

I have no idea what's happening; nomads brush the snow from their bodies and still their weapons. Behemoth stands between my defenseless body and my savage attackers, his growl never ceasing at the base of his throat. I hear several gasps from all around as Behemoth makes himself known, then get even more confused as they drop their weapons and kneel, each of them bowing before Behemoth's feral authority.

"What the fuck is happening?" I call out, trying to reconcile the adrenaline of being ambushed with the perplexity of our attackers surrendering.

Cur wipes the snow from his eyes and stares up, equally as confused as I am. "I think they're... I think..."

They're worshipping me, Behemoth snarls before Cur can finish his thought.

"They're kneeling for him like he's some sort of god," Cur states, trying to decipher what's happening.

"I told you... The people of this land see the polar bear as a mythical creature. His mere presence is enough to instill peace."

Behemoth paces back and forth in front of them, lowering his head to take in their scents. Each nomad he passes over trembles with fear and supplication. They don't appear to be Ra-El from what I can tell. The Ra-El haven't expanded this far east, which is partly why Draven settled here. No, these pelt-covered men and women are likely natives with no objective other than surviving each passing day. I've got to give it to them—their use of the snow dunes as a way to disguise themselves was an effective hunting strategy. I now see what I failed to notice before—scattered beside the holes they emerged from are bamboo shoots they used as breathing apparatuses.

They have us outnumbered by thirty at least. If it hadn't been for Behemoth, the hunters would have caught us by surprise and skewered our bodies for what little meat our bones have to offer.

Tell them they must make an offering in exchange for my forgiveness, Behemoth says.

"An offering?" I ask, "Of what?"

"Who are you talking to?" Cur asks, still hovering over my body like a turtle's shell.

"Behemoth, now be quiet."

You came out here to find food. Instead, you found me. Send them to fetch you wild game for a burnt offering; then, you won't have to do it yourself. It's the least they can do, seeing they tried to kill you.

Ten years I've had these powers, and today I've finally scratched the surface of controlling them for the first time. I touch my stomach, smiling. Two months down, seven to go.

39

MONTH THREE

My soul panics as it returns to my body. It feels as though I'm a dandelion in a hurricane. I vomit immediately, but my body is too numb to feel the hot acid surge up my esophagus. I roll onto my side so I don't suffocate on the regurgitation, coughing uncontrollably. All the while, I cradle my stomach as my body shudders. Something stirs in my womb, reminding me of the fetus within.

"Deep breaths, Drakini," Myre urges. "In through your nose... Out through your mouth..."

But deep breathing cannot save me from the effects Dreamveil has. Having your soul leave your body and transcend to another dimension is not something breathing exercises can easily cure. I let the coughing fits and skeletal chills run their course, then begin speaking as soon as I can. "I saw... these lands," I say, knowing the drill. Memories from the infinite don't transfer over to reality with ease. Just like last time, the visions I've seen flee my mind faster than I can recount them. It is like catching a fly with chopsticks, trying to gather the things I've just seen before they escape forever. "I saw these lands... before they died... before Steppenwolf... I saw them, and they were a paradise..."

"Good," Myre says. "Keep going... As much as you can, speak it into being."

"It was the Death-Defeater's creation that... fractured this world... The world I come from... and the Deadlands... were one nation. But the Creator devoted himself to making... a place where humanity could go... once they died... An eternal chamber for suffering souls, Myre... It was a horrible thing to see. It felt like... like I was drowning perpetually with the water's surface only an inch away from my lips... The waves around me ebbed ever so slightly, allowing me to breathe just before my lungs imploded. But the water would return almost immediately, and I'd drown once more, over and over. That is the only way I can explain how it felt to gaze into this... this Hell... And its creation, Myre... Its creation is the reason these Deadlands were fractured from the Areopagus coast... When the Creator finished Hell's creation, it shattered the crust of the earth and made every inch of the world shake. People all across creation screamed prayers of repentance, but the Creator's wrath could not be satisfied. Two hemispheres fractured, their nerves stretching down to some sinister core—a place to trap and torment souls, and Steppenwolf is the one for whom the bell tolls! As above, so below—mora velan, mora falen—it is the same blood magic the Wendigos use to seduce the weak-minded... Their illusions are built on the shattered dreams of those who died far too soon," I say, wiping an involuntary tear from my eye.

"As above, so below... Steppenwolf will turn this world into hell so the Creator can make it paradise once more. The children of Luna and Solis will look to the heavens and cry out for mercy. Solis will stand still once more, as he did for Sylvian the First's campaign... Eight of the Nine

Harbingers will fight to save creation from the Destroyer's grasp. This world will not end with a bang, but with a whimper. The Reaper will rage against the dying of the light! Huntress will rally those who dwell in the valley of dying stars... The Winged Wolf will mend the broken jaw of our lost kingdom! Under the black fog of a winter dawn, a hellcat that cannot be held by Hell's gates emerges; chains cannot restrain her; where chains imprison most, she turns them into her preferred weapon. The universe birthed her from necessity; absolute evil cannot exist without its eternal foe. The War of Worlds is three-sided, Myre. Enchantress and her Army of Dead—The Creator and his Death-Defeater—and the Reaper who stands firmly between the world of the living and dead, wielding his scythe against any who threaten his beloved world. I saw all of this and more Myre; I know these words make no sense, believe me, I know they make me sound like some crazed prophet. But it is impossible to retain sanity after seeing the way the world ends..."

I watch Myre intently as I prophesy, watching his face twitch ever so slightly as I speak of the end times. There is a prying look in his eyes, as if he knows there's something I'm withholding from my visions.

I will not tell him what I saw inside the gates of Hell...

I will not tell him *who* I saw inside the gates of Hell...

Soon enough, he will find out for himself.

40

MONTH FOUR

"Breathe, damnit," Draven tells himself, slapping himself on the face. He sits across from me with his legs crossed. I'd be lying if I said meditating with Draven is easy. It's been a part of our daily routine since my training with him began, but it hasn't gotten any less hysterical. Draven meditating is like a rooster trying to lay an egg—it's practically impossible.

I feel like I've gotten a good grasp on controlling my thoughts after weeks of doing this consistently, but Draven has practiced the art of breathing for years and still has trouble conquering the maelstrom that riots inside him. I open my eyes and watch him, not hiding my smile as he snorts air violently through his nostrils and forces it from his mouth. Early in my training he told me to imagine my breath as a breeze that sweeps over the surface of my mind, carrying away any distractions that plague my brain, then expelling them from my body with a deep exhale. But it's easier said than done for Draven, I've realized.

He slaps his face with his eyes closed, getting mad at whatever distractions refuse to leave his head. With each blow he delivers, his cheeks grow redder as he attempts to beat away his brain's insubordination.

"Breathe!" Netherwing croaks, entertained by Draven's outburst.

Draven's face looks like he is trying to expel an impossibly big turd from his asshole—it shakes with strain; veins rise to the surface along his temples. Draven whispers under his breath loud enough for me to hear, "Sally sold seashells by the seashore. Danny's dog danced delightfully during dawn. Giggling ghosts grow gloomy grins."

Does this guy ever shut up? Behemoth asks with an annoyed grunt.

I'm afraid not, I reflect inwardly. Meditation is hard enough on its own, but having to do it in Draven's presence is like running uphill during a landslide. Weeks ago, the man's frequent outbursts annoyed me, but now that I've learned how to ignore them, I'm actually thankful for the mental resistance he provides. Learning how to focus during his tantrums has allowed me to control my thoughts in every condition. I'm convinced a tornado could be headed my way and it would not prevent me from closing off this world and accessing my third eye. And so I don't entertain Draven's ramblings as I force my eardrums to vibrate. I focus on my forehead's midpoint, slowly letting a pressure build with each breath I take.

I imagine invisible energy flowing from my brain down my neck and through my limbs. Every time my thoughts wander, which is often at first, I just bring my focus back to the space inside my skull. Gradually, after several minutes, my mind wanders less and less, opening my senses to the world beyond this one. My eardrums continue to vibrate, drowning out my surroundings with thunder. The bitter cold fades as I force my body to generate its own warmth. All these years I've relied on ignisberries to heat my blood, but now I've taught my body how to thermoregulate on its own.

I can feel my heart beating in my chest. My veins dilate as my mind transcends this world, not leaving it completely, but standing with one foot in this dimension and one in the next.

When I open my eyes, I am no longer in the Deadlands. Similar to my visions under the influence of Dreamveil, I'm in a place that exists outside of mortal reality. The Twilight Expanse—the location's name pops into my mind as I recognize it from Dreamveil's dreams. It is an endless abyss of oblivion. No time; no material. Only shapeless void and palpable darkness.

A lone chain lies at my feet. I bend over and pick it up, realizing it is tethered to something in the distance, though I cannot see through the islands of shade where it leads. Without remorse, I push the shadows back beyond cold stars and walk on, following the chain, which has never led me astray.

Sliding its links through my hands, I navigate this world step by step. There is no way of knowing whether peril waits for me, or if it currently converges on my unsuspecting figure. This whole transaction is nearly enough to make me laugh. I've gone from seeing fake monsters to creating entire worlds of darkness in my mind. But I can't doubt the things my mind shows me—that was Draven's first lesson. Doubt is a Seer's eternal enemy. If I succumb to it, I will never master these ambiguous powers. But if I overcome it, I will unlock the powers needed to save humanity.

"Is someone there?" a familiar voice cries out from the distance. "Hello? Does anybody hear me?"

I quicken my pace, turning my walk to a trot, then to a sprint. I yank the chain several arms-lengths at a time, not heeding the possible danger I could be in. I don't respond to the panicked voice, not wanting to give my location away to whatever monsters lurk in this darkness. I've visited the Twilight Expanse before, and although I can't remember why, thoughts of it cause me to shiver. I can't recall if this is an evil place, but I certainly know it is not a good one.

The chain slowly elevates as I continue forward, raising off the ground without me having to hold it, then rising to my midsection, then rising above my head altogether. I slow my stride as the chain reaches a height I can no longer reach. Suddenly, as if I've stepped on a tripwire, a spotlight illuminates my surroundings. I freeze like a deer who's heard a hunter's footsteps.

Though the darkness persists all around me, some transient light has descended upon me and my immediate surroundings, allowing me to look up at where the chain leads. Fear consumes me as I see a thick web above, woven by thousands of metallic chains. The chains sparkle in the spotlight, their form freakishly resembling a spider's web. Trapped in the web's center, covering his eyes from the blinding light, is a single man.

He lets out a desperate scream, as if he's riddled with agony, "No! Not the sun, anything but the sun!" He writhes for freedom, tugging at the chains which bind him. I see instantly why he fears the spotlight—the prisoner is Undead, apparent from his sparkling silver hair. This is likely the first time he's ever experienced a light of this magnitude, seeing he's been condemned to a life of darkness. But this light doesn't come from the sun, that much I know. Its rays are a shade of pure, luminescent white. Because of this, it doesn't harm the Undead fugitive whatsoever, even though it takes him several seconds to recognize it.

Once he stops his screaming and realizes his flesh doesn't burn, he looks around in confusion, his purple eyes furrowed with perplexity. Only then do I get a full look at his face and realize who he is. My heart sinks as I lock eyes with an enemy I hate almost as much as Steppenwolf.

"Ventur," I growl under my breath.

"Bloodbag whore," he spits, pretending he wasn't screaming and crying only moments ago. "I should have known you were behind this sorcery the moment these chains bound me."

Any confusion at his presence here is supplanted by the joy it brings me to see him tied up like a helpless fly in a black widow's web. He's aged into an adult since the last time I saw him, taking on his father's prominent features. Like Count Viren, Ventur is devilishly handsome, which hurts me to admit.

From the look of hatred he holds on his face, I can safely assume he hasn't forgiven me for killing his father a decade ago. His lips sneer at me, exposing his upper fangs as he hisses angrily at his current circumstances.

"What are you doing here Ventur?" I sigh, not sure if any of this is real. That is the crux of my abilities—there's never any telling what's real and what's a figment of my imagination, especially in a sinister place like this. But I won't waste my time asking him if he actually exists. Doing so would only reveal my powers to the only person on this earth I want to hide them from.

"You tell me, damn daywalker! One moment, I'm going to bed in the Areopagus, and the next, I'm caught in this hellish nightmare!" As he screams the words, he thrashes against the chains viciously.

"Wait... You mean to tell me you're sleeping right now?" I ask, putting the pieces together slowly. If Ventur is sleeping in real time, does that mean this trapped version of him is actually his subconscious mind? If so, that would mean he isn't a figment of my imagination!

"Did I stutter?" he mocks, obviously annoyed. I can't really blame him. This is likely his first time dabbling in the world of illusions. I'd be pissed too if Ventur disgraced my dreams with his presence. "I closed my eyes to sleep the daylight away, and when I opened them once more, I was here!"

"Oh what a tangled web we weave, when firssst we practiccce to deccceive," a voice hisses from the darkness above, causing me and Ventur to look up simultaneously. The web of chains shakes as a creature stirs outside of the spotlight. Eight lights which glow red peer down at us, blinking. It takes both of us a moment to register what's happening, but as soon as Ventur does, he resumes his screaming: "You've got to be fucking kidding me! Get me out of these fucking chains Drakini! I'll do whatever you fucking want! Just get me the fuck out of here!"

The red eyes stare at Ventur's struggle whimsically, letting him get out his temper tantrum before proceeding. I, too, savor every moment of the Undead's vulnerability.

We had spiders in Fyrefell. Big, ugly ones; small, hairy ones; ones with long legs and some so venomous they could kill a grown horse with a single bite. I still remember having one that spun its web outside our hut one summer—it had a sinister looking black-and-yellow exoskeleton, and when it stretched its legs fully it was as big as my palm. Its web was strung between our roof's gutter and a sidewall shingle. Father said it was a Writing Spider, teaching me it was commonly known for the beautiful, symmetrical designs it wove in its web, somehow similar to the patterns frost leaves on an ice-crusted window.

I can still remember the day the spider moved in and set up shop. As a little girl, I let out a scream the first time I saw it, running into the house and begging my father to go outside and kill it. But when he saw it was a Writing Spider, he merely laughed at my childish fears. "I know it looks big and scary, Drakini, but these kind of spiders are our friends. Summer is coming, and this spider will help keep the mosquitos and flies at bay. Best to leave it be for now, sweetheart," he said.

But the spider that emerges from the shadows above is unlike any arachnid the Creator has ever conceived. This is the Twilight Expanse, a dimension outside the Creator's control. I don't know how I know this, but I do. Earth is the Creator's domain, but this place is an entity of its own—a realm that existed before the Creator himself.

"In a world of shadowsss and liesss, the truth will alwaysss ssseem dessstructive," the creature above hisses, lowering herself into the light. She has the body of a woman but the features of a spider. Her pale flesh is naked, covered only by the polished exoskeleton of a black widow. Tendrils of hardened, skeletal deposits cover her ribcage, abdomen, and shoulders. Her arms and legs are bare, yet eight, distinctly spider-like legs emerge from her back in the space between her shoulder blades. The legs traverse the web of chains gracefully, allowing her humanoid body to float in the spotlight as she draws closer to her trapped prey. Her eight red eyes never leave Ventur's agonizing body. She wears a sinister smile between the pincers that extend from her cheekbones.

"GET ME THE FUCK OUT OF HERE!" Ventur orders, his fear turning quickly to anger. I can see the veins bulging from his neck as he tries to rip free of the chains. For a split second, I mistake him for his father as my chains snagged his forearm. "What kind of sick, twisted joke is this?" Ventur laughs violently, his anger turning to hysteria. I've never taken pleasure in seeing people be tortured, but I feel a perverse joy welling inside my heart.

"You've been a busssy boy, Count Ventur," the arachnid woman says, hovering over Ventur as he bounces helplessly. "Ssschemesss within ssschemesss. How many people will you ssstab in the back before you're sssatisssfied, I wonder?"

"I don't know what the fuck you're talking about!" Ventur spits a pathetic glob of saliva at his accuser but misses completely.

"Now'sss not the time to play ssstupid, Cccelessstial. I have watched you from the Twilight Expansssse sssinccce your inccception... You have aligned yoursssself with Ssstephenwolf and the Creator; even now, you plan to betray Sssileniusss Sssylvian."

"What is she talking about Ventur?" I call out, seeing how Ventur's face grows flustered at the spiderwoman's words. Instead of denying the accusations, Ventur grows eerily still as he looks up at his captor with venom in his eyes. Innocent people do not react in this manner, I reflect inwardly.

"Stay out of this, bloodbag whore," Ventur growls.

The spiderwoman continues, "Poor, poor Ventur... Neglected by hisss father, boo hoo, nobody lovesss him. Ssso much wasssted potential, it'sss a shame! The Creator plansss on dessstroying your entire ssspecccies, and ssstill you offer him your ssserviccce? Who hurt you, I wonder?"

"You don't fucking know me, demon!"

"I know enough, and ssso doesss she," the arachnid points at me, but Ventur doesn't bother averting his eyes.

"You're... You're serving Steppenwolf?" I stutter, not surprised but still confused at the same time. The Wendigos are directly opposed to the Undead... Hell, it was a Wendigo who killed Ventur's father, along with hundreds of his father's soldiers. The Wendigos will hunt the entire Undead population to extinction if they make it off these Deadlands... So why the hell would Ventur support their cause?

"It's not like I was left any other option, Huntress," Ventur sighs. He catches me off guard. I'm not used to him addressing me as anything other than 'bitch' or 'cunt' or 'whore.'

"You wouldn't understand, bloodbag," he continues. That's more like it, I reflect. "You are one of the Nine, Huntress. Or at least, you will be... Mortal men like me weren't left any other choice. Enchantress has chosen the Sylvians as her champions; the humans have you, and the Creator has his Death-Defeater... There isn't much use for a man like me when the end times come."

"How do you know about the Nine?" I shout. I am one of the Harbingers and even I was unaware of these metaphysical entities until recently. There is no reason a man like Ventur should possess otherworldly knowledge like this. "Better yet, how do you know about the end times?"

"Oh please," Ventur snickers, "Don't act like you're the only one on this earth who has access to the secrets of the universe. You may have a part to play in all of this, but I descend from one of the Nine, the Bat. These secrets have been passed down through Tribe Celestial for centuries—we have based our entire existence on them, human. Everyone must pick a side in the coming war, and my ancestors aligned themselves with the Creator. I am merely carrying out the things they set in motion."

"And then what? You'll watch every man, woman, Lycan, and Undead be wiped from existence—yourself included? Why would your ancestors choose that outcome? Why would you support it?"

"Liesss and deccception," the demon adds.

"Oh shut up," Ventur quips. "Your lisp is unbearable. Both of you, just shut up! This is just some fucked up nightmare... I'm going to wake up in my bed and carry on with my life. Neither of you can stop the Creator, so why bother? If you can't beat him, you might as well join him. We are just a bunch of fucking pawns. I am not betraying my species, Drakini. In fact, I'm countless steps ahead of you... The Bat did not agree to serve the Creator to preserve our species in *this* lifetime; rather, we cut a deal so we can reign supreme in the afterlife. Our fates in this life are sealed—there is no overcoming utter obliteration. But the Creator has made a place for us to dwell after we die—a Hell of sorts, called Draemir. But because of the promises Damon made to the Creator, the Undead will be the rulers of this realm. Humans and Lycans will be our servants for all eternity, and there isn't a damn thing you and your chains can do to stop it."

"Sylvian's sake, Ventur, you've got to be shitting me..."

"He ssspeaksss the truth for oncccce, Drakini. The Twilight Expanssse isss the bridge between your world and the placcce he ssspeaksss of. Thisss very moment, the sssoulsss of the dead sssuffer inssside, cursssing the Creator for hisss betrayal."

"If you won't listen to me, listen to the demon Drakini. I am not living for myself anymore. The weight of a million eternal souls rely on me. The Reaper will lose the coming war. Enchantress doesn't stand a chance. And you... You haven't the slightest clue what the Creator is capable of! I mean look at you—you're pathetic! Ten years you've been trapped in the Deadlands. You already faced off against the Death-Defeater once; look what happened! You got the piss beat out of you and got everyone who followed you killed... You want my advice? Bite the damn apple, Drakini... Arcadia may be fake, but it's sure as hell better than defying the Creator and spending an eternity in Hell."

"Fuck you," I shout, instantly triggered by his words. They cut deep, mostly because they speak the truth, and in a world of shadows and lies, the truth always feels destructive. The advice itself would be attractive to most mortals. The Wendigos present us humans comfortable lies so we don't have to face harsh reality. With our bodies possessed by their curse, we become exempt from the Hell Ventur speaks of, giving us the option to spend eternity with the ones we love instead of under the rule of bloodthirsty bats.

"Are we done here?" Ventur scoffs, directing his question to me and the spider both.

"We will sssee you at the end," the spider hisses. From her wrist shoots a never-ending chain, causing Ventur to scream once more. I stand and watch with detached indifference as the spider converges on Ventur. Her eight legs get to work twisting his body as the chain from her wrist wraps itself around him. Like a fly being spun into an inescapable cocoon, Ventur is quickly mummified by the chain so tight that he cannot resist the restraints. His scream becomes muffled as the metallic links cover his mouth, then he disappears from sight as the makeshift womb envelopes him completely.

"I am Nephra," the spider says, introducing herself as she devotes her full attention to me. Her legs leave Ventur in place as she scurries across the web in my direction, shooting a chain from her wrist as she leaps from the web and slowly lowers herself to the ground.

Without giving me time to process what I've seen or reply to her greeting, she lands on her human feet and tucks her eight legs away, bowing before me in supplication. "I have waited many yearsss for your arrival, Ssseer. Wisssteria told of your coming. It would be an honor to ssserve you asss a shadow sssoldier."

"You know Wisteria?"

"She isss our leader, the mosost feared shadow sssoldier ever created."

"But she's gone," I stammer, unsure if this creature has learned of my hellcat's demise. "Steppenwolf killed her several moons ago..."

"Ha! Wisssteria cannot be killed! Whoever told you that hasss no knowledge of the Twilight Expansssse... Wisssteria will return in due time, Huntressss. But until then, I will help you prepare the way."

I pause to compose myself. If these words are true, and I have no doubt they are, I have no reason to sit around and mourn the hellcat any longer. If Wisteria is coming, I too must prepare the way for her, and to do that, I need to get stronger—need to master these powers...

"Tell me, Nephra... Can you teach me how to create chains from thin air like you?"

"I can teach you that, and much more, Huntressss..."

I smile diabolically as my plans slowly come together.

"Then welcome to the resistance," I announce, closing my third eye as I drag Nephra alongside me into the Creator's reality.

41

MONTH FIVE

I breathe deeply, holding my stomach as I feel something other than
nerves stir. It's been five months, give or take, since Cur and I conceived
the child I carry, and it is already communicating to me with its fiery spirit.
The child Dane blessed me with was always silent, especially this early on.
But Cur's child sometimes seems as if it's doing somersaults inside the little
room my abdomen provides.

Cur still doesn't have the slightest inkling I'm with child, which isn't
surprising. I've learned over the years that men are innately oblivious creatures. I can count on one hand the number of times I cut my hair and
received notice from Dane. It's not that men don't care, it's that they spend
most of their time inside their own heads instead of being present in the
moment. Besides, there are little signs for Cur to pick up on. Though my
stomach shows a slight bulge, I wear mostly loose fitting pelts during the
day and even more at night.

Tomorrow, Cur will leave this place and return to finish constructing the boat. If Myre's prophecy can be trusted, I will face Steppenwolf again by the time I bear this child. Whatever time I don't spend meditating with Draven is spent plotting for that day's arrival, and Cur's boat is an integral part of fleeing this place if things go awry. He protested my orders at first, but he rarely wins any of our heated disagreements. Besides, I'm unsure if I'll be able to hide the baby bump from him much longer.

"Reality is what I say it is," I exhale, focusing on my surroundings and sculpting them to current desires. I repeat the phrase again, "Reality is... what I say it is."

"I swear to the gods, this will never get old," Cur remarks as I open my eyes.

We are no longer in the Deadlands.

Well, technically we are, but just as Wisteria was able to slow time and distend reality for me, I've now cast a domain around Cur and I that makes this place look like paradise. But it isn't actually paradise—it only looks perfect because we've lived in the Deadlands so long that Fyrefell now looks like a vacation destination.

"Say, can't you just use these powers to finish the boat?" Cur asks, looking around at Fyrefell with astonishment. There is sand and clay as far as our eyes can stretch. Instead of snow bombarding our plane of sight, our view is now unobstructed. Only dry, humid air surrounds us. "I mean, you could build the boat with a snap of your fingers... Then, Netherwing and I could stay here and continue to help you with your training."

"That isn't how my powers work," I laugh, though I wish it was. Even though I need to conceal this child from Cur, I don't want him to leave my side for even a moment. In only a few short months, I've grown both weak and strong because of the love I feel toward him. Weak, because he could be leveraged against me by my enemies. But strong, because he's given me more to live for than myself. "My powers can make it seem as though the boat is finished, but the second you put it on the water for voyage, it would sink faster than the Sun Treader. I am not the Creator; the things I create are not real. I merely infect the minds of others with my own delusions. Draven calls it 'fishing for the moon.'"

"Feels pretty damn real to me, just like the Blood Moon Hex," Cur reflects, walking up to one of the many huts inside of Fyrefell and placing his hand against its outer wall. I look past him, into the distance, smiling at the sight of the Fire Mountains that rise from the earth's crust. This isn't the first time I've cast Fyrefell as a domain, but the details get more and more real with each time. I spent my entire childhood in this town, and I've finally reached a point where even I can't tell what separates this hallucination from the real thing. "But go on, tell me what the all-wise Draven means when he says 'fishing for the moon.'" Cur jokes, knowing Draven's lessons are not easily interpreted.

I alter our surroundings, allowing Fyrefell to vanish completely as another scene phases into being. The sun is gone now, and we stand on the edge of a serene lake. Frogs croak in the distance, cicadas chirp, woodpeckers hammer. These are all things I'm particularly proud of. A hallucination is only as real as the details I imbue it with. Seeing is not believing, but adding auditory clips to my viewer's experience adds to the realism of the optical illusion.

I hand Cur a fishing rod, which didn't exist a moment ago but now does because I need it to. He is flustered from the sudden shift in reality, slightly dissociated from being ripped from Fyrefell and planted beside this fabricated lake. I've practiced this power so many times by now that dissociation sickness rarely grabs hold of me anymore. But for Cur, this is merely a reminder of how fickle his mortal mind is and how easy it is to fall prey to a well-constructed lie.

"What's that for?" he asks, staring at the fishing rod, then taking it from me.

"I've learned it's easier to just show you Draven's teaching, rather than explain it. Cast the hook into the water and try to catch the moon."

"I'm not an idiot," he says, pointing up at the sky. "You can't catch the moon from this lake, even if there is a reflection of it in the waters. The real moon is in the sky."

But when he follows his finger and looks up at the starless night, he sees I've cleverly omitted adding a moon amidst the darkness. There is no moon above. The only moon that illuminates this night is the shimmering reflection that dances in the lake's center several dozen yards away from us. "Ah, I see what you did there. So the lesson to be learned is, and correct me if I'm wrong, that those without your ability are all staring at the reflection of something without knowing it is just a cheap imitation of the source that casts the reflection?"

"Something like that," I laugh, thinking back to the demonstration Draven used to teach me this same principle. "Draven took me into a cave weeks ago, before I had the ability to cast domains of my own. He made me stare at the cave's wall and lit a fire behind me, telling me I wasn't allowed to turn around. He sat between me and the fire, casting shadow puppets along the wall, forcing me to announce the things I saw. Using his own Seer vision, he tricked my mind into thinking the wall and its figures were all that existed in this world. The cave around me transformed into a real-life iteration of the play he was performing. The shadow puppets morphed into real creatures, drawing me into their world without me even noticing.

"That's the world we live in, I've gathered. Humans, Lycans, Undead, doesn't matter. We are all chained prisoners forced to watch the Creator's shadow puppets, not knowing we have the power to turn around and leave the cave. But as a Seer, I'm learning how to detach from this illusion... Not only can I leave the cave—I can cast shadows of my own... The shadows I cast may not be real, but I can convince a person's mind that they are... And with enough practice, I'll be able to destroy any domain Steppenwolf casts."

"Then what makes you any different from a Wendigo?" Cur asks. He's somewhat sincere, but he's also concerned. "I mean... They trapped me in my mind for four snotting years... And I'm not saying you'd do that to me, but what makes a Seer any different than them?"

"Steppenwolf and his Wendigos rely on blood magic to access these powers... They draw on the Underworld—a place called Draemir—a resting place for the souls of the dead. That is what fuels the growth of Arcadian Apples. The apples are the shattered dreams of the dead—without Draemir, the Wendigos wouldn't be able to trap humanity in Arcadia. But my powers... I still don't know what allows me to see the things I do... I may never know... It's almost like the universe saw the Creator's intentions, saw Steppenwolf's path of destruction... And created me from necessity... Just as I created Wisteria from my own necessity..."

"The Huntress," Cur says, his voice filled with adoration as he stares at me. He touches my arm, causing me to turn. I'm met by his deep gaze. They catch me by surprise and distract me, forcing me to let go of the world I cast around us. The lake and its surroundings vanish, replaced with the harsh winter of the Deadlands. A gust of spine-chilling wind bombards us, but I can't stop looking in this man's eyes.

He continues, "You're right, Drakini... This world needs you... Now more than ever. Whether the universe made you to protect humanity or for me to love, I don't care. You are my pack. I would follow you to the ends of the earth. Where your chains lead, I will follow. I need you to know this because... because I didn't speak my mind soon enough ten years ago, and by the time I found you again, it was too late. I don't know what will happen when we face Steppenwolf a second time, but I won't let my feelings for you go unspoken."

I press a single hand to my stomach, feeling the life of this man's child swelling inside of me. If there is any moment for me to tell him he's going to be a father, it's now. A storm of guilt and anxiety rises in me. Emotions flood my nervous system, all of them screaming in my brain conflicting actions. Tell him! Tell him now!

If I tell him, Steppenwolf will use him to hurt me, just like he did with Dane. I can't tell him. I mustn't tell him.

I have to tell him!

"Cur, I—"

"It's okay, Drakini, you don't have to make a decision now... But if we both survive what's to come... If I'm able to finish the boat and get us off this desolate rock... I hope you'll consider choosing me when we return home."

"And if we don't make it home?"

"Then I look forward to enduring the agony of the Underworld by your side," he says, smiling painfully.

He starts to turn from me and I blurt, wanting to stall his departure, "You never told me your name, Cur..."

I haven't brought this topic up in several months. It's become a silly joke between the two of us, one that equally entertains me as much as it haunts me. He's saved me, he's fucked me, he's confessed his love for me, he's sired my child, and still I only know him as the same derogatory term the Hunters assigned to him. I owe this man more than I've given to him. I can't help but think that he deserves more than me, a married woman who built a life after he sacrificed himself for me.

He laughs, somewhat happy he's managed to hold this over me all these years. "How about this... You beat Steppenwolf to a bloody pulp, and I'll tell you my name. Deal?"

I nod softly, knowing our time together has come to an end.

When he lets go of me I want nothing more than to scream for his attention. I want to grab his hands and place them on my stomach so he can feel our child kicking inside me. I want to stare in his eyes and watch his reaction the moment he learns he's going to be a father. I want him to hold me while I cry tears of joy for the present and tears of fear for the future. But I don't do any of this.

I bite my tongue as he leaves me. All I can do now is hope I haven't made a monumental mistake.

42

MONTH SIX

I knew I'd miss Cur, but his absence has been particularly painful these past couple weeks.

My training with Draven has been pushing me past the bounds of sanity. It's like I'm in the Areopagus again, except I'm no longer training my body to be fit for battle—I'm training my mind to withstand invasion and manipulation. It's exhausting. Meditating, domain casting, Dreamveil consumption, shattering optical illusions... Any devious drill Draven could devise, he has. His teaching approach is sink or swim, and it feels like I've sunk lower than the Sun Treader at this point.

My brain feels like overly mashed potatoes with the amount Draven's poked and prodded at it. I want nothing more than to crawl into a cave with Cur one last time. To press my face into his side while he runs his hand through my hair. To feel his lips kiss my forehead tenderly.

But Cur is gone, leaving me to deal with my depression alone—Nephra and Behemoth aren't exactly what I'd call emotional support creatures, and Draven lacks in the empathy department.

On this particular night, I find myself on a midnight stroll across the nearby drawbridge—the same one Draven and Cur crossed each month when it was time for a moondance. Whether subconsciously or intentionally, some part of me hopes I will find evidence of Cur on the opposite side of this bridge. I've never taken it upon myself to travel across it—I'm always too exhausted to explore after a long day of training with Draven. But now, I find myself seeking some reminder of Cur. A tuft of Lycan fur, perhaps. Maybe claw marks slashed in a tree's bark. I'd even settle for the carcass of an animal he hunted some previous full moon.

I shouldn't have let him leave, I think to myself as I cradle my swollen stomach. Dagon's sake, what if he misses the birth of his own child because of my secrecy? It's hard to be confident in my decision as this baby gets closer to term. As my stomach has grown, so too has the pressure this secret exerts on me. This isn't a path I want to walk alone, despite how well-intentioned my decision to do so was.

The bridge beneath me creaks, causing me to pause in my stride. I hear a thump, followed by a thud. Something grunts as the rusted metal that holds me up clangs. The drawbridge shakes ever so slightly, instantly filling my mind with fear. There's no telling how long ago this bridge was built; what are the odds that tonight of all nights is when it decides to collapse beneath my feet?

The shaking grows. I throw myself to the side handrail, bracing myself as my feet shuffle on ice. Nausea floods my throat—a mixture of this near-death experience and my recurring pregnancy sickness. I grit my teeth and swallow repeatedly, trying to hold the vomit at bay.

A dark figure catapults itself over the opposite side of the bridge, flipping several times through the air like an acrobat, then landing gracefully only a few strides from me. I get my feet under me as the figure rises from a low crouch. I take in the creature's appearance as it stands on its hindlegs, whooping and hollering excitedly like a toddler not old enough to speak. Its proportions are all wrong, I notice. Its legs are short and stocky while its arms are long enough to scrape the icy bridge.

"Monkey see, monkey do!" the ape shouts excitedly, throwing himself up against the same handrail I cling to. I flinch slightly away from his enthusiasm, which causes him to flinch slightly away from me.

Monkey see, monkey do? I ask myself, pondering the primate's words. I've heard of monkeys before, but I've never seen one in real life. Truth be told, I don't even know what region of the world monkeys call home, but I know this animal sticks out in the Deadlands like a snowflake in the Scorpos desert. I squint my eyes at him, inching my face closer. Astonishingly, without any hesitation, the monkey mimics my movement flawlessly.

"Erm... What... Or who... are you?" I ask, pointing my finger at my guest.

The monkey straightens himself and lifts his own finger at me, pointing as he whoops excitedly, "Monkey see, monkey do! Monkey see, monkey do!"

"I heard you the first time, but what is your name, monkey?"

The animal twists his head in confusion. I take a step toward him, and he moves to take a step toward me. I leap back, jumping away from the ape as he does the same. Then, partly because I want to test my theory and partly because I want to entertain myself, I slide sideways across the ice, which prompts the monkey to do the same. I laugh at the animal's antics, and he laughs too. It's like staring in a glass mirror, only the reflection that stares back is a hairier, more primordial version of me.

I raise my hands to cover my eyes, then crack the space between my middle and ring fingers, peaking at the monkey to find he's cleverly done the same. He whoops, "Monkey see no evil!"

I move my hands to my ears, and he whoops once more, "Monkey hear no evil," as he does the same.

Then, I cover my mouth and listen to his muffled speech recite, "Monkey speak no evil," from behind his palms.

"Well aren't you quite the oddball... You might be weirder than Draven, my friend."

The monkey smiles so wide that I can see his back molars.

"Simon says jump!" I shout, jumping once. The monkey's feet land from the jump at the same time mine do. "Simon says sit!" I command, laughing as I plop down on my pregnant ass and watch as the monkey cannonballs against the icy bridge. "Stand!" I say, pushing myself back to my feet, panting as my back aches from the weight of my stomach.

For the first time since meeting him, the monkey defies my order and remains sitting, staring up at me with a stupid smile.

"Well, well, well, aren't you a clever monkey," I say, offering him a hand. "I think I'll call you... Simon."

43

Month Seven

"Time to put two and two together, Piss Eyes!" Draven shouts, clearly amused by this outlandish plan. "I've heard you're a half-decent fighter, and now you've taken your first steps as a Seer, so let's put 'em together and see what you've got!"

"Remind me one more time why I have to do this with a blindfold on?" I ask, tightening the thick cloth around my eyes. The sun was hardly visible from behind the dark clouds anyway, but blinding myself completely feels... like something only Draven could devise.

Instead of answering my question straightforwardly, Draven recites a riddle: "I see without eyes, and know without proof; I glimpse what's ahead, though the future stays aloof. Some call it a gift, some say it's a curse; a window to time, both forward and reverse. What am I?"

"For like the 500th time, I don't know! We've got to work on your communication skills. Seriously, not everything needs to be a riddle."

"Clairvoyance! I'm clairvoyance!" he shrieks, disappointed.

"Well I don't even know what that means, so I hope you didn't put too much thought into that... wonderful delivery."

"Class is in session, little chickpea!" Draven shouts. I hear his feet crunching in the snow in front of me, then hear him fidgeting with something. My vision is black, but I can still see my shadow soldiers gathered around me clear as day. Behemoth stands at my side; Nephra and Simon float in the air, though I know they are actually hanging from tree branches that are now invisible to me. Nephra hangs upside down, clinging to a chain like a spider lowering itself on a single thread of webbing. Meanwhile, Simon swings himself back and forth on the same branch like a gymnast who's mastered the art of horizontal bars.

My pulse slows as the air vibrates. The hairs on the back of my neck raise. It used to take Wisteria's intervention to slow time, but now I do it of my own volition. Behemoth's fur is blown by the winter wind slower. Simon's swinging is half the speed it was. Nephra's eight eyes pause much longer before blinking.

Time is a manmade construct heavily tied to perspective, but after months of Draven's teachings, I know how to make it a construct of my own mind.

I sidestep, sensing an incoming projectile before it reaches me. The snowball Draven threw at me wizzes by my ear, missing me by a fraction of a second. I can hear him laughing in slow motion, overjoyed to see I've dodged his attack. But this is only the beginning of whatever lesson he intends on teaching me.

Draven storms me; I can't see him, but I can feel his movement nonetheless. Reality is no longer something I need to see. Countless hours of meditating has taught me how to open my third eye, which is not an eye that needs sight in order to see. I hold my hand out to my side as Draven sprints at me, though I've slowed his stride in my mind to a crawl. The air tingles around my open palm. I close my fist on a chain that wasn't there a moment ago. The chain dart materializes from thin air, conjured into existence by nothing more than my willpower. I have not created it—it doesn't actually exist, just as Simon and Behemoth and Nephra don't actually exist. But nevertheless, it is real in my mind, and the pain Draven will feel from its lashes will be real to his mind.

I stagger my feet defensively as my muscle memory windmills the chain vertically on either side of me. For a brief moment, I almost feel bad for Draven. All these months, he's had his fun testing me mentally. But he's never tested my physical prowess, which means I'm about to teach him his first lesson.

The chain lashes out and wraps around his feet, binding him like a bull at a rodeo. I marvel inwardly at my ability to hit my target despite my blindness. Thanks to my third eye, I'm able to see him without seeing him. It was a gut instinct, something I never listened to before training with Draven. His lessons will be his downfall, literally.

I yank the chain hard, expecting to feel my opponent's feet be pulled out from beneath him. But just as I manipulated reality to summon this chain dart, so too does Draven manipulate reality to overcome its grip on him. The links around his ankles vanish, causing my chain to rip free as I yank it in my direction.

All I can hear is Draven's reverberating laughter as he reaches me, raising his fist to deliver a punch to my gut.

Suddenly, something inside of me snaps as thoughts of my child's safety enter my mind. Draven has no idea I'm pregnant; there is no malevolent intent behind the punch he plans to deliver. He is an innocent hiker who's stumbled upon a grizzly bear cub, not knowing its mother lurks nearby. Like a mother bear faced with her cub's peril, I enter a zone of frenzy and panic I've never experienced.

Even though I'm blindfolded, I can see everything crystal clear now. My surroundings are so clear that I nearly forget a piece of cloth covers my eyes. I can see the snow falling around us and the surrounding forest of evergreens. I can see Draven's hysterical face as he convinces himself he's moments away from defeating me. I hyperfixate on the frozen perspiration that gathers along his forehead. His fist is inches away from committing an unforgivable sin. I have to stop him before it's too late.

I act without thinking. This is no longer a training exercise to me. My baby is in real danger, and I respond accordingly. I sidestep his pathetic punch, wrapping my chain around his wrist, then wrapping his wrist around his body. Once more, he manipulates reality and makes the chains disappear, but as he does so, I melt the permafrost beneath his feet, causing the ground to swallow him immediately. Draven falls into the puddle of water to his waistline, and before he can lift himself from the hole, I freeze the ground once more, effectively cementing him in place.

The snow crunches behind me, causing me to turn. I'm now surrounded by an entire army of Dravens, just as I was the first day I met this man. All of them have the same, overly enthusiastic smile Draven had before I beat him. There are so many of them, far too many to count. They creep toward me steadily, each one of them snickering as they await my response.

But I see through the illusion.

I don't need to overcome these puppets in battle.

I just need to defeat their master.

I turn around swiftly to face the original Draven as he melts the permafrost that traps him. Before he can lift himself from the hole, I deliver a swift, devastating kick to his head, knocking him unconscious.

When I turn to face the army of Dravens again, they are no longer there.

I'm safe for now, as is my child. But in the back of my mind, I now realize what the cost of losing to Steppenwolf is. If I can't beat him, it not only means I lose. It means I risk losing the only being in this world I care about more than myself. Despite any doubts I had in my capabilities before, losing is no longer an option.

44

MONTH EIGHT

"Aₛ above, so below," are the only words I remember as the Dreamveil's mirage of visions leaves me. I peer up at the full moon above; this is the eighth time I've traversed Grimspire Peak—the eighth time I've met Myre along the mountaintop in order to unlock the secrets of the universe.

"Finally," I gasp, no longer forced to fear the unknown. Hell is only so terrifying because we humans don't know what awaits us within its patient gates. I smile as the illusion fades as fast as it arose, looking up at Myre. He waits for me to prophesy on the things I've seen. "I've seen what Hell awaits us... Draemir... A realm that exists past the Twilight Expanse... Not only that... I saw the death of Steppenwolf! I know how to kill him..."

"How? How does Steppenwolf die?" Myre asks, almost fearfully. "Well, what did you see?"

He almost sounds desperate, like he has some personal stake in my revelation. For the briefest moment, his face twitches, then spasms. He swiftly slaps his cheek as if he is trying to rid himself of a fly. Oddly enough, his cheek isn't the faintest tinge red when he lowers his hand, despite it being cold enough to freeze boiling water. His eyes flinch ever so slightly as he locks gaze with me again, knowing that I saw the slip in his facade.

"Are you okay Myre?" I ask. This is far from the first time he's struggled composing himself. Every month I meet him atop this mountain, his seizures grow worse. But something was different about this one...

Myre is a shadow soldier—a figment of my imagination, sure, but when his face convulsed, for the briefest second, it was like I could see something inside him. I've never seen one of my shadow soldiers glitch, even in the early years of knowing Wisteria.

"I'm fine," he replies, almost defensively. "Just got... overwhelmed, I guess... when you mentioned Steppenwolf's demise... Is it true? Is there really a way to defeat him?"

I look at him skeptically, then dismiss the lapse from my mind for the moment. "This entire continent, all that we see, was built on the misery of those suffering inside Draemir," I say, closing my eyes so I can focus on the Dreamveil premonition. "That's what the Ra-El mean when they say 'As above, so below'... The Creator has given Steppenwolf's legion the power to feed off the eternal turmoil of Draemir's prisoners... Hundreds of thousands of souls tormented so the Creator can achieve his end goal... But my powers can defeat him; I saw it clear as day."

"How can this be?" Myre seethes, almost as if he's angered to hear these words. "Your powers? Where do they come from, if not from Draemir?"

"I don't know..."

"Oh, come on," Myre says, noticeably annoyed. "Eight months you've come up this mountain; eight times you've consumed Dreamveil! Surely you must have some idea where your powers come from?"

"Calm down, Myre... I've learned so much these eight months; who cares where my powers come from?"

"I do, damnit!" Myre shouts, his face twitching again. "You're a human! An insignificant speck of dust, and yet you've been given the powers of a Seer? Defeating Steppenwolf depends entirely on where your vision comes from—*who* your vision comes from!"

Something isn't right. Alarms ring in my head, warning me that I'm in danger. My child kicks violently inside my stomach, almost as if it's reaffirming my senses. This isn't the Myre I knew. Still, his face continues to twitch... No, not twitch... His whole head contorts and convulses now. Myre tries to slap his cheek again to end the spasm, but this time it does little to end the jerking. He doubles over, moaning to himself, "Stop... fighting!"

I smile, realizing that it's finally time to unleash my grand plan. After months of conspiring, I will finally tell him what I saw inside Draemir's gates, and it will be this imposter's undoing.

"You know, it's weird... When I finally dared to open the gates of Hell, there was someone waiting for me... I doubt they would've ever found me if it hadn't been for Wisteria..."

"What do you... mean?" Myre grunts, fighting some otherworldly pain in his bowels.

"Well, the souls of Draemir are damned to suffer for all eternity, but once Steppenwolf killed Wisteria, it seems she descended to the Underworld in search of one soul in particular."

Chunks of Myre's face start to illuminate, then fade from existence. But there is something, someone, behind the cracking face. I flinch away from him as he loses total control of his body. His limbs flail; his clothed midsection cracks like a thin sheet of ice; he bites on his tongue so hard that blood pours over his lips. A panicked voice screams from inside his diaphragm, "Drakini... It's a... Trap!"

"Shut up, cretin!" Myre yells at himself, punching himself in the face. He stares up at the sky, his entire body coming undone with each passing second. "How? How is this possible?"

"Maybe this will make you feel better?" I suggest, extending my hand to Myre. In my hand is a glass of orange juice—a rather bizarre object to distract Myre with momentarily.

His hands cradle the cracks in his face, but his eyes glare at the orange juice like I've just told some rotten joke. I continue, "Personally, a refreshing glass of orange juice always makes me feel better." I laugh, not because I want to set Myre at ease, but because after all these years, I have finally gotten my revenge against Steppenwolf.

Myre stammers, "What are you... Where did you... There are no oranges..."

"Looks like the jig is up for both of us," I say, releasing the distortion of reality that clothes me. A veil of light shimmers around me, melting away Drakini's features to reveal my true identity.

Steppenwolf, clothed in Myre's shattering facade, stares at me in horror, then screams, "You! It's... How can it be... It's you!"

"In the flesh, old nemesis! My friends call me Draven, but you can call me The-One-That-Got-Away! Say, how 'bout a riddle? You like riddles? I'll spin you a yarn, a tale, or a fib, but catch me red-handed, and I might ad-lib. What am I?"

Steppenwolf releases Myre's appearance entirely now—shadows pulse around him, shedding the false skin he wore to trick my apprentice now that I've revealed my charade to him. We've both put our cards on the table, each of us playing each other for the fool. But I, Draven Daybane, the Wolf

Who Howls At The Sun, have always been called a fool, whereas this is an extremely painful realization for Steppenwolf.

The Wendigo straightens himself fully, seething violently as foam bubbles from his rabid mouth. He's a feral skeleton covered in decaying, frozen moss and and fraying thickets. His fangs are icicles; his horns are ivory spears. There is no blood, no beating heart, no human emotion inside of him. It has all been burned away by frost and greed. Though his eyes are emotionless specks of white ice, I can feel an entire world of hatred radiating from him, enough to shatter the mountain we stand upon.

"I broke your mind, fickle Lycan!" the Wendigo growls vehemently, enraged at the prospect that he's been outsmarted by a neanderthal like me. I haven't been this happy since plucking an orange from the sky; oh how I want to savor every moment of this interaction! The Wendigo points up at the moon and demands an answer: "How are you here when the moon is full?"

I follow his pointer finger to the moon's mantle in the sky, playing dumb merely to increase the amount of pleasure I get out of my clever lie. "Hmm, you make a good point, Steppenwolf... The only problem is... The moon isn't full."

Call me a fool, call me butt-licker, call me a fleabag, fine; but there's certainly one thing no one has the right to call me, and that's a goddamn dummy! I've been preparing for this night since the day Drakini returned from Grimspire Peak speaking of a childhood acquaintance she met. At first, I didn't voice my suspicions to her, but as she told me about the "shadow soldier" continually wanting her to divulge the secrets of her visions, I became more and more mistrustful. Things weren't adding up; all of Drakini's other shadow soldiers follow her around like flies on dung. So what made this mysterious Myre different than them? Why was he too good to leave this mountaintop, huh?

I started manipulating the moon's appearance in the sky without telling Drakini, setting my plans in motion without her permission. I didn't want to worry her before I confirmed my theory. Then, one morning she returned from Grimspire Peak with news that this "Myre" was glitching, almost as if there was something defective with his existence, even though none of Drakini's other shadow soldiers suffer such infirmities. I made her tell me everything, and that's when I told her my suspicions...

This wasn't a shadow soldier she was seeing at all... It was the Death-Defeater, Steppenwolf, using her to learn where her powers came from in order to snuff out the threat she presents.

At first, Drakini pushed back—she's quite the little firecracker, yes she is! "He showed me a vision from when we were kids that no other person in this world would know," she said, ever the clever little cookie. "I remember it like it was yesterday; two bullies were beating Myre up for the money his parents gave him! Then I showed up and put the bullies in their place! There's no way Steppenwolf would know about that memory; this shadow soldier is definitely Myre."

"All that's good and well, Piss Eyes," I told her, "But there's just one thing you're overlooking... He said you're a Seer, not a Necromancer... And yet, search your feelings... Your friend—Myre, the real Myre—died years ago..."

Steppenwolf looks up at the moon and sees it is, in fact, far from full. My months and months of hard work have paid off! I cast my conscience every night to alter a detail as insignificant as the moon's fullness just so I could appear on this night and face off with Steppenwolf one last time.

"Who's the fool now, eh?" I laugh, thoroughly pleased with myself. "I applaud you, Death-Defeater—you would've had the clever girl fooled if she didn't have crazy 'ole Draven in her corner! Wanna know where you went wrong?"

"Where is the girl?" Steppenwolf growls, closing the gap between us. I don't move; I knew very well what I was getting myself into when I staged this trap.

"A fine question, good sir, but I'd rather answer mine first... You see, I can tell you're getting weaker as time passes. You must be, or else fooling you would've been impossible! That's when it occurred to me, and your inability to control your illusion tonight only confirmed it! You've sucked all the marrow the Deadlands have to offer, and I think we both know you're running out of souls to torture in Draemir. The longer your precious Creator makes you wait, the weaker you get! That's why you had to choose the identity of someone as weak as Myre to appear before Drakini, my star pupil. But even Myre, Lord of the Losers, was too strong an opponent for you to conquer!

"You killed Wisteria, allowing her to peruse the depths of Hell with a VIP ticket! The clever hellcat found Myre's soul and freed him from your torment, allowing him to fight back against your manipulation! I could hear his soul communicating from the afterlife just moments ago! Even after death, the brave boy won't tolerate bullies like you, and why should he? After all, deep down, a bully is just a—"

Steppenwolf's claws close around my neck, crushing my trachea and choking my words. It's for the best, I was beginning to run out of words to stall with. My part in this plot is finished; all I can do is hope I've bought Drakini enough time to finish the mission.

"Did I stutter?" Steppenwolf asks, then screams, "WHERE IS THE GIRL!"

Steppenwolf pulls me in so close that I fear he intends on kissing me. My legs kick in the open air as he moves to the ledge of the mountain, holding me over the cliff's edge. The distance beneath me is enough to kill me ten times over if he decides to let go. But I no longer fear death—I welcome it.

For most of my life, I've been mocked by those who failed to understand me. Now, my neck kisses the claws of the monster that shattered my mind. But there is no greater feeling than looking in his eyes and seeing that he knows I thwarted him. The only thing that could make this moment better would be a sip of ice-cold, refreshing orange ju—

I smile as he drops me. In the several seconds it takes for me to hit the mountain valley below, I slow reality and live an eternity.

45

DECEIVING A DECEPTOR

A sharp pain rises in my chest, prompting me to look to the sky. Draven has sent the signal—the moon is no longer full—Steppenwolf has discovered our trap, which means Draven's fate is sealed. I pause for a silent moment of mourning, closing my eyes. Eight months ago, I thought Daybane was crazier than a crowing goose. But I was wrong about him.

Draven wasn't crazy... He was a crazy genius. This night wouldn't have been possible without him. He did the impossible; he deceived the Ultimate Deceiver... He saw through Steppenwolf's disguise, something I should've seen through myself but was swayed too easily by his rhetoric. "Don't mistake a parrot for a prophet, Piss Eyes," he said. "Damn Death-Defeater is a chameleon, and a chameleon is never underdressed."

I know Draven died with a smile on his face. It's just who he was, and now it is my turn to pick up the baton and finish the race.

"Nephra, you take Dane. Behemoth, you're on Pip duty. Simon, you've got Katana," I order, looking at the three remaining soldiers from a once unstoppable force. I've returned to the place where it all started—Teufelshörner, better known to natives as Devil's Horns, the place where the dead don't rest. It's been less than a year since Steppenwolf destroyed everything I know and love. Less than a year since he broke me, forcing me to question everything I thought I knew about myself. But now I've returned, and I am no longer playing defense with powers I don't understand. This time, I am bringing the attack to him.

Monkey see, monkey do! Simon whispers urgently, hopping into action, approaching Katana's cold corpse. Katana, a soldier I previously thought impossible to best in battle. But Steppenwolf does not fight fair, and a warrior's physical prowess doesn't matter once pitted against the Death-Defeater.

I rub Dane's blue-stained cheek, well aware that his mind, like Pip's and Katana's, is trapped in some foreign dimension. And yet, they are still human... Whatever vision Steppenwolf shows them, they've rejected comfortable lies in favor of harsh reality. Eight months they've clung on to their lives, stuck in a comatose Hell where paradise is within their grasp, yet they fight the lustful urge to reach for it.

These three were stronger than Calico and Wasp and Lullaby. Though Calico was smarter than any man I've ever met, intelligence doesn't grant the wisdom to defy a Wendigo. Though Wasp has likely poisoned more men and women in secret than even Ventur, Arcadia poisoned his mind in return. And although Lullaby's lips could send a man to death with the whisper of a curse, nothing could prepare him for the curse of false paradise.

There's no telling I'll be able to bring these men back from their vegetative state. And if I can, there's even less certainty what the state of their minds will be. Cur was prisoner to the Blood Moon Hex for several years, but he had Wisteria's help breaking free from his delusions. Without some external influence, my husband's mind might be lost forever.

I look around at the unconscious bodies that litter the cavernous fortress. Devil's Horn is home to the largest Arcadian Apple orchard in the Deadlands, meaning it's home to the greatest population of Ra-El east of the frozen ocean. My shadow soldiers were able to find the cave entrance with relative ease, allowing me to enter this underground citadel unencumbered.

The Ra-El never saw me coming once I collected their minds in a temporary domain. All these months, Draven has been my mental sparring partner, so tricking a few hundred humans was comparatively light work. All humans have desires and fears. Create the right lie and they will absent-mindedly walk right into my trap and lock the door behind themselves.

Steppenwolf's army of Wendigos, however, were a different story. I look up at several dozen Wendigos who stand scattered in the distance, each of them standing before a projection of myself—false clones I cast, each of which stare at Arcadian Apples in their palms as predatory Wendigos watch them intently, completely blind to the fact that they're trying to deceive a deception.

They are so hellbent on consuming the minds of my puppets that they can't even see me, nor can they see the fact that I've single-handedly disarmed their entire cult of Ra-Ellian followers.

I almost want to pat myself on the back, realizing I've managed to trick Steppenwolf, his Wendigos, and the Ra-El all in a single night. But this night is far from over, so I cut the rope that binds Dane, Pip, and Katana, then step out of the way so my shadow soldiers can retrieve their bodies.

"Take them to Cur and get them on the boat," I order as we exit the cave together. As my face is hit with the freezing cold front of an incoming blizzard, I release the illusions I cast all at once. If I'm going to face Steppenwolf, I can't have my third eye preoccupied and divided between the remaining Ra-El and Wendigos. Instead, I free them from their mental shackles and cast a different illusion altogether, one that takes much less mental fortitude to sustain. I whisper into the night: "Your cave is collapsing; there is no way out, the exit is blocked; the only way to survive is if you pat your heads and rub your bellies. If anyone stops and says the patting and rubbing is foolish, kill them."

46

REMATCH

Steppenwolf lumbers forward from the dark forest as his legions are consumed by insanity below.

We've switched places, I realize. Eight months ago, I stood where he currently does, and I now stand where he did. Darkness clings to the elemental beast's frame as he stalks toward me, equally furious and impressed. His skeletal mask and white eyes are as terrifying as they were before, yet I feel no fear as I greet them a second time. We humans fear the unknown, but this monster is all too familiar to me now. Call it delusion, call it cockiness, call it whatever you want... I am the one who deserves to be feared now.

"So glad you could join me, Myre," I say, smiling at the demon's obvious frustration. "Or are you going by a different name today? It's hard to keep track of the truth when you are such a clever liar."

"Your deception has accomplished nothing, Seer. Your lunatic friend is dead, and you will soon join him," Steppenwolf growls.

"So I'm guessing your offer to mentor me has expired?"

"I'm glad this is funny to you. Let's see if you are still in the mood to make jests when I damn you to Draemir and use your powers to fuel the destruction of all you know and love, plebeian!"

"Ooooo, that's very tempting! But I'm afraid I'll have to pass. Let's try things my way first, and if that fails, I'm totally down to explore the whole destruction option," I say, snapping my fingers. The Deadlands vanish in the blink of an eye, replaced instead with a battleground where the home field advantage shifts in my favor. "Welcome, Steppenwolf, to The Twilight Expanse," I announce, my voice echoing through the darkness.

47

THE BOY WHO CRIED WOLF

A single spotlight illuminates Steppenwolf as he takes in his surroundings. I observe him with detached neutrality as I fortify the walls that imprison us both.

The hulking Wendigo now stands in a labyrinth of mirrors that I've carefully placed in a way that will make him question his every move. I watch him take in his surroundings, seeing nothing but different iterations of his own distorted reflection. At first, he spins slowly, peering into each piece of glass. It doesn't take him long to catch onto what I'm doing.

"Do you feel that?" I ask, my voice echoing through the palpable silence. It's the same question he asked me as my chain turned to a snake and choked the life from me. I continue, still quoting the words that are etched on the surface of my brain, "That's fear... Suck it in, Steppenwolf... Linger in it... Let it undo your soul, if you even have one anymore..."

Steppenwolf approaches one of the mirrors, breathing heavily like a bull that's just been taunted. He stares at his demented image, then punches the glass, shattering as he screams, "COME OUT AND FACE ME, HUNTRESS!"

"Once again, it's a tempting proposition... But I'll pass," I say as Steppenwolf steps through the shattered mirror's frame into a long corridor of crooked, angled mirrors that make it impossible to discern which direction is forward. His claws scrape the glass walls next to him as he marches onward, all while I fill the silence with my narration:

"You know, my parents told me as a child that lying was a sin, can you believe it? I know, I know, it sounds like that is a lie in and of itself, seeing how we all lie from time to time... But it reminds me of a story they used to tell me... It was called 'The Boy Who Cried Wolf.' Have you heard it before? No? Well it goes something like this... There was a boy, I believe he was a shepherd, and for some reason, he thought it was funny to shout that the town's flock of sheep was being attacked by a wolf! No one really knows why crying wolf brought the child joy, yet he did it time and time again, each time getting the same reaction from the townsfolk, who came running to chase the wolf away...

"Well, one day, when the boy was shepherding the flock, a wolf *did* come, for real this time, and it attacked the sheep. Naturally, the boy cried wolf, knowing the townsfolk would come running and help him save the sheep from being slaughtered... The only thing was, the town's citizens had been fooled by the boy so many times that they instantly dismissed the boy's alarm as another foolish lie! So, as I'm sure you are able to predict, no one came to save the boy's sheep even though the danger was real this time. All the sheep died, and lying finally lost its appeal in the boy's mind. In the end, ironically, it was the wolf who got the last laugh.

"I'm sure you're wondering why the hell I'm rambling on at this point, right? Well, I've gotta hand it to you—you're a clever fox, Steppenwolf. You've built yourself quite an empire off lies and deception. But now, I am the wolf who's arrived on your doorstep, and no one will come to save you as I destroy your empire bit by bloody bit."

"Spare me your lectures, pathetic woman," Steppenwolf counters as he bumps face first into a panel of glass that he thought was the way forward. I can feel his cold-blood boiling as his claw raises to touch it, scratching its surface slowly so the screeching noise rings out. A reflection of me, his hunter, flashes in the mirror panes all around him. Enraged, and perhaps a little startled, he turns around to face me. But I am not behind him; my reflection in the mirror was merely another illusion planted in his deteriorating mind. "ENOUGH OF THIS! SHOW YOURSELF!"

His body succumbs to a tantrum. All at once, his limbs shatter glass that surrounds him in every direction. His fists punch and his legs thrash as he spins, making the immediate walls around him reduce to fallen shards. But the Wendigo leader isn't as clever as I thought. His incessant spinning not only makes him forget which direction he came from and which way he was going, but it merely opens the labyrinth up so another layer of mirrors is revealed, further distorting his sense of direction.

I appear before him, positioning myself so he can see me in several dozen panes that circle him. There is no way for him to know which me is the real me, or if any me is the real me. For him, it's maddening. But for me? For me, it's peak entertainment.

"We Hunters have a saying," I say, smiling as he rotates, trying to determine which Drakini to attack first. "Hunt... Or be hunted."

"How is this possible?" Steppenwolf howls miserably. I can hear something in his voice... Doubt, the destroyer of worldviews. Since my arrival, he's struggled with my existence. It's likely his Creator told him he was the only one who possesses these powers. But when he encountered me, he learned that belief was an illusion in and of itself.

Steppenwolf couldn't bring himself to kill me eight long months ago. He, the Ultimate Deceiver, had to know the truth. Without the truth, a liar finds no meaning in their life. No, he couldn't kill me. I was something he needed to study, a tool he needed in order to discover the truth. That is why he appeared to me as Myre, so he could divine meaning from the visions revealed to me as I learned to wield my powers month by month.

"I am pestilence..." I say, quoting his words from eight months ago. Steppenwolf recognizes his words and lashes out irrationally, shattering the mirror closest to him in an attempt to silence me. But behind that mirror is another, so my image remains displayed before him, grinning. His arms and legs bleed as several hundred glass fragments pierce his flesh and cling to his decaying fur. I continue, "I am famine... I have seen the Twilight Expanse; I have seen Draemir's Gates; I have visited the inside of Hell itself... I have seen the Dawn of Creation, and I have seen its End. You ask how this is possible, and I have only one answer for you, Steppenwolf. Though this world is your Creator's domain, there exists a higher power beyond his tyrannical rule, and it demands that your evil be balanced. It sent me, to accomplish that balance, and so we will now see which force wins in the end—Good, or Evil.

"Letting me live will be your downfall, Steppenwolf. Letting me learn how to use these powers, your greatest mistake. You had the chance to be the Hunter, but instead, you awoke the Huntress."

I release my control over the mirrors. All at once, they explode in a single, ear-shattering sonic boom. Steppenwolf falls to his knees and cradles his devilish face. A storm of microscopic daggers settle around him, revealing what the mirror-laden labyrinth hid this entire time. When the dust settles, Steppenwolf will see that he kneels before the gates of Draemir—the same gates I plan to cast him into for all eternity.

48

Cur (Pt. 3)

"I hope that was entertaining for you," Steppenwolf grunts, standing from the dune of razor-sharp dust I've created. His long, spindly claws pat the glass from his fur.

I stand behind him, opposite from Draemir's opening. The Wendigo studies the gates astutely, then turns to face me. "Go ahead, savor this moment human. Because when this world collapses around you—when I reduce your species to ashes, I want you to remember that you are the one who provoked my wrath."

"Look around, Skinwalker... It's over for you. I'm going to open those gates, and there isn't a damn thing you can do to save yourself from joining the souls it holds."

Steppenwolf doesn't have the face of a human, but my warning causes his corroded lips to smile beneath his bonelike exoskeleton. He straightens himself, sighing with a chuckle as he puffs his chest and cracks his menacing knuckles. Slowly, he lifts a single hand for me to see. His bony thumb touches his middle claw, as if he intends to snap this nightmare away. Menacingly, Steppenwolf growls, "Never forget, Drakini of Fyrefell, that I was the first to congratulate you on your pregnancy."

My heart drops as he snaps, its echo ringing out in the surrounding darkness.

My hands shoot to my stomach as a sharp pain jolts in my midsection. I let out an uncomfortable wheeze. I feel the space between my legs pop, then look up at Steppenwolf as a trickle of fluid runs down the inside of my thighs. My lower abdomen cramps and spasms, sending shockwaves of pain down my legs strong enough to steal my breath. I whisper to myself, "No... I still have... It's only been eight months..."

"Perhaps," Steppenwolf revels as I languish in silence. "But no child is born in my jurisdiction without my say so, Huntress. So, I say we speed this up and deliver the child here and now." Steppenwolf stalks toward me while I limp backwards slowly, my concentration struggling to focus on anything other than the sharp pain of rapid contractions.

"No... None of this is real," I say, trying to convince myself to see through the illusion. "I'm not due for another month... This is just another one of your lies..."

"Is it?"

"I just need to... Just need to shatter the illusion..."

"Be my guest," Steppenwolf urges, waiting for me to walk the walk.

"Fuck you!" I shout, "My body is not yours to control! This is just a pathetic attempt to distract me!"

"Or, and listen carefully, perhaps it isn't... You see, you were right about me—I am a diabolical liar; my species itself can only be preserved by preying on the many regrets and guilts of human swine. But I've grown terribly bored of crying wolf; it has lost its humor to me... So, eight months ago when I met you, I decided to play the long game. Because anyone can tell a lie, but it takes a true liar to make someone fall in love with one... And speaking of lies, no delivery is complete without the father being present!"

Again, Steppenwolf's claws snap, and their echo reach through time and space to summon the person in this world I want to see the least right now—Cur.

The tan-skinned Lycan appears from thin air before the Wendigo, looking around dazed and confused as he looks around the Twilight Expanse. He sees me as I limp in pain, both hands cradling my stomach as tears form in my eyes. "Drakini?" he calls out, taking a step toward me.

Steppenwolf's claws grab a chunk of his hair and prevent him from proceeding any further. "Ah ah ah, not so fast, Lycan." The claws twist Cur's head until he sees the beast that lurks behind him.

"Steppenwolf..." Cur murmurs, no fear to be found in his voice, but instead... sadness?

"Ah, you don't seem excited to see me! Hopefully you didn't get so caught up in your little romance that you forgot we had a deal?"

"What's he talking about?" I cry out, my heart aching at the sight of my lover trapped by my worst enemy.

"This isn't what it looks like!" Cur cries as Steppenwolf throws his body into a pile of shattered glass.

"He's right," Steppenwolf chuckles, cracking his knuckles all at once. "It's actually much worse than what it looks like, I assure you... Now, would you like to tell your little lady friend about our deal, or should I?"

"Fuck you!" Cur shouts, ripping pieces of glass from his bloody skin as he stands.

"Please tell me you're real," I cry, my mind racing with a million thoughts a minute. "Tell me you weren't some fucking illusion Steppenwolf cast to trick me!"

"Oh please, I like to think I'm a little more original than that!" Steppenwolf scoffs, "You would've seen that coming—to use your own words against you, you would've known I was 'crying wolf,' pun intended... No, I assure you, this selfish fleabag you've fallen for is real, though I suspect you'll soon wish he wasn't."

"I'll fucking kill you!" Cur screams, charging Steppenwolf in a futile attempt to keep the truth hidden. Cur leaps at the Wendigo and is met with a violent backhand that sends his body flying through the air. The Lycan thuds amidst the broken glass once more and slides several feet through the shards, slicing his back open enough to leave a trail of blood.

Cur covers his crying eyes as he whimpers, "I'm so sorry Drakini... I just... I wanted it to be real... I wanted you to love me... I wanted our daughter... I wanted to make the lies a reality... I didn't know what I was doing!"

"Shut up!" I scream, covering my ears and squeezing my eyes shut tight. "Everyone shut up! I need to think!"

My entire midsection burns with pain as cramps contract faster and faster. I can barely stand. The pain is unlike any wound I've incurred on the battlefield—it feels as if the baby inside me is trying to kick and tear its way to freedom.

I need Wisteria.

I need her now more than ever.

"Please, Wisteria, if you can hear this prayer, I need you," I whisper to myself. "You said you were born from necessity. If you're out there—if you can hear me—I fucking need you!"

"In a world of shadows and lies, the truth will always seem destructive," Steppenwolf sneers, his figure somehow using my fear and panic to grow. "So, Huntress, would you like to know the truth?"

"Drakini, you have to believe me, I didn't know what I was doing! He tricked me!" Cur wheezes as his bloodied body picks itself up once more.

"What deal is he talking about Cur? And don't you dare lie to me..." I hold my swollen stomach as something inside me fights to free itself by any means necessary. Cur sees my pregnant belly, then wipes tears from his eyes with the back of his hand.

"Go on, tell her," Steppenwolf snickers, more than happy to postpone killing us so I can discover my lover's betrayal.

"That night, eight months ago," Cur begins, struggling to speak the words that will inevitably destroy my love for him. "I told you I saw our daughter, the one we had when I was cursed by the Blood Moon Hex... The truth is, I did see her, which is the only reason I found you... But she wasn't the reason I was able to break through Steppenwolf's domain..."

"What do you mean? How were you able to... Oh gods," I exhale, looking back and forth between Cur and Steppenwolf.

"When I found you, I couldn't break through Steppenwolf's barrier... You were so close, yet so far... Even with my Lycan strength, I couldn't reach you... I could see you struggling; I could see you losing, but there was nothing I could do to save you... Until... I... Steppenwolf... We cut a deal... He agreed to let me in so I could save you, then showed me a vision of our daughter... He promised everything I lost when I broke free from the Blood Moon Hex could be mine once again... You, our daughter, our life together... And I... I believed him..."

"Oh Cur," I sob, falling to my knees as the emotional pain grows too great to bear.

"I sold my soul for a chance to save you, Drakini," Cur says, sniffling built-up mucus from his tears. "He offered me the chance to save you—save our daughter—save the world... And I fell for it..."

"This is why I love humans," Steppenwolf cackles, "And to think they say chivalry is dead! Can you blame the man, Drakini? He sold his moth-erfucking soul to save you—does it get any more romantic than that?"

"Damn you," Cur growls, then whispers to me from a world away, "You have to believe me, I wasn't even sure if the deal I made was real, Drakini... I was in my Lycan form; the whole night was a blurry haze... When I woke the next morning and saw you, I didn't know what to think! And I was afraid to tell you the truth—afraid that if you learned about the deal you wouldn't want anything to do with me... It was so fucking selfish of me, I can see that now... But I couldn't bear the thought of losing you again... If you want the truth, I'd do it all again if I had to—my soul is worth nothing without you..."

"How long have you known?" I growl, staring at him through tear-blurred vision. "How long have you known I was pregnant?"

"I didn't know... I had suspicions, but I wasn't sure... Not until now."

"Don't blame him, Drakini," Steppenwolf says sarcastically. "You of all people should know it's in his nature to sacrifice himself for those he loves most. Hell, he wouldn't even be here if he hadn't taken the fall for his murderous brother!"

A shriek escapes my mouth as something claws my insides, forcing me to fall on my back. Cur sprints across the Twilight Expanse as I remove my breastplate and rip the pelt that covers my stomach. I gasp as I see my abdomen is purple and black with internal bleeding. "No no no no," I stammer, touching the flesh tenderly as a paw print beats against my bellybutton.

Cur crashes to his knees beside me, placing his hand behind my head as I hyperventilate. In his eyes are a million unspoken words. His scarred lips tremble uncontrollably. He wants to comfort me but doesn't know how to. Each of us knows something is wrong, very wrong. We are both old enough to know this isn't how labor is supposed to go.

"This is my favorite part," Steppenwolf sighs emphatically, his shadow creeping over us as I fight to keep a scream of agony inside my throat. "This is the part where my plans come together... Like I said, it takes a master of manipulation to make someone fall in love with a lie, and now I get to watch both of your realities fall apart at the seams! Your Lycan lover sold his soul just for me to revel in this moment, and now I will get to watch him lose everything he loves in this world a second time!"

Claws pierce my stomach lining from the inside, slashing my stomach open diagonally as Cur's monstrous Lycan pup delivers itself. I let out a feral scream so loud that the gates of Draemir shake. Blood pours from my slitted stomach as a glob of bloody fur peaks through.

I can't feel my legs anymore; my entire lower half has gone numb from the monster's efforts. Cur is an emotional wreck as he tries to stop the bleeding, holding what appears to be my entrails as a bloodied wolf pup sheds my flesh.

I'm light-headed from the blood loss. I can barely make out what's happening anymore. I hear a high-pitched whimper as Cur lifts our child from its ravaged womb. I can only see its silhouette in Cur's arms. One second, it looks like a wolf pup, its black fur covered in my blood as it stretches its snout to the air and howls. I blink several times, then see a human child cradled in Cur's arms, crying desperately for its mother's embrace.

"How marvelous, it's a girl," Steppenwolf snickers. "Now, perhaps the Seer's daughter will be willing to help me conquer this world, since her mother refused. Don't make this harder than it needs to be, Cur. Hand the child over to me."

"I'd rather die!" Cur shouts, provoking our baby girl to cry even louder.

"Suit yourself," Steppenwolf cackles.

A loud thud sounds from behind Steppenwolf as the gates of Draemir tremble, causing Steppenwolf to pause in his malevolent stride. With the fleeting life I have left, I stare at the gates as they shudder a second time, as if some demon is trying to break free from within. Chains rattle in the distance. Something stirs in the shadows around us.

Monkey see evil, a voice echoes as a chain flies from the darkness, aimed directly at Steppenwolf. The Wendigo tries to bat it away but the chain wraps itself around his forearm. *Monkey see, monkey do!* Simon shouts, emerging from the shadows atop Behemoth as the two charge into battle. Simon twirls a single chain in his hand like a cowboy ready to wrangle a bull. Mimicking Nephra, Simon throws the chain with masterful aim and manages to snag Steppenwolf's other wrist. Behemoth and Simon cheer simultaneously as they pull the Wendigo's arm tight. Nephra lowers herself from the pitch-black sky on a web of chains, pulling Steppenwolf's opposite wrist taut.

Writhing with frustration, the Wendigo growls, "It's going to take a lot more than three of your pathetic shadow soldiers to beat me, Huntress!"

Suddenly, almost as if it was timed to perfection, the gates of Draemir shudder a third time, then explode open, revealing a set of glowing, golden eyes.

A voice purrs, *How about nine pathetic shadow soldiers?*

"Wist... errrr... ia..." I wheeze, my heart aflame as I hear her voice for the first time in eight months.

Behind the hellcat's blurry outline stands five figures I am able to recognize, even on death's door.

Wisteria purrs, *To the almighty Huntress that resides inside...*

Lu Bu continues, *We ask for the serenity to accept that which we must abide...*

Havik adds, *Give small gorl courage to fight...*

Grite recites, eager to deliver his line, *Make it hurt whenever she bite!*

Osprey chirps, *Let her see through the enemy's lies...*

Dyran finishes, *Give her the strength to bring about his demise.*

"Amen," I whisper, watching as all nine of my shadow soldiers join forces.

"I'll kill all of you!" Steppenwolf howls, shattering the chains that bind his arms as Nephra slings six more in his direction to replace them. The chains wrap around his body as Dyran, Grite, and Havik reach him, each one of them dealing lethal blows they've been storing for eight months. "I'll... kill... every last... one of you..." Steppenwolf grunts between the scattered punches.

Wisteria grabs a single chain between her teeth and yanks it, ripping the Wendigo's feet out from under him. Osprey descends from the darkness and grabs another chain. Six chains, Nephra bound Steppenwolf with, and each of the six shadow soldiers that escaped Draemir grabs hold of them, combining their strength as they drag Steppenwolf toward Draemir's open gates.

"I love you both so much," Cur sobs, kissing our daughter's forehead, then leaning over my dying carcass to kiss me. I am too weak to speak—too weak to ask what he's doing. His warm lips press against mine, giving me a spark of life to hold on a moment longer. "Forgive me," he whispers in my ear.

I scream inwardly, unable to protest the thoughts he withholds from me.

"This isn't over!" Steppenwolf screams, causing the walls of the Twilight Expanse to shatter. "Trapping me in Draemir will only delay the inevitable, Huntress! Those walls cannot hold me forever! I will escape, and when I do, your entire species is doomed! All of creation is doomed! The Creator will free me, and when he does, I won't stop until I've destroyed everything you've fought to protect!"

"I have to go," Cur whispers, staring at our daughter as he holds back tears. "Daddy has to go, baby girl... But mommy will take care of you, I promise... She is the best human I've ever met..."

"Cuh... Cuh... er..." I am screaming his name inwardly, but my lips can only manage a desperate whimper.

"My name isn't Cur," he says, smiling at me through a world of pain. He shifts our daughter into my arms and whispers something in my ears. "Crixus," he says. "My name is Crixus."

He kisses my forehead delicately, then stands heroically, admiring our daughter one last time, as if she is the only thing that can give him the strength to do what must be done.

"I know you won't understand why I'm doing this, but so long as that monster lives, your life will be in danger Drakini. I will go to Draemir to hold him back as long as I can. You have my word, so long as my heart beats, our daughter will be safe. I owe her that—I owe *you* that... I love you. Don't forget that, and don't forget me."

I watch as Cur agonizes over his decision, then walks off, joining my shadow soldiers as they reach Draemir's threshold. In a matter of minutes, I've gotten everything I've ever wanted—Steppenwolf has lost, Wisteria returned, I've delivered a healthy child—yet at the same time, I've lost the person I love most in this world.

Wisteria blots my view as she lays by my side, purring as the chain that tethers my heart to this world shatters. Her ribcage vibrates as she licks my daughter's cheek, causing the baby to wail with laughter. It's a beautiful noise to hear; I only hope Cur can hear it as he closes the gates of Draemir behind him.

EPILOGUE

"You sure 'bout this? Somethin' ain't sittin' right with me," Pip says, staring at the swaddled baby I offer him.

"I'm sure," I reply, locking eyes with Wisteria for strength. "These lands are no place to raise a child. She will be safer in the western world."

"Then come with us," Pip scoffs, choking up on his emotions. "Lil' tyke deserves a mother, an' I sure as shit don't know nothin' 'bout raisin' a kid…"

"Every day I spend by her side is an endangerment. Steppenwolf will return Pip; Hell can only hold him for so long…"

"These lands ain't got nothin' for you anymore," Pip stammers, trying to persuade me against my decision. "I didn't sew you up and heal that stomach just so you could go get killed on some aimless mission!"

"You're right, these lands have nothing for me. But I'm not staying here. It's hunt or be hunted, so it's time to go on the hunt, Pip."

"The hell does that mean? You trapped the Wendigo in Hell!"

"Which is exactly why I'm going to enter Draemir."

"Bullocks, yer outta yer snotting mind! Is this about Dane? If he's the reason you don't wanna join us, we can leave his sulking corpse here for all I care!"

"This has nothing to do with Dane," I say, staring up at the boat as the masked leader leans over the hull, intentionally turning his back to me. The man will never forgive me for my adultery, of that I'm sure. He intentionally waited for me to awake from my coma to take his wedding ring off, just so I could see him do it. There is nothing I can say or do to earn his forgiveness. He likely curses the gods that Pip was able to heal my body in the first place.

He hasn't said a single word to me, not even a simple 'thanks' for saving his life. Since coming to, I've gathered it wasn't until the gates of Draemir closed on Steppenwolf that Pip, Katana, and Dane were freed from the Wendigo's hold on their minds. I can understand the thoughts of treachery he feels, though. Eight months he fought back against Arcadia with the intention of returning to me, only to discover I spread my legs for another man and bore him a child. More than that, he's likely bitter the child he sired in me died before reaching term, yet Cur's child had the strength to claw its way to life—literally.

Maybe with time, he will realize it wasn't as simple a betrayal as he's making it seem. The wound in his heart is too fresh to see things with reason, but I can hope he will find the power to forgive me as time passes.

"People get cheated on all the time," Pip says in my defense, though I didn't ask for him to side with me. "Lover boy up there will get over it... Besides, who's going to row our boat all the way back to Areopagus?"

"The oars are all yours this time, my friend."

"Then I'll row harder than ever before and pray the gods send us wind when my body fails," Pip says, sniffling silently as he hides his sadness from me. Slowly, against his wishes, he grabs hold of my daughter and pulls her tight, smiling slightly as she grabs hold of his beard and gives it a tug. "She's got yer feistiness already! She'll be a damn salmon in no time, I'm sure of it... You decide on a name for the lil booger yet?"

"Crixus... After her father," I whisper, afraid that if I speak any louder the words won't come out.

"A fine name indeed," Pip exclaims, holding Crixus up for closer inspection. His short, stubby fingers tickle her armpits, causing her to wail with laughter. I look to Wisteria once more for strength, my heart shattering.

You will see her again, Wisteria reassures. *This is the only way to keep her safe. You must be strong for her.*

"You'll be the feistiest lil Lycan pup out there, of that I'm sure," Pip chuckles, pulling Crixus in and rocking her diligently.

"She has a family in the Scorpos Desert; grandparents, if they've survived this long, but an uncle for sure. If you can't raise her yourself, all I'd ask is that you find them, please."

"Consider it done," Pip says. "But don't be too long in Draemir... Slay the snotting Wendigo and get back here, ya hear? She'll be waiting for you..."

"I'll be back," I say, not sure if I'm telling the truth or another lie. "And if the gods are with me, I'll return with her father too."

"Good, cuz I'd like to give that fleabag a piece of my mind! Ain't no world out there where I'm a more fit father than him—shoulda been ole' Pip that went to Hell in his place; at least fighting demons is somethin' I'm good at."

"Take care of her, Pip," I say, kissing her forehead one last time. I don't dare look in her eyes as I turn away. It's taken every ounce of courage I have left to make it this far. Instead, I look to my shadow soldiers. All nine of them stand opposite the boat. Though my heart is empty, I'll never be truly alone with these nine by my side. Together, we prepare ourselves for the journey to Hell and back.

"So long as I have breath in my lungs, not a single hair on this precious babe's head will be harmed!" Pip shouts, boarding the docked boat that Cur built for my escape. If it wasn't for my daughter's father, there's no telling how long our child would be stuck in this godforsaken place. The ark sways in the icy water as a testament to his love for me.

My eyes hyperfixate on the ground at Wisteria's feet as the boat departs, its oars sloshing through the slushy waters. There, where the hellcat's feet wait, sprouts a single white rose. The flower stands defiantly along the plains of the Deadlands, likely the first budding bloom this land has seen in decades. Steppenwolf's hold over this nation has come to an end, and with its end, comes new life.

"Cur!" a bird squawks, flapping its wings loudly as it descends from the snowless sky. For the first time in over a decade, there is no longer a chill in the air, and the sun beams its radiant rays without interruption from clouds.

"Netherwing," I say, smiling as the raven lands on my shoulder. I stroke her neck feathers, then whisper in her ear, "I miss him too... Maybe you can come along to help me find him, eh?"

"Come along!" she repeats, bobbing up and down excitedly.

"Once more into the fray, I suppose," I sigh.

You've changed in my absence, Wisteria says, though her tone suggests it's a good thing. She walks up to me and rubs her fur against my side, purring like a stray cat who's found its home.

"How so?"

You're less serious... The Drakini I knew lived for the approval of others. But now, you have a sense of crazed indifference.

"She's got me to thank for that!" a voice shouts from the thawing wilderness. A beaten and battered Draven emerges from a thicket of briars, panting and laughing at the same time. "Sorry I'm late, so terribly late! If you recall, I threw away my only sundial, though I'm not sure it woulda been much help even if I had it... Well well, who do we have here? Nine shadow soldiers! I'm impressed, Piss Eyes! That's thrice the amount you had when I saw you last!"

"Draven!" I shout, sprinting to the withered man. He lets out a grunt of joy as I throw my arms around him, squeezing him tightly. "I thought you were dead!"

"Thought peed his pants and thought he was sweating, pupil," Draven laughs. His body is covered in bruises and cuts, and if I had to guess, he probably has a few broken bones.

"Draven, this is Wisteria and the gang," I whisper excitedly, releasing him so he can meet my shadow soldiers in full.

"Howdy, Wisteria and gang! Name's Draven, but my friends call me Draven. Any friend of Piss Eyes here is a friend of Draven's... Say, y'all like riddles?"

I like moccasins and fur hats, Grite giggles.

Havik like fighting! Havik exclaims.

"All admirable ambitions, I'd say, but try this on for size... Why do hellcats make good shadow soldiers, eh?"

I run my hand through Wisteria's fur as she thinks through Draven's riddle. As Pip and Dane row for the Areopagus with my only daughter, I feel a sense of contentment wash over me. I will see Crixus again, of that I'm sure. Until then, I have only the gods to thank for the family that surrounds me now. Though we are a delusional group of utter misfits, I wouldn't want anyone else by my side as I make the descent into Hell.

It's up to me, and me alone, to save this world from Steppenwolf's destruction. Eight months ago, he broke me. But several nights ago, I proved to myself I have what it takes to defeat him. Soon, I will find him again, and we will break this tie so that only one of us stands victorious.

No amount of lies and deceptions will protect the demon from me. I am the Huntress, one of the Nine Harbingers, created by an eternal ethos that is far more powerful than the Creator and his Death-Defeater.

It is the Creator's fault for making this world a place where I must hunt or be hunted. Now that I've learned how to control these powers, the Creator will see the dangerous web he's weaved. So long as I'm alive, Steppenwolf will never prevail. So long as I'm alive, I will hunt.

"I think I know the answer," I reply through a thinly pursed smile.

"I knew you had it in you," Draven says, jumping with excitement, then grabbing his injured ribcage with regret as he lands. He wheezes, "Go on... Tell us why Steppenwolf couldn't beat our beloved Wisteria!"

"Because hellcats have nine lives."

ABOUT THE AUTHOR

You likely saw this book has been dedicated to Draven, a Rottweiler my family rescued in 2018. From the beginning, he was a dog we planned on fostering short term, but quickly realized his aggressive temperament wouldn't be suitable for rehoming under any circumstances. For the first two years of Draven's life, he was owned by a truck driver, who would leave him in a dark basement for days at a time while on the road. Because of this, Draven was raised in an environment where he viewed any and all affection as a threat. Even the act of petting him would trigger his fight-or-flight instincts, causing him to attack.

Unfortunately, by the time Draven was given away, he was too old and dangerous to have these habits broken. Because of this, Draven was going to be euthanized. That is, until my family rescued him and brought him to our small homestead farm. Although we couldn't break Draven completely of his aggression, we've spent the last eight years teaching him that affection is not something that needs to be feared.

As I said in the dedication, I'm sorry that humanity failed you Draven. I hope more than anything that we have shown you a slice of Heaven in these last eight years.

www.ingramcontent.com/pod-product-compliance
Lightning Source LLC
Chambersburg PA
CBHW020307200626
46814CB00006BA/2132